THE BENGAL BRIDEGIFT

Anne Cleeland

ISBN: 0692662774
ISBN 13: 9780692662779

For Johan's mom, who was braver than she knew; and for all others like her.

1

Juno aimed the blunderbuss at the gentleman's chest and warned, with all the confidence she could muster, "You must leave, now; I should not like to shoot you." She wedged the heavy weapon between her hip and her ribcage because she didn't think she could lift it to her shoulder, and hoped she gave the appearance of someone so familiar with such a weapon that she would handle it rather casually.

Unalarmed, the gentleman's dark eyes rested upon her, and then upon the weapon trained on him. "You cannot shoot. The frizzen, it is fixed."

She looked at the lock plate of the gun in confusion—although she had no notion of which he spoke—and while her attention was thus diverted, he took the weapon from her with a swift movement.

Horrified, she waited for whatever was to come, but he merely inspected the metal mechanisms on the stock, and removed a small piece of cork that was wedged between. He then handed the weapon back to her.

Having the unhappy conviction that she had lost all advantage, she faced him wordlessly for a moment and then managed, "I will not hesitate to shoot, you know." She did not bother to lift the gun again, fearing that her hands would not obey direction.

Her companion made an apologetic gesture toward the weapon. "Not this day—the gun, it has no shot."

Acutely aware of the foolish picture she presented, Juno regarded the ancient weapon in exasperation. "No? I was assured it was primed and loaded."

He reached for the blunderbuss again and, fearing a trick, she gasped and did not relinquish it, stepping back.

"Me, I will show you," he explained in a patient tone, his hand outstretched. The depths of the dark eyes were guileless and indeed, held a gleam of amusement that was at odds with his fearsome appearance. He was tall, and seemed immensely broad-shouldered to her; thick and muscular as he held out his hand, palm up. "Come, come."

Because it seemed rude to refuse him, she allowed him to take it from her. Shaking the barrel slightly he met her eyes and declared, "Empty." His spoke with a heavy accent—Dutch, she imagined, which only verified his identity; not that there was any mistaking. With an air of polite deference, he handed it back to her, the movement causing his long braid, glossy and black as a raven's wing, to fall forward over his shoulder.

Juno wanted to throw the stupid gun into the under-brush, but instead, she rested the butt of the weapon on the ground and tried to conceal her extreme annoyance—it was heavy, and she had struggled to carry the wretched, useless thing all this way, thinking it would protect her. Faintly, the voices of shouting men could be heard in the distance, and she raised her head in alarm, only to remember that her worst fear stood before her.

Her companion cocked his head, also listening. "Come, come; I will take you back. You would not make it to the fort."

Juno had already come to the same conclusion, but she felt she should at least make an effort to avoid such an escort. With what she hoped was a confident air, she bowed her head in a gesture of dismissal. "I thank you, but it is not necessary—I know the way."

Reaching to lift the blunderbuss, he ignored her. "Do you wish to bring this?"

Juno decided to abandon any protest—in truth, she'd rather not re-trace her steps alone, and it seemed she had little choice, anyway. "It is not mine, so I suppose I must bring it back. Useless thing—I feel like an idiot."

"No, no," he assured her in an earnest tone. "Me, I was very frightened."

To her amazement, Juno found she very much wanted to laugh, but managed to refrain. "Yes," she agreed gravely. "I could see that you were."

With the blunderbuss negligently suspended in one hand, the gentleman began to walk in the direction of the convent school with Juno at his heels—she noted with some unease that he seemed to know the way. Looking back at her over his shoulder, he urged, "Come, come; make haste. The sun, it will set."

Reminded that she was alone with a strange man in a hostile area, and that darkness was fast approaching, she announced in a firm tone, "I am betrothed," just so he was aware there would be retribution, if he tried anything untoward.

He glanced back over his shoulder again. "He is careless, this man."

Finding she had no real desire to defend her suitor, Juno admitted, "He is on his way to England, actually."

"And yet you are very much in Bengal."

Juno debated how much to reveal. "I was supposed to leave for England two days past—on an East Indiaman frigate—but instead the fighting broke out; the Mughals." She paused and noted she could no longer hear the shouting in the distance—hopefully the raiders had gone up-river, after having found the fort impenetrable.

"There has been the fighting for two days?"

"Three days, now." There seemed little harm in telling him; apparently he was a new arrival.

They walked a few more steps. "You are a little foolish, I think."

But the criticism was too much for Juno's bruised sensibilities, and she defended herself with some heat, as she swept a mangrove branch out of the way. "You have *no* idea, and cannot lay blame. And I must get to Horry—if he is not already dead of the stupid, *miserable* fever." Hearing the thread of hysteria in her voice, she firmly pressed her lips together to calm herself—no need to let him know she was at her wit's end, although it was probably evident, anyway.

At her outburst, her companion halted and faced her, his manner sympathetic. "Your brother, he has the typhoid?"

"No," she corrected, struggling to regain her composure, "Malaria." Keeping her gaze downcast, she noted with some alarm that her strange companion was aware that Horry was her brother.

The braid fell forward again as he tilted his head toward her. "You will see him in the morning, yes? You must not go now—it is too dangerous."

He waited, seeking her agreement, and she nodded to show she understood. The twilight was fading, and the Bengal night, with all its dangers, came quickly. They resumed their journey, he cautioning her to stay away from the undergrowth for fear of venomous snakes—as though she had not lived here nearly all her life, and knew very well what was venomous and what was not.

Still stinging from his comment about her foolishness, Juno was unable to resist further defending herself as they trudged along. "I left the school because I was afraid the Mughals would return; I would just as soon take my chances trying to reach the fort, than to stay there, and I wanted to see if Horry was sickening still."

"You are alone?"

Castigating herself for a fool, she then decided there was little point in prevaricating about it; it was obvious that she was unprotected. Besides, his manner did not seem at all threatening—quite the contrary, in fact, and she was cautiously heartened. "Yes. I was to be escorted to England by a visiting priest, but unfortunately, he was attacked by the Mughals."

This caught his attention, and he slowed to walk beside her on the graveled path, his gaze thoughtful upon her. Juno was not short, but she came up only to his shoulder. Glancing up to him, she saw he wore a gold earring, and there were colored beads woven into his braid. She quickly looked away again.

He tilted his head, the wide brim of his black felt hat shielding his face from her. "Tell me of this, if you please."

She obliged him—in a way, it was a huge relief to speak of it. "The girls and the staff left for Fort William, once there was word of fighting—it happens, from time to time." She glanced up at him, and he nodded in awareness of this unfortunate fact. "Jacob was to escort the priest and me directly to the docks, but then the school was attacked. It was unprecedented, you see; the Mughals have always been careful not to harass the school for fear of the consequences, so we were caught quite unprepared." Glancing at him sidelong, she tried to gauge his reaction to this disclosure, but he gave no clue as to his thoughts.

She paused, remembering the shouts and crashing as she hid, terrified, under the pantry table, then crawled on her hands and knees to slip out the back door, expecting to feel a rough hand seize her at any moment. "I hid in the chicken coop—under the roost—until they were gone."

"Ah," he nodded. "The chickens, they did not object?"

"I cleared them out," she assured him, "—and left the door open, so none would think it worthwhile to enter."

This subterfuge apparently met with his approval and he nodded again. They walked a few more yards, until he halted and held his hand up, cautioning her to stay silent. They listened as faint sounds—shouting and gunfire— could be heard in the distance, up the river. "The priest and this Jacob, where are they now?"

"The priest was beaten and stabbed—left for dead, but he was still alive when I found him. He died shortly afterward." She tried to keep her voice steady, but was not entirely successful.

He touched her elbow, gently, in sympathy. "And this Jacob? Where is he?"

She drew a steadying breath. "Jacob wished to flee, but I could not just abandon the poor priest—" she looked up at him, seeking confirmation.

"Assuredly not," he agreed.

"—and so Jacob left me this wretched weapon, and said he would go to get help." Remembering it, she could not disguise her scorn.

"But you do not think so," he concluded.

"No. I think he fled."

"If I meet this Jacob," he offered diffidently, "I will slit his throat for you."

It was exactly the right touch to settle her emotions. "I thank you," she said gravely. "I would appreciate it."

They walked in silence the remainder of the journey, and the convent school came into sight just as the darkness settled in. I have no idea what is to happen now, Juno thought, and I am almost past caring.

"This priest," asked her strange companion. "He was a Frenchman, yes?"

Juno looked at him in surprise. "Yes, he was. From Normandy."

"And he is now dead—you are certain?"

"Yes. I buried him as best I could in the garden; I didn't want the tigers to get to him." Juno firmly quashed the picture that threatened to rise in her mind—of gleaming white fangs and outstretched claws coming toward her at a terrifying pace, whilst she could feel her heartbeat in her throat.

"Me, I will bury him." He nodded in approval. "You did well, I think."

Pleased by the compliment, she nevertheless demurred modestly, "Truly—I had little choice."

He faced her and held out a hand. "Me, I am Jost Van der Haar."

"I am pleased to meet you, Mr. Van der Haar," she replied in form. "I am Miss Juno Payne." She took his proffered hand and winced. "Blisters," she explained, turning her hand over to show him. "From the shovel."

"You did not wear your gloves?" He indicated her work gloves, folded at the belt of her school uniform.

There was a pause. "Oh; oh—no," she stammered, and hoped he didn't notice her rising color. "I had mislaid them at the time."

He nodded, studying her thoughtfully. "You will stay here, if you please; I will have a look-about."

She waited, watching with some trepidation, but it didn't appear that he expected to discover any hidden dangers as he approached the building in a casual fashion, without a weapon drawn—she had noted that he carried a brace of pistols, and a sword. As he circled around toward the back, she stood beneath the spreading branches of the breadfruit tree, watching her unusual escort and remembering the dying priest's warning to her. In his delirium, he would lapse into unintelligible French but occasionally he would recall himself and clutch at her hand, nearly frantic in his urgency. "Tell no one of the diamonds."

"I will not," she agreed, and hoped it was not a grave sin to lie to a priest.

"There is a Barbary pirate—a Dutchman—he is a devil! He—he will try to take them. You must not allow it—it is his people who did this." Wild-eyed, his fingers dug uncomfortably into her arm.

"You must lie quiet, Father," she soothed, thinking this concern a product of his delirium. "I promise I will repulse all pirates."

"You must not allow him to seize them—take them to the Nabob, I implore you—it is of the utmost importance."

After lapsing in and out of consciousness for a space of time, the poor man had finally died. Juno had rolled him on to the parlor rug so as to drag him to the garden burial site, thinking it a shame he spent his last hour on earth worried about pirates, of all things. Therefore, her extreme dismay at being confronted by the very picture of a Barbary pirate was unfeigned and sincere. Although to be fair, thus far he did not seem bloodthirsty in the least—and certainly did not appear to be bent on wresting the diamonds. In any event, there was no point in trying to escape; he would track her easily, and the dangers presented by the Bengal night were even more fearsome than a pirate who may or may not have an eye on her virtue.

Her companion returned, and indicated with a gesture that it was safe to proceed inside. "You are hungry?"

"No," she lied, worried about spending the evening alone with him. "Perhaps you should sleep in the rectory."

"Me, I am hungry," he pronounced, ignoring her suggestion. "What can you feed me?"

She hesitated, trying to decide how firm she should be, and whether it would do any good to be firm, as she was clearly outmanned.

Watching her, he explained patiently, "If I wanted to kill you, Juno, you would be dead. And I will not take you to bed—unless this is what you desire?" He raised his black brows at her as if this would be more of an inconvenience than anything else.

The perfunctory offer quelled her concerns. "No," she replied with a small smile, and then added, "No, thank you."

"Then we are comfortable, yes?" He indicated she was to proceed.

When Juno crossed the yard toward the steps, she startled some small creature so that there was a rustling in the undergrowth to the left. She quickened her pace, but her companion responded by raising the blunderbuss to his shoulder and firing with a report that sounded like a thunderclap. Agape, she watched him walk over to retrieve a dead chicken riddled with buckshot, which he held up by its claws. "Dinner," he pronounced with satisfaction, and walked ahead of her into the school.

2

An hour later, they were seated before the hearth in the kitchen, the chicken roasting on a skewer over the fire. Juno's role had been confined to plucking the feathers after she was forced to confess that she had no experience in the dressing of poultry.

Her companion had cocked a black brow as he took over the task, deftly gutting and cleaning the bird at the wash basin, while she watched. "What is it they teach you, here?"

"Sewing." She glanced up at him, a teasing light in her eye. "And watercolors."

He had shaken his head in disapproval. "Me, I think it would be better to know the chickens. Or the weapons."

"I think events have proved you right," she'd agreed, watching him remove the small pieces of shot with probing fingers. "Although it was unkind of you to make me believe I had no ammunition."

"Me, I was afraid you would hurt yourself—so I must take it without causing you to be anxious."

As he had not succeeded in this aim, she had diplomatically made no comment, and was now watching him roast the chicken over the crackling fire. When they had first entered the deserted school, her companion had rested his hand on his hips, silently reviewing the scene Juno had left behind. It was in wild disarray—the intruders had smashed furniture and slashed upholstery so that little was left intact. Dark bloodstains on the settee and parlor floor were the only testament to the death of the visiting priest, and Juno averted her gaze because the terrible memory was still too fresh. The convent school was a small one, meant for the education and refinement of the female offspring of those English traders who served the East India Company out of Calcutta. Juno had in fact graduated the year before, but stayed on as an instructress, because her father had given no other direction and continued to pay for her board, apparently unaware the school had fulfilled its purpose, and that her future should instead be arranged elsewhere. Juno had been unsurprised by this lapse, and hurriedly turned her mind to other matters, not wanting to think about her father, just now.

Recalled to the present, she moved her gaze from the fire to glance at her companion, only to see him quickly look away—so; he had been watching her covertly. She had taken her own covert assessment, and had noted that his face was not unhandsome; he had rather an intriguing bump in the bridge of his nose—as though it had been broken—and the dark eyelashes were almost ridiculously long for a man. His skin was of a mahogany hue very familiar to her; the result of prolonged exposure to the tropical sun. The dressing of the chicken had helped them settle into a polite companionship that was as comfortable as it was strange, and so she was not alarmed by his scrutiny— that he was already aware of her identity seemed evident, and she very much feared she knew why this was. Thus far, however, he had not mentioned the one topic she dreaded. Until now, that was.

"Do you know what they searched for, these men?" The dark eyes met hers.

"I imagine they were looking for valuables," she replied evenly.

After a brief moment, he looked to the chicken and turned the skewer, chuckling to himself.

"What is it?"

"You do not make a good liar, Juno," he observed without rancor.

Her color high, she admitted, "No, I suppose not— there's another useful skill I was never taught."

He shrugged in mock-regret. "Me, I was never taught the watercolors."

Aware that her reaction had given her away, she looked to the sizzling chicken and waited with some anxiety for the next question, but it did not come. Instead, he moved to remove the bird from the skewer, protecting his hand from the hot metal with a rag. The crockery in the kitchen had all been broken when it had been thrown down from the shelves, and so they had cleared away the shards on the floor, and decided to use the wooden trenchers normally reserved for bread. While Juno perched on the only joint stool that remained intact, her companion settled cross-legged on the floor beside her as they ate their makeshift meal. "It is quite good," she complimented him. Having had nothing to eat this tumultuous day, she found she was indeed hungry.

"Take care for the shot; there may be some pieces I did not catch."

He ate and seemed disinclined to converse, but she couldn't like the silence, especially because his unspoken question hung in the air between them. She had the un-easy conviction that he was awaiting a confession from her, but she was made of sterner stuff, and changed the sub-ject. "Do you hail from Holland, Mr. Van der Haar?"

"Haarlem," he acknowledged. "Although I have not vis-ited in a long time."

"No, I imagine not." Holland had been occupied by the French during Napoleon's recent war in Europe, which had caused no end of trouble for those whose livelihood depended on the East India Company. War was never good for trade, and the Dutch were traders of the first order. "Is your family safe? Have you had word?"

"I no longer have family there." He offered nothing further.

Hoping she hadn't mis-stepped, she volunteered, "I have only Horry, myself."

"And your betrothed." His dark eyes slid in her direction.

"Of course," she conceded, her color rising. "But he is not family—not as yet."

"Of course," he echoed her words, and she shot him a suspicious glance, but his expression seemed sincere. "Me, I will be wed soon." He took another bite of chicken.

Hiding her surprise, she offered, "My congratulations," and thought this announcement entirely unexpected; there had been something in his manner toward her that had led her to believe he was unattached—aside from the fact he did not seem to be the marrying kind. His poor sweetheart will be led a merry chase, she decided a bit crossly—she must be a very poor specimen.

To turn the subject from his beleaguered country and his beleaguered sweetheart, she ventured, "I have lived here in Bengal most of my life; I have little recollection of England." Her mother, never a strong woman, began to decline after giving birth to Horry, and when she died, their father had done the most expedient thing and moved his two young children to Fort William, because he was a sea captain with the East India Company. Even so, he was rarely at Fort William and small wonder, if the terrible news she had learned about him was true. Again, she put a stop to this particular line of thought, and tried to think of something else.

"And now you will return to England." Her companion interrupted her thoughts, his thoughtful gaze on her face.

"It will be strange, but I do think it will be for the best. There are some matters that are pressing—" she hurried on, not wanting to think about those pressing matters, "—and I would like to take Horry to see a specialist. I understand there is a physician in London who has established a bank for the tree bark that is used in treating malaria."

Her companion nodded. "The chinchona bark."

"Yes—that is it," she exclaimed, pleased that he knew of it. "They say it helps to control the fever, but unfortunately the source trees are rare in India." She contemplated the fire for a moment. "Horry is not going to die."

"Assuredly not," he agreed.

Realizing that she sounded over-fearful, she subsided. They had not had an easy time of it of late, and she had taken to holding the belief—a fanciful one, perhaps—that if she and Horry could only make passage to England, they would be safe; safe where there were no tigers or murderous brigands or sudden deaths from miserable diseases. Or at least not in the same numbers as India, one would hope. She only wished—oh, how she wished—that she had someone to support her in this weighty endeavor; she was not very brave, which was probably the main reason she'd even considered the Nabob's unlooked-for offer of marriage. Almost without conscious volition, she glanced at her exotic companion, but then firmly reminded herself that here was no rescuer, but only another in what seemed like an unending supply of persons who should not be trusted. She concluded, "It would be well worth the trip, if Horry could obtain a supply of the bark."

"And you are to be wed." The expression in the dark eyes was openly amused that she tended to overlook this momentous event.

Making a wry mouth in acknowledgment of her lapse, she admitted, "Yes, I suppose I shouldn't keep forgetting, should I?"

"You do not wish to marry this man?"

She met his eyes, feeling she should disclaim as a matter of form, but then remembered that she did not make a very good liar. "We shall see," she equivocated. "I have to decide what will be for the best."

He nodded and looked to the fire. "He is a trader?"

As much to convince herself as to tell him, she replied, "He's very important—indeed, he's a nabob, and made his fortune financing the East India Company."

"Ah—many congratulations."

Not liking the implication, she defended, "It is not as though it's a cream-pot marriage; he was my father's financier, and kindly offered for me when he saw how things were, with no one to help us, and Horry so sick. To observe the proprieties, he engaged the priest to escort us home, and then sailed ahead to hire a house in London. I was at my wit's end, I assure you, and I am ever so grateful."

The Dutchman seemed unconvinced, and shrugged a muscular shoulder. "This man, he makes a good bargain, if he will take your bridegift."

She looked at him in confusion. The reference was to *vardakshina*, an Indian tradition among the upper classes by which a father would bestow an enormous sum of money upon his daughter's new husband, the thinly-disguised bribe meant to attract a suitor of the highest caliber. "No; I have no bridegift—the Nabob is acting out of kindness."

They sat together in silence for a space of time while the firelight flickered. Now that she had eaten, Juno realized she was weary to the bone, but the thought of making her way to the deserted dormitory was not a welcome one. "Do you suppose there a danger they will return—the Mughals?"

"No."

But his certain answer also made her uneasy, and she was reminded that the dying priest claimed that it was her companion who had sent the brigands in the first place. Whether it was true or not made little difference, since she could not defend against him, and in any event, she sincerely believed he meant no harm. She glanced at him, and found that once again he was watching her, only this time he did not look away, the expression in the dark, liquid eyes unreadable. The moment stretched out as the fire crackled, and Juno could feel her color rise. To cover her confusion, she offered, "There are some eggs in the chicken coop, for the morning."

"Ah. I must cook the eggs, too?"

"If you would," she replied with a smile, and the confused feeling passed.

He indicated with a gesture. "It is best if you sleep here on the floor by the fire—I will fetch a pallet and a blanket for you." He did not indicate where he would sleep, and she did not ask. "In the morning, if it is safe, we will walk to Fort William."

"Thank you," she said sincerely. "You have been very kind."

"Can you sleep without a candle?" With a nod of his head, he gestured toward the exposed windows where the curtains had been torn down. "It would be for the best."

"I will be quite all right," she assured him, and hoped this was true.

He stood to bank the fire with a few expert thrusts of the poker. "You will call if you need help, yes? And you have your pistol."

Surprised, she shook her head and disclaimed, "No—I have no pistol."

He leaned to indicate her work gloves, folded at her waist, and illuminated by the waning firelight. "There is a pistol here, no?" There was indeed a lump that betrayed the presence of an object—hidden in the inner glove so that it wouldn't be apparent to the casual observer. Apparently, her companion was not a casual observer.

Juno's mouth went dry, and she said as steadily as she was able, "No—it is my father's pipe. I keep it with me, for sentiment."

The dark brows rose in interest. "A Meerschaum pipe—a dragon?"

She stared at him in utter amazement, unable to speak for a moment. "Yes; how—how do you know of it?"

He smiled, his teeth flashing white in the dimness. "Me, I gave it to him."

Juno could feel the color drain from her face, as her heart sank within her breast.

"Good night, Juno." Her companion bowed his head, and made his way out of the room.

3

The next morning, Juno woke early, and stared into the ashes in the grate for a moment, surprised she'd slept as well as she had. Propping herself up on an elbow, she listened, but did not hear any indication that her companion stirred. A pirate who was Papa's cohort, she thought with some dismay; it wanted only this.

Stretching tentatively, she decided she would very much like to wash and make herself a bit more presentable before coming face-to-face with Mr. Van der Haar, regardless of his questionable allegiances. With this aim, she pulled on her shoes, and found a tin pail amongst the rubble, then made her way outside to the garden well. As she turned the corner, she came upon the sight of the Dutchman, stripped to the waist and digging with the shovel so as to rebury the dead priest. Upon sighting her, he paused to catch his breath, taking off his hat and running the back of his arm over his forehead. "Good morning," he called.

You must close your mouth, Juno, she told herself, and suited action to thought. His bare chest was well-muscled and broad, with tattooed markings up and down the length of his arms and on his torso, which was of a considerably lighter hue than his face and neck.

"You should not approach." With a gesture, he indicated the corpse.

"I won't," she assured him, striving mightily to keep her gaze on his face as opposed to the rest of him, but finding that she was not entirely successful. She lifted the bucket. "I will fetch some water for washing."

He nodded. "Can you start a fire?"

"Of course," she replied, and hoped this was true.

"Leave some water in the bucket, and set it near the fire when you are finished—I will cook the eggs."

"There is a mango tree just over there," she indicated helpfully. "Shall I fetch one?"

"Very good." After replacing his hat on his head, he bent to continue with his endeavors.

I should move, now, Juno thought, and tore her gaze from his muscled torso, chastising herself for shamelessness. But he was a fascinating sight, and he didn't seem at all concerned about the proprieties—which made the entire situation less awkward, all in all.

By the time he entered the kitchen, Juno had managed to slice the mango, and coax the water to a boil in the bucket. He carried the eggs in his felt hat, and it was apparent he'd washed at the well—his hair was wet, and his shirt clung to his skin where it was still damp. Genuinely curious, and deciding that he wouldn't mind the question, she asked, "The markings you have—are they significant for any reason, or just fanciful?"

"They are for sentiment," he teased, reminding her of what she'd said about Papa's pipe.

"Oh—oh, I see." She decided it wouldn't be appropriate to ask him to enlarge upon the subject—she very much feared he wouldn't hesitate to pull off his shirt again, and she truly shouldn't encourage such an action. Truly, she shouldn't.

After he'd soft-boiled the eggs, they took their wooden trenchers up once again and began their breakfast. The atmosphere had changed subtly; the Dutchman's trace of amusement—always present, it seemed—was no longer in evidence. Cracking her eggshell, she glanced at him, and found that he was contemplating her, his expression grave.

"When did you last hear from your father?"

So—he was afraid she didn't already know. She answered quietly, "I know he died of the cholera, in Madras."

Nodding, he lowered his gaze and she was suddenly aware, for reasons she could not explain, that he did not believe this to be true. A bit shocked, she ventured, "Is this not what you have heard?"

His met her eyes again. "It is what I have heard. I am sorry."

She gazed into his dark eyes for a long moment. "Thank you." She hadn't wept for her father—not yet, and perhaps not ever.

"The pipe—he gave it to you?"

"No." With conflicting emotions, she contemplated the trencher in her lap. "He mislaid it, when last he visited—I was going to give it to him when he returned." Unbidden, she had a sudden vision of the pipe in its usual waistcoat pocket, her larger-than-life father laughing in the loud way that he did, his thumb hooked in that same pocket. Overcome, she bent her head and began to cry, her hand covering her eyes; wholly embarrassed.

"Ach, Juno." Her companion slid over to sit beside her stool, and take her hand in his. "I am sorry—I should not have said."

After weeping silently for a few moments, she wiped her cheeks with the back of her hand and took a shuddering breath to steady herself. "No, no—it is only so hard to believe, I suppose; he—he always seemed so invincible."

"Me, I do not know what this means," he confessed.

She contemplated him through her tears, thinking about it. "It means it seemed nothing could harm him."

He nodded, thoughtful. "Yes. He was a good friend. I will not find another one like him."

The sincere accolade gave her pause; it did not gibe with her assumptions about the relationship between her father and this man. Noting that he still held her hand, she gently withdrew it, and decided she may as well ask. "Did the two of you have business ventures together?"

Ah—she could see that he became wary, all of a sudden, and he answered carefully, "Your father and me, we shared many adventures."

Yes, she thought with some bitterness—I imagine you did. She thought of the diamonds, and of her journey ahead, and the wrongs that must be made right, and wished she could go back to how things were before that terrible, terrible morning; when the Lloyd's investigator came to tell her of Papa's death, and that there were a few questions, if she wouldn't mind answering them as best she could.

"We go to see your brother, yes?"

She broke away from her melancholy reverie to answer him. "Yes, please."

"You should bring your things," he directed. "We will not come back."

This was not a concern. "I'm afraid all my things were destroyed by the Mughals."

They regarded each other, and Juno was aware he knew very well why the looters had ripped up her valise, and shredded all the clothes within. Lifting her chin, she stood and brushed off her skirts. "I shall have to purchase some clothes at the commissary, I suppose, to replace what was lost."

Donning his hat, he indicated she was to follow, as he walked out the door into the bright sunlight. "Me, I will pay for these clothes."

Following him down the front steps, she disclaimed, "Thank you for such a kind offer—" she'd seen no indication he carried any money "—but it will not be necessary; Horry should have some funds at the fort—enough to tide us over, certainly."

"Do not be so foolish." He glanced sidelong at her, the amused gleam back in place. "The money, it will be a loan."

"I'm afraid I cannot allow you to buy my clothes." She followed him as they made their way across the yard, to the path that led to Fort William. "It would not be decorous."

He cocked his head, thinking; the long braid falling over his shoulder. "I do not know what this means."

"It means—it means it would not be proper," she explained, her cheeks a bit pink.

The look he gave her was dubious. "If it was my child, your father would do the same." He idly picked up a branch and broke off the leaves, fashioning a walking stick.

Knowing her father, this was indisputably true—but it was also indisputably true this man was not her father's age, being perhaps in his early thirties, although it was difficult to judge, due to his exotic appearance. Therefore, it was an entirely different matter, but she decided she didn't want to delve into further explanations. "As a loan," she conceded. "A private loan." She emphasized the adjective, and hoped he knew enough not to speak openly of such matters. "You must give me your direction, and I will make certain you are repaid."

"There is no need," he said easily, slicing at the underbrush with the stick, as they walked along the pathway. "Once we are in London, you can repay me."

She stared at his back, and found she had wildly conflicting emotions within her breast. "You are going to London with us?"

He spoke over his shoulder. "Assuredly. I must speak to your nabob."

Juno's acquaintanceship with this man was not long-standing, but his meek tone was enough to set off a warning alarm in her mind, and she nearly stumbled to catch up to him. "And why do you need to speak to my nabob?"

He turned to look down at her, his eyes wide and guileless. "You are ruined."

Utterly shocked, she was brought up short, but he continued walking. "Come, come," he chided over his shoulder, gesturing with his stick. "Make haste."

Hurrying to catch up once again, she said with a great deal of emphasis, "I assure you, Mr. Van der Haar—I am not ruined."

"Ruined," he repeated matter-of-factly, his gaze focused upward on the sunlight, filtering through the forest canopy.

"I think—" she offered, "—that this is another word you do not understand."

He cocked his head to contemplate her. "Yes? What does it mean?"

She could feel herself blushing hotly, and struggled with the explanation, all the while aware that he was enjoying himself hugely. "It means I have will have granted you a husband's rights, even though we are not married."

He looked forward again. "Ah. It is the wrong word, then."

"Compromised, I think, is the word you seek." Juno realized her error the moment she said the words.

"You are compromised," he corrected immediately, without breaking stride. "And now I must marry you."

"I am not compromised, either," she assured him firmly.

"Juno, Juno," he chided. "We stayed the night together—we ate, and we bathed."

Completely nonplussed, she stared at him, trying to decide if he was teasing her. "No one knows of this," she reminded him. "And no one need know."

He cast her a baleful glance. "Ach, Juno—I am the honest man." He couldn't quite contain a smile at this out-and-out falsehood, and she decided with some relief that he was indeed teasing.

"And what about your poor betrothed?" She tried to match his mock-serious manner. "You cannot marry the both of us."

"Me, I have no betrothed." He tossed the stick from hand to hand as though it were a sword. "I do not know why you say such a thing."

She didn't know whether to laugh, or be outraged. "You said so yourself just last night—you said you were to be wed."

"Me, I was speaking of you," he explained, as though speaking to a simpleton. "You must pay attention, Juno."

They walked a few more steps in silence, whilst she struggled with her emotions.

"I must explain this to your nabob," he continued with a serious air. "And allow him to thrash me, if he chooses."

The idea that the Nabob could thrash the dangerous specimen that walked beside her proved too much, and Juno placed her palms over her eyes and started to laugh, leaning over and unable to proceed until her merriment had ceased. "You are the most *absurd* creature," she gasped.

He stood and watched her, a smile playing around his lips. "You have a very sweet laugh," he observed. "I am glad to hear it."

Still smiling, she addressed him. "Mr. Van der Haar. . ."

"Jost," he corrected.

"Jost," she agreed, humoring him. "I beg of you—say nothing of this to anyone."

He contemplated her for a moment. "You must agree that we will wed, yes?"

Juno decided she would agree to no such thing, and that it was past time to throw him off balance, for a change. "I am worried that you only seek to lay your hands on my Papa's pipe."

But if she thought to disconcert him, she was to be disappointed. "Me, I wish only to see what you do with it," he replied easily. "If I wanted to lay my hands on it, Juno, I would have."

Her brow knit, she regarded him, bemused. "I wish I understood all this better than I do."

"You are doing very good," he offered kindly, and resumed walking.

4

"I've no idea how much the diamonds are worth," Juno concluded her recitation to Horry in a low voice. "But there are more than a few."

"May I see them?" Her brother, an apprentice clerk with the Government House, was recovering from a recent bout with malaria, and lay on a cot in the fort's infirmary. He was sixteen, and tall for his age, which only accentuated his too-thin, lanky frame. His hair—a darker brown than Juno's—lay damp against his forehead, and Juno had to hide her alarm; usually when the malaria-induced ague had run its course, Horry was restless, and refused to stay in bed. This time, he continued listless--even though the fever had broken--betraying only a small spark of interest when informed of the cache of diamonds. It seemed to his concerned sister that his fits of fever were more frequent of late, leaving him alarmingly weakened. It was this un-happy conviction that had fueled her desire to take him to England with all speed, and by any means necessary—even if it meant marrying the Nabob.

"I am afraid to show the diamonds to anyone," Juno admitted. "The priest was nearly beside himself, and I think the Mughals were after them—you should see what a shambles the place is, Horry—so I think it best to keep them out of sight, until they are delivered to the Nabob." She paused delicately. "And perhaps if we make the delivery, the Nabob will see his way to repaying the underwriters at Lloyd's—surely he will not begrudge us a diamond or two."

Her brother's brows drew together, and he stared at Juno in shocked disbelief. "You are not going to believe that those lies about Papa are true, are you?"

Unwilling to agitate him, Juno nevertheless ventured, "It does not look well, Horry—"

"No," her brother interrupted hotly, making an abrupt gesture with his hand that reminded Juno of their late father. "It is not true, Juno."

Dismayed, Juno dropped her gaze and contemplated her hands in her lap. "I know, Horry—I did not want to believe it either; but apparently the evidence is irrefutable."

"You didn't know him as well as I did," Horry insisted. "Papa would never have cheated anyone."

"But the investigator from Lloyds of London—the admiralty insurers—he told me of it himself, Horry. He said Papa sank his last two ships—or pretended to—so as to collect on the insurance money. Then he sold the ships and the merchandise for a secret profit. Why would the investigator create such a shocking tale, unless he was certain?"

"Then where is the money?" Horry asked with undeniable logic. "There would be a fortune somewhere, and there isn't."

But Juno was already well-aware that this was a mystery. "The investigator seemed to think that I knew where the money was, and threatened to make a scandal if I didn't lead him to it immediately—he hectored Sister Marie about it, too, unable to believe there was no fortune set aside somewhere for me. He was so disagreeable, Horry—I felt that for two pence he would have put me on the rack, until I confessed."

"Ridiculous," scoffed Horry. "You are teaching at a girl's school with a passel of nuns; obviously you have no fortune."

There was a pause, while the Payne siblings considered their bleak circumstances. Juno ventured, "It does seem providential that—out of the blue—I am entrusted with a fistful of diamonds to deliver to the Nabob. If he would help us—and as Papa's financier, I am certain he would— we could make amends, and scotch any scandal within the Company." This was a sensitive subject; Juno was hoping Horry would agree to stay on in London as a provisions clerk for the East India Company, but her brother wanted to be a sea trader, like their father. In light of the current state of his health, however, this seemed to be a recipe for a quick death, and Juno could not even begin to contemplate how unbearable life would be if she lost Horry, too.

But her brother was puzzling over another aspect of her tale. "Why would a priest be smuggling diamonds to the Nabob?"

"I haven't the first clue—he didn't say. But he was killed for his pains, so someone else must have known of them." Reminded, she asked, "Did Papa ever speak of a man—" she tried to decide how best to frame the subject "—a friend who was a pirate?"

Horry glanced up with interest. "Sir Jost?"

Juno blinked. "*Sir* Jost?"

"I've never met him, but Papa spoke of him often. I don't think he meant he was an *actual* pirate, Juno—it was a figure of speech; if he holds a title, he can't very well be a pirate."

As Juno had no doubt that Horry would soon discover the error of this assumption, she didn't correct him, but instead considered her brother with a knit brow. "What do you know of him—do you think he could have been involved in the scheme to defraud the insurers?"

"There was no scheme," Horry corrected her, exasperated. "And it sounded as though they were good friends, and sailed together, from time to time. Why do you ask?"

Deciding that Horry probably should not be regaled with the particulars, Juno explained vaguely, "Only that he has arrived on the scene, and I do not think it a coincidence." She realized that she was reluctant to explain to Horry that the Dutchman had known of the diamonds, or that the dying priest had implicated him in the attack.

The reasons for her reluctance did not bear scrutiny, and so she did not scrutinize them.

Bending an arm behind his head, Horry leaned back on the cot. "I hate to disabuse you, Juno, but if the diamonds belong to the Nabob, it seems unlikely he will give any of them to us out of the kindness of his heart; he's not a nabob for nothing."

Her color rising, Juno made her reluctant confession. "He did raise the topic of marriage."

Horry stared at her in frank astonishment. "To you?"

Unable to resist a smile at his evident horror, she chided, "Yes, to me—for heaven's sake, Horry, am I so repulsive?"

Horry was motivated to sit upright again. "More like *he* is repulsive, Juno—don't tell me you are considering such a thing; I'll not believe it."

"Please don't vex yourself, Horry, and lie down." Best not to confess that she had indeed been considering it— or was, as late as yesterday evening. Nor did she mention that suitors appeared to be thick on the ground, here in Bengal. "But you must admit the Nabob could be very helpful in dealing with the Lloyd's investigation, Horry— he is very powerful within the Company, and I didn't want to antagonize him."

Horry stared at her for a moment, then couldn't suppress a grin. "Good *God*, Juno."

She couldn't help laughing in response, and they laughed together, unaware they were no longer alone, until they were interrupted by the infirmary physician, who cleared his throat at the door. Juno looked up to see that the man was accompanied by Mr. Van der Haar—Sir Jost, more properly—who quite filled up the doorframe and the sight of whom inspired a breathless feeling within her breast. He looked no less out of place in the infirmary than he did in the convent school, but Juno was nonetheless aware that she had been unconsciously marking the time until she was once again in his company—not that she had any intention of considering his offer, of course. Nevertheless, she'd been inspired to purchase some perfumed scent, at the commissary.

"I *say*," Horry breathed in wonder.

The physician himself appeared a bit unsettled by this turn of events; he was a humorless man, with a brusque manner that Juno found at odds with his professed calling. "I understand you are acquainted with Sir Jost, Miss Payne."

He sounded as though he half-hoped she would refute such a claim, but Juno only smiled and replied, "Yes—Sir Jost was a friend of our father."

Impatient with these preliminaries, Sir Jost shouldered past the man to pull up a stool and shake Horry's hand. "Yellow jack?" he asked in a negligent manner.

This remark prompted a grin from Horry, as yellow fever was a deadly disease, and acutely contagious. "Only malaria, I'm afraid—I am pleased to meet you, Sir Jost; my father spoke of you often."

"You have the look of him," said the Dutchman, and Horry flushed with pleasure.

"Horatio and Juno," the physician observed in his dry voice. "A hero, and a goddess."

"Our mother admired the classics," Juno explained, rather wishing that she hadn't.

"That is all," Sir Jost abruptly addressed the physician. "You will leave us, now."

That worthy appeared startled at being thus dismissed, but bowed and retreated with a measured tread. Horry met Juno's eye with an expression that conveyed his intense admiration for someone who could so easily dispense with polite behavior, and Juno could not resist an answering gleam.

Jost then turned back to Horry. "So—can you eat?" He leaned in to lift Horry's eyelid, and check the white of his eye in a matter-of-fact manner.

"Not yet," Horry admitted, blinking in surprise.

Sir Jost leaned back, and regarded him thoughtfully. "Your sister, she is not a good cook."

Juno sat, horrified that he was going to expound on their stay together, replete with references to ruination and compromising, but no such exposition was forthcoming. Instead, Horry offered with another grin, "No. If she is pressed, she can make toast."

Their guest stretched his long legs out before him and pushed his hands into his pockets. "What is it you like to eat? The best thing?"

Horry considered. "Papa and I would go fishing off his skiff, when he was in port. Sometimes we would catch a skipjack tuna."

"Ah," Sir Jost nodded. "That is good fish."

Remembering, Horry continued, "If we caught one, we'd pull the skiff on shore, and cook it over a pail of hot coals—it was the best meal imaginable."

"Me, I like the tuna with the pepper sauce." Jost contemplated the wall for a moment, dwelling on this imaginary meal. "Juno's toast—maybe it needs the pepper sauce."

"I shall hear no more of your aspersions," laughed Juno. It occurred to her that Horry's spirits had risen considerably since their guest had walked into the room, and she cast him a grateful glance, only to find his own gaze warm upon her. He doesn't know that he shouldn't look upon me in such a way, she thought in confusion—or he is aware and doesn't much care, which is more likely the case. To cover this breach, she announced, "Sir Jost will accompany us to London, Horry."

"Capital," said Horry, surprised, but willing to be enthusiastic. "What's the ship?"

"Me, I will tell you soon." In his abrupt manner, Jost rose to take his leave. "Come, Juno, we must be busy."

He doesn't know he shouldn't use my Christian name, either, thought Juno as she bade goodbye to Horry—and I should explain this to him, or people will believe that we are indeed betrothed. She glanced at him sidelong, as they made their way to the infirmary's entry. I can't very well be betrothed to a pirate, she thought firmly, and I definitely dare not trust him—not until I find out how he's involved in all this, and what he knows about the diamonds.

"This way, Juno." Her companion walked outside, into the bright Bengal sunlight.

Without demur, she hurried to follow him.

5

After leaving the infirmary, Juno waited beside Jost, whilst he stood for a moment in the dirt yard outside the garrisons, apparently lost in thought. Several passersby in the immediate area stared with frank curiosity, but he seemed unaware of their scrutiny, and Juno strove to be as unconcerned as he, as though keeping company with a Barbary pirate was something completely routine for her. The day before, he'd escorted her only as far as the exterior gate, and then had excused himself, citing his intention to see to some arrangements on the dock. This had relieved Juno to no end, as she had been trying without much success to come up with an explanation for his accompanying presence. After this morning, however, it all seemed rather moot. She could always claim him as a friend to her father, but that may not be the best course to take, either—although she would very much like to see the Lloyd's investigator try to harass Sir Jost.   She had little doubt as to who would emerge the victor from such an altercation.

"Your brother," her companion interrupted her thoughts, his hands on his hips as he gazed into the distance. "He is sicker this time, yes?"

"Yes—and I am longing to take him to England; how soon do you think we can leave?"

"Very soon." A passing soldier tugged at the brim of his hat, and Jost nodded in acknowledgment. "Come, we go to the Purser's Office, now."

She fell into step beside him, finding that she was more than willing to accompany him on whatever errand he contemplated. "Do you have business with the Purser?'

"You do," he replied in his easy manner. "We will ask questions about the money for you and your brother."

She thought this over as she walked beside him, hurrying to keep up with his long strides. "Do you think there may be a pension, of some sort?"

"I know not," he replied. "But we will see."

This did seem prudent, considering they would be leaving for England soon, and so she asked no further questions, but instead apologized, "I was not aware that you held a title."

"I did not mention?" He glanced down at her in surprise, his expression guileless.

"No," she confirmed, hiding a smile. "You should have corrected me, when I addressed you improperly."

He shook his head, chiding her gently. "Juno, Juno; you must not be impressed by such things; the Nabob's riches, the titles."

Struggling to maintain her countenance, she insisted, "It is not that I am impressed by such things—it is the proper protocol."

He tilted his head toward hers. "Me, I do not know what this means."

"It means the right way of doing things, I suppose. The rules."

"Ah," he said. "Decorous."

"I think—" she opined as they walked past the garrison wall, gleaming white in the mid-morning sun "—that you enjoy teasing me."

"Yes." He turned his head to observe her with his flashing smile. "The color, it comes to your face."

Blushing hotly, she could only look away and try to control her smile, which seemed irrepressible, when in his company. Another soldier passed by. "Cap'n," the man said, tugging on the brim of his hat in a respectful fashion.

"You are well-known," Juno observed as they walked along. "Are you indeed a captain?"

"When I sail a ship. Me, I have sailed many ships—some with your father."

"Do you have a ship docked here, in Calcutta?" She realized she was asking a great many impertinent questions, but found that she could not seem to help herself and besides, he was a pattern-card of impertinence, so it hardly mattered. She wished he would slow his pace; truly, it was a lovely day, and should be enjoyed at leisure.

"My ship, she is in Algiers, now."

This comment put a halt to Juno's idle questions, and reminded her that she needed to temper her inclination to tarry with him. Algiers was the bane of shipping in the Mediterranean—a hotbed of pirate activity, and infamous for its slave trade.

They entered into the Purser's Office, a small, fortified building that handled the fort's treasury and other monies on deposit. The young clerk behind the counter looked up, and smiled upon viewing Juno; she had met him previously, when he'd delivered her father's payments to the convent—on those occasions when her father remembered, that was. "Miss Payne, are you quite safe? I heard there was some unpleasantness at the school."

"Indeed I am," said Juno, thinking that "unpleasantness" did not even begin to describe it, but that it was very like the military to understate things. "It will take some work to set it back to rights, unfortunately."

"Allow me to aid you in any way I can—I stand at your disposal." The young man managed to drag his gaze from Juno long enough to give Sir Jost a perfunctory greeting.

Juno decided it would be best to turn the topic to the object of their visit, before the young man declared himself. "I would like to make an inquiry as to whether there are any funds on deposit for me or my brother—whether my father had any money, set aside."

"I already know the answer." The clerk shook his head with regret. "Mr. Finch was asking the same thing last week; he was very concerned about your future."

Mr. Finch was the Nabob, and Juno concluded, "There is nothing, then?"

"I'm afraid not—or at least, not here; I cannot speak for any arrangements that may have been made in Cutler Street." Cutler Street was the address for the East India Company's headquarters, in London.

Sir Jost spoke up. "There is no account for Juno? You are sure?"

"No, sir," the clerk confirmed. "I am sorry."

Juno thanked him and then, under Jost's amused eye, responded to the young man's shy inquiry by explaining she was temporarily residing at the women's quarters in the fort. They then took their leave, and once more Juno noted that her companion seemed distracted, as he stood for a moment on the stone steps, lost in thought.

But Juno had pieced together an explanation for his unusual interest in these matters, and prompted, "Are you searching for the bridegift you spoke about? Is that what this is all about?"

If she had surprised him by the question, he hid it well, and instead, indicated that they should walk forward, away from the building. Once in the courtyard, he replied, "Yes, I look for the bridegift—it is important that it be found."

Shaking her head, she said with all sincerity, "I can't believe there *is* a bridegift; surely my father would have mentioned it to me."

He met her eyes. "It is a secret, Juno. Even from you."

This seemed unlikely, as the whole point of a bridegift was to attract a husband. And besides, her father was not one to put money away; indeed, there were times when her boarding fees had been many months in arrears, with Sister Marie shaking her head over Juno's lackadaisical parent.

Her brow knit, Juno puzzled over her companion's acute interest—it was evident he was not best pleased by what the clerk had disclosed. She reminded herself that he was a pirate, and perhaps had been involved in the insurance fraud scheme—although Horry did not believe there was such a scheme, in the first place. Indeed, all things considered, it would not be surprising if Sir Jost was bent on stealing the bridegift—if it indeed existed. She glanced up at him, briefly, and was almost embarrassed to realize that she trusted him completely, and would stake her life that he intended no evil purpose. Surely the fact that he hadn't already wrested the diamonds from her proved this; and he'd been a friend to their father, and kind to Horry, just now. Truly—it all made little sense.

He interrupted her thoughts. "I must ask the promise from you, Juno."

His tone was serious, and she lifted her face to his in trepidation, wondering if he was going to start pressing his suit again.

"You must stay in the fort, today, yes? Do not walk outside."

So—apparently he wasn't going to start pressing his suit again, which was annoying in its own way. For a man who had proposed on such short notice yesterday, he certainly wasn't very lover-like today—and the perfumed scent had been rather expensive. With an effort, she focused on his request. "Do you think there is still a danger of attack, then?"

"It is the best to be safe," was all he would say, his hands clasped behind his back as they began to walk forward again.

"Then I do promise. I have no plans to leave, anyway— I thought to visit Horry later, and play cards, to pass the time."

But he could not like this plan, and raised his chin to contemplate the high turrets that flanked the fort's entrance. "You must not visit the infirmary again. Not today."

She teased him, "Then you leave me no choice but to go out walking with the Purser's clerk."

But she could not provoke a display of jealously, and instead, he threw her an amused glance. "Me, I do not worry."

She subsided in confusion, wishing she could be a bit less transparent. Truly, he shouldn't be so certain of her— after all, she wasn't even certain of herself. As they paused before the women's quarters, he soothed her sensibilities by bending his head to hers, and saying with a world of warmth, "Me, I would like to go walking with you, Juno, but I must be very busy, today."

Mollified, she asked a bit shyly, "I should like to hear your story, some time."

"Assuredly." His teeth flashed white as he contemplated her. "Although there are the parts I must not tell you." He tilted his head, thinking about it. "Maybe, I will tell you after we are married."

Juno found that she was unable to deny this assumption outright, and so instead she cautioned, "I'll remind you that I have not yet agreed to such a course."

"You will." With a parting gleam, he walked away, leaving her to gaze at his retreating form in bemusement.

6

"**J**uno—*lieve*, you must be quiet," Jost whispered from behind her head, as he held her struggling form against his chest.

In response, she kicked out wildly as he held her aloft, one hand over her mouth, and one arm clasped around her waist, like a band of iron.

"You must listen, yes?" he insisted, near her ear. "It is important."

She subsided, mainly because she was having trouble drawing breath, between his hand over her mouth, and the paralyzing realization that she had misjudged her man. Gauging her moment, she brought her heel against his shin with as much strength as she could muster.

Grunting, he shifted his hold so that she could not repeat the attack. They were in her room at the women's quarters, where she had awakened to the terrifying sight of his form looming over her in the darkness; his breath on her face. On instinct, she'd scrambled out of the bed to make a dash for the door, and the current wrestling match had ensued, although it was more properly a mismatch, as she was now suspended helplessly.

"I am not going to hurt you, *lieve*—my promise."

Closing her eyes, she drew a long breath through her nose, and forced herself to calm down, her heart still hammering.

"We must go, and make haste," he said quietly into her ear. "Horry, too."

She placed her hands on the muscular forearm wrapped around her waist, and tapped her fingers to indicate he could put her down. Carefully, he complied, watching for her reaction, and ready to recapture her, if she showed an inclination to escape.

After drawing several gasping breaths, she turned to face him. "You frightened me," she accused, a bit ashamed by her overreaction.

"You frightened me," he returned, very much put-upon. "My leg, I think it is broken."

She had no sympathy, and rubbed her bare arms with her hands. "What has happened? Is Horry all right?"

"Horry is leaving this place tonight—it is not a good place for him."

She stared up at him in the dimness, completely astonished. "But—but he is not well enough to travel."

Her companion set his jaw a bit grimly. "He will never be well again, if he stays. You must gather your things and we will go. Make haste."

Nonplussed, she faltered, "You cannot mean that his physician is—is poisoning him, or some such thing; why, that is absurd."

But he'd moved over to stand beside the window, moving the curtain aside to take a cautious look down below. "There is no time to argue. Come, come; gather your things, and we go out the window."

She stared at him. "I—I can't go out the window in my nightdress."

"It is not a good nightdress," he pointed out. "You must find a better one."

Blushing to the roots of her hair, she noted with some irony, "I beg your pardon; I did not foresee that I would be entertaining anyone in it."

"We have no time to discuss the bed sport," he chided her. "Make haste."

Bewildered, and very much fearing she was going to do whatever he asked, she ran her hands through her disordered hair. "Where do you mean to go?"

He fixed his dark gaze on hers, completely serious, for once. "Me, I am going to find out who killed your father."

She stared at him for a few stunned moments, as the words hit home. "Well then," she said briskly, "let us make haste."

Stepping over to the narrow cot, he pulled the pillow case from the pillow. "If you wish to dress, do it quickly." He then crossed over to the wardrobe, and pulled the only two dresses she owned off their hooks, so as to stuff them in the pillowcase.

"I'll wear that one," she indicated, and when he tossed it to her, she decided she should cling to whatever shreds of propriety that were left. "You must turn your back."

He did, and whilst she scrambled out of her nightdress and into her linen shift, he asked, "Where is the pipe?"

"I have it in my glove, still."

Considering this, he decided, "Me, I will put it in my boot."

This did not seem wise; and Juno knew a moment's qualm—although certainly, if his intent was to steal the diamonds, there was no need even to wake her. "I—I promised the priest I would not entrust them to anyone," she explained diplomatically. "It is not that I don't trust you, but I should not break a promise to a priest."

"He was no priest," her companion replied, but made no further argument. Between them, they managed to securely tie the glove on a shoestring around her neck. Although she stood in her shift for this procedure, he betrayed no consciousness of this fact, and efficiently lowered her frock over her head at its conclusion, leading her to believe he was well-versed in the dressing of women.

Having no time to comb her hair, she ruthlessly twisted it into a knot at the nape of her neck as he approached the window, and lifted the sash as far as it would go. He then held up a cautioning hand to her, and listened with his head out the window for a few moments. "We go," he advised, and threw a leg over the window sill, the pillowcase with her clothes bundled under his arm, and dropped to

the ground. He gestured to her from below, and after closing her eyes tightly, she leapt into his waiting arms.

"You must follow and stay quiet, yes?"

She nodded, and did as he directed, expecting him
to head toward the infirmary as they skirted the walls of
the buildings, staying in the shadows so as to avoid any
patrolling soldiers. Instead, however, he seemed intent
on reaching the perimeter wall that surrounded the fort.
Once there, he pressed close to the wall and hurried toward the water gate entrance, the one nearest the dock.

As she tried to keep up with him, Juno wondered how
he planned to extract Horry, and was acutely aware that
she was not cut out for this sort of adventure—she was very
much afraid that they would be discovered, and seized at
any moment. On the other hand, this type of skulking
seemed very natural to Jost, so perhaps she should become
accustomed—if she planned to accept his offer, at some
point. Not that there seemed any chance that anyone else
would have her, after this latest compromising—not even
the Purser's clerk.

Her distracted thoughts were interrupted by the realization that they now approached the water gate, manned
by soldiers who—one would think—would not allow Juno
to pass unremarked. She hurried closer to Jost, awaiting
instruction, but he only kept up his progress in the shadows, and boldly approached the soldier who stood at the
pass-through door, that allowed for foot traffic.

Juno stood behind Jost as the soldier, wooden-faced,
opened the door for them without comment. Glancing up

as she passed, she saw the sentry exchange a significant look with her escort.

"Was that a friend?" she asked in a whisper, after they'd cleared the dry moat that surrounded the fort. It seemed that they were headed to the river, and the air began to stir, and feel cooler.

"Me, I have many friends," he explained in a low tone. "You must say no more until I tell you, *lieve.*"

Silently, Juno followed him, staying to the edge of the vast maidan, as they crossed toward the River Hooghly, with the moonlight illuminating their progress, and the night insects making their usual racket. Ahead, Juno could see several soldiers guarding the dock, and blushed to think how it would look—what with her creeping out of the fort with Jost in the dead of night—but before they came to the dock, he deviated from the path, and descended the bank toward the river. Turning, he offered a hand to her, so that she didn't slip down the grassy slope, and then did not release her hand as he led her to the water's edge.

A small skiff was secreted among the reeds, and Jost first saw her seated in the stern, and then pushed off and climbed in himself, taking up the oars. Juno decided she could remain silent no longer, and whispered with some anxiety, "I cannot leave Horry behind, you know."

"You will not," he assured her, and then motioned for her to be quiet, as he rowed away from the shore and up the river, the oars making a lapping sound. If Juno hadn't been having second thoughts about the wisdom of her actions this evening, she would have enjoyed it very much—the moonlight on the placid river, with the plying of the oars the only sound. As it was, she could only sit in silent anxiety, fingering the pipe beneath the fabric of her dress, and hoping it wouldn't be necessary to leap out of the boat, and swim to shore. After a few minutes, she realized that their destination was an unlit schooner, anchored off-shore in the river ahead. Once they came alongside, Jost instructed her in a low voice to climb up the rope ladder that hung against the hull.

Juno swallowed hard and obeyed, balancing in the skiff as she grasped the ropes, with Jost standing astride behind her. I hope, she thought as she made her way up the ladder whilst he held it steady, that I am not making a monumental mistake. For reasons that cannot withstand scrutiny, I am reposing complete trust in a man who can only be described as piratical, and who has abducted me twice, thus far.

Her fears appeared to come to immediate fruition when the man at the gunwale who helped her on board was revealed to be her nemesis, the Lloyd's of London investigator. "Miss Payne," the man greeted her in an ironic tone. "Welcome aboard."

Acutely dismayed, Juno nodded, and then looked to Jost, who vaulted onto the vessel to stand beside her. "Where is Horry?" she asked in a small voice, fervently hoping she had not walked into a trap.

"He is below," the Dutchman assured her. To the investigator he said, "There will be time for questions tomorrow—let us be underway."

"Where—where are we underway?" faltered Juno.

"Madras." Jost indicated she was to follow him, and they clambered down the companionway stairs toward the small cabin that was situated at the bow of the schooner. Upon opening the cabin door, she beheld the welcome sight of Horry, already asleep on one of the two narrow berths.

Relieved beyond measure, she watched her brother sleep for a moment, Jost standing silently beside her. She asked in a whisper, "What is in Madras?"

"Many questions—perhaps a few answers."

She met his eyes and, after a moment, nodded, although she wasn't certain to what she was agreeing.

"We will talk in the morning, yes?" He leaned down to gently kiss her mouth, as though it was the most natural thing in the world. "Good night, Juno."

7

"**A**re you awake yet, Juno?"

She wasn't, but she could hear in Horry's voice the desire that she wake up forthwith, and so she made a mighty effort. Opening her eyes, she gazed at the cabin ceiling, and felt the boat's movement. "I'm awake."

Turning her head, she saw Horry, propped up on an elbow and regarding her from across the narrow space between their berths, his brows drawn together. "Sir Jost thinks Papa was murdered."

Dismayed that Horry was privy to this unsettling theory, and wishing she had been given a few more minutes to gather her sleepy wits, Juno replied, "Yes—although we don't know why, and we mustn't jump to conclusions, Horry."

But Horry was not yet done, and added in outrage, "He thinks that someone may have been trying to kill me."

"That does seem unbelievable," she cautioned faintly. "Pray do not upset yourself."

"It's beyond *anything*," her brother flashed. "Despicable."

"I cannot imagine the fort's physician—" Juno ventured, but was interrupted by her brother, who could no longer be described as listless.

"Are you all right, Juno? He said you've had a rough time of it."

A bit taken aback, she assured him that she had managed to survive the various perils to which she had been exposed over the past several days.

Her little brother reached over and clasped her arm with his hand. "He reminded me that—with Papa gone—I am now responsible for you."

Juno assimilated this change in his attitude with some bemusement. "I appreciate it, Horry—truly I do."

He swung his legs over the edge of the berth. "Let's go above, shall we?" He paused, considering his new responsibilities. "I'll wait outside, and allow you to dress first."

"Do you feel well enough?"

"Juno," he admonished, filled with new resolve. "We don't have time to rest; we have to find out what is afoot."

When they emerged on deck, it was to see Jost at the helm, in quiet conversation with the investigator, their heads bent together. Two other sailors were manning the sails, and looked upon Juno with barely-concealed curiosity.

Shading her eyes against the bright sunlight, Juno reviewed the lush shoreline to the starboard side, as the schooner skimmed along, on its way down the east coast of India toward Madras. In this area, the subtropical forest came all the way to the shoreline, and the day birds could be heard chattering in the canopies—a familiar sound to anyone who'd lived in the region. She and Horry went over to join the two men, and with palpable reluctance, Juno introduced her brother to the tender mercies of the Lloyd's investigator. "Horry, this is Mr. Landon."

But the lean, saturnine gentleman rose and replied with some stiffness, "Miss Payne, I must apologize if my manner was a bit overbearing, when last we met."

Nonplussed by this turnabout, Juno refrained from sliding a speculative glance at Jost. Instead, she said graciously, "Pray think nothing of it, Mr. Landon—I understand that it is a vexing problem."

As they settled into the cockpit, Horry asked Jost, "May I take the helm?"

"You may not," the other replied easily. "To the stern, there is a fishing line. Catch us a skipjack, if you please."

"Capital." Horry needed no further encouragement, and moved toward the back of the schooner, steadying himself by grasping the shrouds along the way.

"Boy needs to eat," commented Landon, watching him go.

Juno nodded in agreement, having suppressed an urge to ask Horry to sit quietly and rest; apparently, she was not to fuss over him, any longer. She thought about Jost's theory—that Horry was being poisoned—and found she had to take her gaze away from her too-thin brother, because she couldn't bear thinking about it.

"Landon would ask a question of you, Juno."

Juno blushed, aware that she should have already put an end to Jost's use of her Christian name. Hopefully, he wouldn't compound the transgression by invoking the endearment he had used multiple times the night before.

The investigator fixed his gaze upon her. "Have you married, Miss Payne?"

Juno blinked, thinking this entirely unexpected. "No, sir."

"Are you certain?" the man persisted.

Perplexed, Juno pointed out, "I believe I would be not be in any doubt, if such an event had occurred, sir."

The investigator drew his brows together and regarded her for a moment. "Can you tell me when you last spoke with Mr. Finch?"

A bit confused by this reference to the Nabob, Juno answered, "It was about a week ago. He came to the school shortly after your own visit, when you told me of Papa's death. He did speak of marriage—he explained that the protection of his name would go a long way toward helping to scotch any scandal. But I assure you, there has been no wedding ceremony."

"Did he express an intention to travel to Madras?"

Juno shook her head in puzzlement. "No—he claimed pressing matters in London, and he traveled ahead, to lease a house for Horry and me. Did he indeed travel to Madras?"

The man leveled a stern look upon her. "I will ask the questions here, Miss Payne."

Jost turned his head to consider the investigator dispassionately, and after a few moments the other man cleared his throat and capitulated. "Yes—he did travel to Madras. And I have received word that a marriage license has been filed with the British authorities at Fort St. George."

Thoroughly astonished, Juno could only look from one man to the other in disbelief. "Why—I know nothing of this."

"The license indicates the marriage was performed by the priest who was killed at the school, but my investigation reveals that the deceased man was not, in fact, a priest."

Juno recalled that Jost had said as much, and exclaimed in bewilderment, "I suppose you believe this was an attempt to lay claim to the bridegift, but it makes little sense—it would be a simple thing to disprove such a plot. Why, I need only attest that no marriage took place, and the Nabob would forfeit any bridegift—real or imagined."

"Unless—" the investigator offered gravely, "—unless you were deceased, and unable to make such a refutation."

There was a small silence whilst Juno tried to assimilate what was meant as the schooner swept through the water, and the birds could be heard chattering on shore. "You think—you think Mr. Finch meant to have me *killed?*" With no small alarm, she looked to Jost, who met her eyes, the expression in his own very serious. "The Mughals were sent to kill me? No—the Mughals killed the priest, so surely they were not complicit in the scheme."

"No; I believe the Mughals were not aligned with Mr. Finch," agreed Landon.

But Juno was distracted, finding the man's accusations implausible. "But surely—Mr. Finch is one of the East India Company's Directors, and a wealthy nabob. It is hard to imagine he would resort to such despicable measures, to lay hands on any paltry bridegift."

"There is nothing paltry about your bridegift, Miss Payne," corrected Landon.

Juno looked from one man to the other but neither spoke, and she was given the impression they were reluctant to impart any more information. Nevertheless, she managed to drawn her own conclusions. "You believe the bridegift is connected to the insurance fraud—that Papa was depositing the fraudulent funds under my name, so that it could not easily be found." This seemed evident; as Horry had pointed out, if Papa was fleecing the insurers out of a fortune, then where was the fortune? Unfortunately, this also indicated that Papa was indeed involved in the illegal scheme, and her heart sank. "And—and I suppose if the Nabob is willing to have me killed to secure the bridegift, that means he knew about the insurance scheme, and seeks to hide his own complicity."

"Best not to speculate, Miss Payne—"

But Juno had leapt ahead, and was now staring at Jost. "You think the Nabob murdered Papa—murdered him for double-dealing, and hiding the money from him."

Juno could see Landon shift uncomfortably, as though concerned about what Jost would disclose, but Jost confirmed her suspicions with a nod. "The Nabob, or someone else, on the Nabob's orders."

Juno held her hands to her face, horrified by the dawning realization. "I would have married my father's murderer."

Awkwardly, Landon offered cold comfort. "There, there, Miss Payne—chances are you would have died before you ever found out."

"No—he would have died first," Jost assured them. "Very slow."

While Juno could appreciate this bloodthirsty sentiment, she was still trying to come to terms with this disturbing news. "Why on earth would someone like the Nabob become involved in such a fraudulent scheme? And risk everything he has?"

Landon answered smoothly, "I'm afraid we can only speculate until further information is discovered; however, it would be best to present you at the court in Madras without delay, to refute any professed marriage."

She nodded in understanding, trying to hide her extreme dismay. Clearly, she stood in grave danger, since only she could denounce the marriage, and apparently there was a great deal of money at stake. And in addition, her testimony would immediately put the Nabob under suspicion—perhaps even expose his dark doings. Small wonder Jost had swept them away in the dark of night, and had hired this swift schooner, instead of a more comfortable vessel.

Horry re-joined them, barefoot and brandishing his catch. "Only a paltry carp so far—worse luck."

"Jairus, he can dress a carp to taste like a cod," Sir Jost assured him, and called to the sailor to perform this feat. The short, merry-looking man was revealed to be a cook, and he took the carp from Horry with such a show of mock-reverence that Horry laughed, and cuffed him.

Juno noted that Horry looked a bit weary, and patted the bench, resisting an urge to advise him to rest. Willingly, he settled in beside her, stretching his legs out before him and leaning his head to rest on the back of the bench, so as to feel the sun on his face. His color was much improved already, and she ran her hand over his head in a fond gesture.

Jost indicated a white scar that was exposed on the boy's bare leg. "Shark?" he asked in his negligent manner.

His eyes sparkling, Horry slanted him a glance. "No—tiger."

Impressed, the Dutchman raised his black eyebrows. "In truth, you outran a tiger?"

"No such thing," Horry grinned. "Juno killed it."

8

Both men turned their heads with one accord to stare at Juno, and neither attempted to conceal his astonishment. "Me, I will hear this tale," said Jost. "It is a *capital* tale," Horry pronounced with enthusiasm.

"Horry," Juno demurred, embarrassed.

But her brother had warmed to his role, and leaned forward, resting his forearms on his knees. "It was last spring, and we had just visited Chandannagar—up river— to see Papa, who was trading there. We were returning in the cart through a mangrove forest, when the monsoon started—you know how it is sometimes; a horrific deluge. The lightning cracked—" here he made a dramatic gesture with his hands "—and the poor horse panicked, and jumped over the traces. We were all overturned in a heap, and I broke my leg." He paused, grimacing in annoyance at the memory of such an inconvenient turn of events.

"Bad luck," Landon noted.

Recalling himself to the story, Horry continued, "The cart's axle was splintered, so Jacob unhitched the horse, and rode to get help, while Juno stayed with me under the umbrella." He shook his head, remembering. "It was *teeming*. Then we saw the tiger—my leg was scraped, and he must have smelt the blood, even in the rain." Horry's eyes glowed at the memory. "He was *huge*—-there was nothing like it. He circled 'round, growling, and Juno opened and closed the umbrella at him, trying to frighten him away, but he didn't flinch, and crouched to strike." Pausing, he candidly confessed, "I thought we were done for."

"Assuredly," agreed Jost.

"So Juno closed the umbrella, and when he leapt, she planted the hilt in the mud, and impaled him on the point."

There was a small silence. "*Verdomme*," Jost exclaimed.

But Horry was not yet finished, and added with great relish. "He landed on top of us, dead, and we were completely pinned—he was so heavy. There was blood *everywhere*."

"Horry," Juno cautioned faintly.

"She wouldn't let me keep the pelt," he added with deep regret. "I wish I'd taken it."

"There will be other tigers," Jost assured him.

Horry laughed at the unlikeliness of this. "I thought Jacob would faint, when he finally returned, and they had to roll the carcass off us."

Jost said to Juno, "This is how you came to have the scar on your arm, yes?"

"Yes," Juno admitted. There was a scar on the under-side of her upper arm—he must have been paying closer attention than he seemed, when she was in her shift. She hoped neither of the others paused to wonder how he knew of it.

Landon asked, "And your leg, Horry? Did it knit well?"

Horry lifted it to demonstrate, and flexed his foot. "It was a clean break—I was on crutches for a few weeks, and then I was up again—my scar is all that's left of that episode."

"There will be other scars," Jost assured him.

"I sincerely hope not," laughed Juno. "One is quite enough, if you please."

"Ach, Juno," said Jost in mock reproach. "The scars—they have the great interest for the women; it is the same as the tattoos." He slid her a meaningful glance.

Blushing, she hurriedly disclaimed, "Horry needs nei-ther scars nor tattoos, and you mustn't encourage him."

"Spoken like a sister," noted Landon, while the men folk—including Horry—exchanged amused glances.

Heavens, thought Juno; who is young man, and what-ever has happened to my little brother? She could not be alarmed, though—the change in his condition and out-look was nothing short of extraordinary, and the quick recovery only seemed to support Jost's theory that he had been deliberately poisoned. Wishing to discuss these mat-ters, she shot Jost a glance that hopefully conveyed her de-sire for private speech.

"Go—eat your carp," Jost directed Horry.

"I'd like to take the helm," Horry reminded him.

To Juno's surprise, Jost leaned forward so that his face was inches from Horry's. "You will obey orders. Now, go eat your carp."

Flushing, Horry nodded. "Yes, sir."

Landon rose to follow Horry down to the half-galley, and Juno offered in apology, "Horry's a bit headstrong, sometimes."

"On my ship, there are no strong heads," her companion replied in a mild tone, and glanced up to gauge the sails.

Aware that she was no longer to defend Horry, Juno conceded this point, and instead asked in a quiet tone, "I don't understand how Horry's being poisoned is connected to the search for the bridegift. He would have no claim to it, after all—it would go only to my husband."

"Horry, he would know you did not marry, so he must not be the witness."

"Oh—I see." It seemed such a callous calculation, but then it was clear they were dealing with evil people, who held life in little account. Nevertheless, she shook her head. "It seems a great deal of trouble to go to, when it is not at all clear that the bridegift truly exists."

"The bridegift, it exists." He lifted a tendril of her hair where it had caught on her cheek, and smoothed it back behind her ear. "We are sure of it, and so is the enemy."

This seemed a strange turn of phrase, and she frowned. "Who is 'the enemy'? Someone other than the Nabob?" He didn't answer immediately, but tried to tame the same tendril of hair that had escaped again—she could see that he debated whether or not to tell her. "Can't you say? You are very mysterious, for a suitor."

He tilted his head. "Me, I do not know what this means."

"A man who seeks marriage—and do not change the subject, if you please."

"The French," he said.

She knit her brow. "Who is French?"

"The French, they are the enemy," he explained patiently. "You must pay closer attention, *lieve*."

Staring at him, she wondered if she had misheard. "The French? The French are trying to poison Horry?"

"Do you know who Napoleon is?"

This seemed a non sequitur, and she struggled to keep up. "For heaven's sake—of course I do." She paused. "Hasn't he been executed, or something?"

With a grave expression, Jost explained, "He has been captured, but it is believed he will escape soon. His people are collecting money to make this happen."

But this was too implausible for Juno, who regarded him with stark disbelief. "The Nabob is collecting the bridegift for *Napoleon*?"

"Assuredly," said her companion matter-of-factly.

Juno watched him for a moment as he adjusted their heading, but try as she might, could not find the logic in this theory. "Why would the Nabob do such a thing? He isn't French, certainly—why, it would be treason, and he would be hanged."

"The French, they hold his debts. The Nabob continued to trade when it was stopped—" the Dutchman made a gesture indicating he could not think of the correct word in English.

"The embargo," offered Juno, beginning to understand. "He traded in violation of the embargo, the French secretly financed him, and now—now he cannot risk exposure." She frowned, thinking this over. "Nevertheless, to think that an Englishman would do such a thing—it defies belief."

"He is not a good man," Jost offered. "Me, I am not surprised."

Reminded, Juno suddenly gasped. "The dead priest was French—and he wanted me to bring the diamonds to the Nabob."

"Yes," her companion agreed. "But he was not a priest, *lieve.*"

It was so fantastic as to be almost unbelievable, except for the fact that it had indeed happened; her father had died, everyone thought there was a fortune hidden in her name somewhere, the faux priest was desperate to smuggle diamonds to the Nabob, and Horry had been the victim of a poisoning attack. Much shaken, Juno tried to assimilate these ominous events, as Jost absently stroked the back of her head, even though the calluses on his fingers kept getting caught in her hair. Leaning away from him, she said gently, "You mustn't, you know."

"Ach, Juno—" he protested, "—we are nearly wed."

"No, we are not." She smiled, to soften the rejection. "And you mustn't kiss me, either."

The dark, guileless eyes widened. "Did I kiss you?"

She decided it was past time to match him at this game, and copied his negligent shrug. "Well, it wasn't much of a kiss—I am not surprised at all that you do not remember."

In response to this challenge, he leaned forward, and met her eyes. "The next time," he assured her, "you will not complain."

She had not reckoned on the effect that his intense, heated gaze would have on her midsection, and she very much feared that if he wanted to demonstrate an unforgettable kiss, she would have gladly allowed him the liberty on the spot. Instead, this promising discussion was curtailed by Landon, who cleared his throat as he rejoined them. "Boy's eaten, and now he's asleep."

"Oh—oh, is he? I am so glad," Juno stammered, blushing.

"A likely lad," Landon observed as he sank down into the cockpit across from them. "Full of juice—he'll make captain, someday."

But Juno shook her head. "He has malaria, I'm afraid; instead I am hoping he will be apprenticed as a provisions clerk." With some disquiet, she noted that both men regarded her with amused sympathy.

"If you say," agreed Jost in an indulgent tone.

Juno subsided, and gazed out over the water as the vessel skimmed along close to the wind, her emotions mixed. It was evident that she no longer had the order-ing of Horry, and she very much feared the others had the right of it—her brother was no clerk. He loved the sea, as had their father, but it was a perilous existence and she wished—oh, how she wished—that they could live one of those lives one reads about; a safe, comfortable life in England. I would like to grow roses, she thought wistfully, having seen pictures of them.

She glanced at Jost, who'd looked up to gauge the sails again. The movement exposed his thick, muscular throat, and she had to look away quickly, lest she sit and stare. She was fast coming to the conclusion that she would not object to a mutual future with this man—even though the very thought had been nothing short of incredible, when he'd first broached the subject. With an inward sigh, she admitted that there was not the smallest chance that Sir Jost Van der Haar would acquiesce to a safe, ordered life in England. Or even worse—that he would do so just to please her, and she would never forgive herself; it would be akin to keeping a tiger in a cage. I am not cut out for any of this, she thought, a bit crossly. I am constantly be-ing called upon to do something courageous, even though I am not at all brave. And I need to be a bit more cau-tious when it comes to him—there is always the chance that he is another one, like the Nabob, whose only aim is to take the bridegift for himself. His gaze met hers, and she acquitted him of such a motive—if he wanted to seize a fortune, he would simply do so; he was nothing if not straightforward.

"What is it you think of?" he asked in a soft tone.

"I am wondering what is to happen," she answered honestly.

He leaned forward to cover her hand with his, even though Landon watched. "All will be well, slayer of tigers. Me, I will see to it."

"Do we stop for provisions at Vishakhapatnam?" Landon asked. "We'll be running low, by then."

Jost shook his head. "Kakinada, instead—I must pick up a stray."

There was something in his tone that indicated to Juno he did not look forward to the task. "What sort of stray?"

"A troublesome one," was all he replied as stood to loose a sheet, and adjust the jib.

Adding a troublesome passenger at this juncture did not seem well-advised, and so Juno ventured, "Because, I suppose, we haven't enough troubles already."

He flashed his white smile. "Assuredly not."

9

J ost held Juno tightly, her back against his chest, and an arm around her throat, whilst Horry watched with interest from his position seated cross-legged on the deck. "Now, what is best?"

"The eyes," she responded dutifully, and made a tentative movement with her fingers behind her head, toward Jost's eyes.

"Very good." Jost was giving Juno a lesson in self-defense, having determined that she was deficient in this area after abducting her from the fort.

"I don't know if I could truly gouge out a person's eyes," Juno confessed.

But Jost gently squeezed the arm around her throat, for emphasis. "You must not delay; once he knows you mean to do this he will stop you—so you must blind him before he knows what you mean to do."

"Heavens," said Juno faintly.

Horry was skeptical, his chin resting on his hand. "I don't know, Sir Jost—Juno's not a fighter."

But Jost disagreed with a shake of his head. "There is a bruise on my leg the size of an egg. Your sister, she is a fighter—she only must learn what is best to do." Bringing his head forward, he advised her, "You should have gouged my eyes, that night at the fort."

"Next time," Juno promised, and Horry grinned.

Juno was released, and then turned by her shoulders to face the Dutchman. "Now, what is best?"

"The eyes again?" she guessed, making a gesture toward them. She would hate to do injury to them, though— they were so very attractive, especially when they were intent upon her.

"No, he will see you and stop you. Take your knee—up hard like this." Pulling her close, he indicated she was to bring her knee into his groin.

"Oh," exclaimed Juno, hot with embarrassment whilst Horry crowed with laughter. "I'd rather gouge the eyes, I think."

"You hit him here, and he will drop to the ground," Jost assured her, and looked to Horry for confirmation.

"I certainly would," Horry agreed, and Juno didn't know where to look.

"You will stay here, and practice with Horry," directed Jost. "Me, I must go ashore." They had anchored at the inlet near Kakinada the night before, and Landon had left in the skiff to replenish their provisions—although how this could be done in the dead of night remained unclear;

Juno suspected the new provisions had been stolen, as opposed to paid for. She was fast coming to the conclusion, given what she now knew, that Landon's talents were not necessary constrained to investigating insurance fraud—and neither were Jost's, for that matter.

"I will go with you," Horry announced, his eager gaze on the shoreline.

"You will stay with your sister." Jost pulled a pistol from his belt, and handed it to him. "Me, I do not expect trouble, but you and Landon are to set sail if anyone tries to approach. I will catch up to you."

After he visibly struggled with an urge to protest such a passive role, Horry nodded.

"You can obey orders?" asked Jost, not moving.

"Yes—yes, sir."

Jost nodded, satisfied. "Can you shoot?"

"Yes, sir—Papa taught me."

Jost raised his brows in approval. "Your father, he was the good shot; I know of only one who was better."

Pleased, Horry nonetheless confessed, "I am not as good as him."

"Landon has the command while I am gone." He gave Horry a level look, and the boy nodded his agreement, but Jost apparently believed more emphasis was needed, and bent his head to look into the boy's eyes. "It is important you obey orders, yes? A ship can only have one captain—even though Juno is your sister, and not Landon's."

"Yes, sir," Horry affirmed, chastened.

Jost took hold of the back of Horry's head and shook it slightly, to show there were no hard feelings. "You have the hot head, I think—you must learn, if you wish to be a captain."

"Yes, sir," Horry repeated with a small smile.

Satisfied, Jost turned to Juno. "Come, Juno—I will give you a pistol also."

Pleased that he was willing to entrust her with a weapon, Juno followed him down the companionway and into the half-galley. Once there, he swung her out of sight against the bulkhead, lowered his head, and kissed her very thoroughly.

Completely surprised, she nevertheless responded—after a slight hesitation—by moving her hands over that impressive chest and softening her mouth against his; nearly melting with new and overwhelming sensations. It was a heady, heady experience, and it was he who broke away first, whilst she looked up at him in a breathless haze.

They gazed at each other for a long moment, and then he said softly, "Me, I could not sleep last night, thinking of the better kiss I must give to you."

"That was a better kiss," she assured him, struggling to recover the strength in her legs.

"Good." He leaned in to kiss her again, this time his lips gently tracing hers. "Me, I will practice."

"You mustn't," she reminded him automatically, and then ruined the effect by rising up on tiptoe so as to allow him to kiss her again. He smelt wonderful; like sea and sun and man.

"Me, I must go. Do not kiss anyone while I am gone."

She nodded, bemused. "Where is my pistol?"

"I have no pistol for you, *lieve*," he explained patiently. "Me, I wanted to kiss you."

She laughed, and he laughed in return, then laid a hand against her cheek and left. She stayed where she was for a full minute, hoping her color would return to normal before she confronted the others again. When she went to rejoin Horry, it was to find he had decided to do some more fishing from the stern, in the relatively quiet inlet. At her approach, he glanced up. "It's not a good time of day for it, but perhaps I can snag a sturgeon or two for supper."

Settling down beside him, Juno ruched up her skirts, and dangled her legs off the stern to watch as he baited the hook and dropped the line into the water. "Horry, did Papa ever speak to you of a bridegift—or any sort of account set aside for me?"

"Landon has already gone over this with me." Horry played with the line between his bare toes then glanced over at her, his eyes sparkling with mischief. "Are you going to need a bridegift, soon?"

Her color rising, Juno did not dignify the question with a response, but instead related to Horry what she had learned from the men that morning; she felt he had the right to know. She concluded, "They seem to think the Nabob was behind the plot against your life, and that he was going to seize the bridegift and murder me, also; it appears the bridegift is actually the money from the insurance fraud scheme."

Horry had fixed his gaze upon hers during this recital, and now issued a low whistle, as he turned back to watch the fishing line. "Infamous; Papa always said the Nabob was a curst rum touch."

"Did he? Well, it gets worse—Sir Jost seems to think the whole scheme was a means to funnel money to Napoleon."

Drawing his brows together, Horry looked to her with an expression of incredulity. "Napoleon's in exile, Juno—little help the money would be to him."

Almost afraid to speak it aloud, Juno revealed, "They think he will attempt an escape soon."

Horry stared at her. "Well, that tears it; Papa definitely would have no part of anything that helped the enemy—no matter how much they paid him. He must have been trying to stop them; I imagine that is why he was killed."

"Why, yes—yes, of course; you are right." Feeling slightly ashamed, she lowered her gaze to watch the sunlight reflect off the shifting surface of the water. "I should have known; I should have trusted Papa, instead of assuming the worst."

Horry was silent for a moment, fingering the fishing line. "It is so hard to believe that he is gone. I keep expecting him to appear the way he used to—with no warning, and wanting to go fishing."

Juno put a hand on his arm and squeezed gently. It was true; Horry had spent more time with him than she, and the loss was more acute for her brother. "I miss him, too."

Pensive, Horry continued, "I wish I had something of his—his pistols, or the skiff we took fishing; just to remember him."

Juno rubbed his arm in sympathy. "Recall I have his pipe, Horry—it is yours, once the diamonds are delivered."

"The diamonds." Horry turned to her, reminded. "You can't take the diamonds to the Nabob, Juno."

"No, of course not—not now that I know what he is."

Thinking about this, Horry asked, "If you aren't going to give them to the Nabob, then what are you going to do with them?" Her brother jerked quickly on the line, hoping to make a snag, but it appeared no curious fish were lurking around the hook.

Juno had been thinking about this herself. "I don't know, Horry—I suppose I must turn them over to the authorities."

"Could you ask Sir Jost? I think he could be trusted to help—perhaps you should ask him."

"He already knows of the diamonds," she confessed. "He guessed that I had them."

The fish forgotten, Horry stared at her in surprise. "However did he guess such a thing?"

Focusing on the rippling water, Juno realized she had no answer. "I am not certain, but I think he was in Bengal in the first place because he was looking for them."

In the time-honored tradition of brothers, Horry teased, "Oh? It seems more like he was looking for you—and he can't seem to stop, I might add."

As gratifying as this observation was, Juno felt she should disclaim for form's sake. "Nonsense, Horry—he was Papa's friend, and so naturally he has an interest in us."

Her brother slid her an amused glance. "Well, he doesn't ask many questions about me, but he asks plenty about you."

Betraying her true feelings on the subject, Juno cautioned, "Don't tell him anything off-putting, for heaven's sake."

With a smile, Horry turned back to his line. "I'm glad you like him; he's a great gun—he is going to teach me how to throw a knife."

Juno thought this an unusual aspiration, and asked in surprise, "How is this? When did he throw a knife?" There was a small silence, and she could see that Horry debated whether or not to tell her, so in the time-honored tradition of sisters, she pressed him mercilessly. "Horry—confess."

"We did have a tight moment during the escape from the fort—I've been cautioned not to relate the particulars to you."

With an effort, Juno suppressed her alarm. "I see."

"He's a great gun," Horry repeated, as he tugged on the line again. "Papa liked him." It was clear that for her brother, this was enough.

"I imagine they were kindred spirits," Juno agreed—even though the similarities between the merchant captain and the Barbary pirate were not obvious at first glance. "I wonder how they became acquainted."

"He turns the subject when I ask; he says he will tell me when I am older."

Juno raised her eyebrows, considering this. "He is rather mysterious."

"I'll bet if you asked him, he'd tell you." Her brother shot her a look. "He thinks you are something like."

"I *am* something like," Juno agreed, teasing.

Horry laughed and then re-focused his attention on snagging their dinner. They lapsed into companionable silence, the lapping of the water against the hull the only sound.

10

Juno was struggling to school her features, and she could hear Horry make a strangled sound, beside her. They were being introduced to Jost's stray, a young woman named Aditi, who was making no attempt to feign any pleasure upon making their acquaintance.

She is very young, thought Juno with some surprise; indeed, the girl appeared to be younger than Juno. But more unsettling was the clothing she wore—or more accurately, did not wear. She looked to be of Indian descent, and wore a cotton sari so thin as to be nearly transparent, with a sleeveless blouse that seemed an afterthought, as it was cut low in the neckline, and cropped so that her midriff was bared, leaving little to the imagination. The girl's heavily-kohled eyes were a striking amber color, and her lips were rouged so that they were the color of ripe berries. It seemed evident she was a concubine of some sort—not that Juno had ever met a concubine, of course—but it did seem evident.

Their new passenger appeared to be supremely uninterested in her new shipmates; her unreadable gaze rested for a moment on Horry, but passed over Juno and Landon with little curiosity.

Juno dragged her attention back to Jost, who was speaking to her. "—you have a dress for Aditi, yes?"

"Of course," Juno replied, while at the same time Aditi glanced at him sharply, and protested in another language. The Dutchman replied in a firm tone, and the girl subsided, sulking.

"Do you speak English, Aditi?" asked Juno, making a mighty attempt to pretend that being presented to a concubine was quite within the ordinary course of events.

"Yes," the girl admitted reluctantly, and offered nothing further.

"Come below with me, then, and I shall find you a dress." Juno gestured for the girl to follow her down the companionway steps.

"You will sleep with the crew," Jost directed Horry. "Aditi will sleep with Juno."

Juno noted that the girl glanced at him in disappointed surprise, her brows drawn together in a scowl. Surely, she hadn't planned on sleeping with Jost? A bit alarmed by the implications of this byplay, Juno descended into the cabin, and pulled one of her commissary dresses from the cupboard, shaking out its folds. "I understand you will travel to Madras with us, Aditi."

This caught the newcomer's attention, and the amber eyes deigned to focus on Juno. "He said you travel to England."

"Yes—after we first visit Madras."

Aditi lifted her chin in defiance. "I will *not* go to England."

At a loss, Juno replied, "I see."

The girl paused, considering the small porthole with narrowed eyes. "Does he?"

Oh, dear, thought Juno. "Why, yes—I believe he does."

Her companion was silent, but picked up Juno's brush without asking leave, and began to unbraid her long hair so as to brush it.

"I shall leave you to change your clothes," offered Juno, and as no answer was returned, she left the girl to herself, sliding the cabin door closed behind her. Once on deck, she let out a long breath, and looked about for Horry and Jost, but as they were deep in conversation on the aft deck, she decided not to disturb them. Instead, she made her way to the bow to join Landon, who was whittling a stick, and leaning against the railing.

He glanced up at her. "The cat's among the pigeons."

She had to smile, and decided it wasn't in bad taste to ask, "Who on earth *is* she?"

"Not a clue," was the man's abrupt reply. Casting a shrewd glance at her, he added, "I wouldn't jump to conclusions."

Striving not to blush at the implication, Juno decided to be honest. "No—I believe Sir Jost is not best pleased that she has joined us."

"Makes it interesting," he observed, and went back to whittling.

Juno left him to it, and settled in to sit on the deck with her legs tucked beneath her, looking out over the water. One thing about living on a boat, one needn't be too particular about the usual rules of protocol—not that the crew seemed to feel bound by such considerations in the first place. The four men evidenced an easy camaraderie—with Jost as their commander—and little was needed in the way of instruction, as though they all performed very familiar roles. Juno had also noted that Landon—the ostensible insurance investigator—deferred to Jost on the matter of the missing diamonds, even though he would have no cause to do so. Now that she was aware that the underlying impetus was to thwart Napoleon's plans for escape, she'd formed a tentative theory that they were all spies of some sort—although it seemed a bit too far-fetched to broach this theory to Horry. Certainly, if they did work for the Crown, Landon's pose as an insurance investigator and Jost's experiences as a Barbary pirate would be useful for infiltrating enemy schemes, such as the one they presently faced.

Absently, she pulled off a hanging thread from her hem, and dropped it onto the water so as to watch it drift away in the slow current. In light of this theory, she could find little sense in the addition of Aditi to their group; Landon did not know of her, and the girl did not appear to be one who would be useful to their cause. Indeed, it appeared quite the opposite—when Jost called her 'troublesome,' it seemed an apt description. *I fear I have little in common with the only other female on board,* Juno thought—*except for one thing.*

The one thing crouched down beside her, and as Juno glanced up at him, she noted that Landon had discreetly disappeared. "Hallo," she smiled, not wanting Jost to think she was yet another sulking female.

"She is the sister of a dead man," he began without preamble, settling in to sit cross-legged beside her.

Juno assimilated this. "What should I do to help?"

He tilted his head. "Do not choke her, if you please."

Juno pulled up her knees to clasp them, and smiled. "I will do my best, then."

"Look at me, Juno."

Juno complied, and saw he was completely serious; the dark eyes grave. "There is nothing between me and this girl. She is young, and has known me long; she has the feelings—" he struggled to find the right word.

"A *tendre,*" Juno suggested.

"*Oui,*" he agreed. "Me, I will bring her to England, and away from here; this is not a good place for her."

Diplomatically, Juno refrained from expressing her opinion of the type of reception Aditi would inspire in England, and instead offered, "Well, then; we shall have an interesting journey."

A gleam of amusement appeared in his eyes. "In Madras, I think we must find a bigger ship."

"That would be to the good, I think."

He leaned in, so that his face was very close to hers. "If we have a bigger ship, there will be more chances to practice the better kiss—yes?"

Deciding that she'd best look lively, what with a half-naked concubine on board, Juno did not hesitate. "I hope so."

His teeth flashed as he smiled in appreciation. "You will take away my sleep again, *lieve*." With a fond gesture, he caressed her hand with his own callused one.

Deciding to take advantage of his soft mood, she grasped his hand lightly. "I would ask some questions of you, and be given straight answers, if you please."

A smile still played around his mouth. "To you, Juno, my answer is always yes."

"How did you know of the diamonds?"

"Me, I cannot tell you," he answered immediately, completely at ease.

A bit taken aback, she contemplated him silently.

"Maybe when we are wed," he compromised. "Then, I will tell you."

With some consternation, she pointed out, "I cannot marry you until I know I can trust you; surely you must understand this—I hardly know you, after all."

"What is not to trust?" Leaning back on his hands, he contemplated her with an amused expression. "I see you among the trees, you try to shoot me—"

"Unfair," she protested, laughing. "I did not."

"—and I think to myself, 'there is a girl who has eyes the color of the sky over the sea, when it is early in the morning. I must marry her.'"

"You are an impulsive man," she observed, pleased by the compliment. Privately, she thought her eyes were her best feature.

He continued, "I perform the rescue of you; I perform the rescue of Horry—"

"I understand this involved the throwing of knives."

"You must not interrupt," he chided her gently. "Now I forget where I was."

"You were going to tell me how you knew of the diamonds."

But he would not be dissuaded, and shook his head. "I cannot."

Gathering her courage, she asked, "Are you the one who ordered the attack on the school?"

"No." Serious, all of a sudden, his eyes met hers. "The attack, it was the Rajah's men."

Juno blinked. "The Rajah? Which Rajah?"

"The Rajah of Sattara."

The reference was to a powerful Indian potentate, with whom the British had a somewhat rocky relationship, it being believed that the Rajah often stirred up the Mughal rebels in order to advance his own interests. "Heavens, this is a complicated story," Juno noted, her brows knit.

"And you are at its center, *lieve*," her companion pointed out with some pride, as though it was a rare compliment. "But you did not know this."

"I have no desire to be at this story's center," she retorted in mild exasperation. "I'd much rather be safe as houses in England, thank you very much."

He was silent for a moment, regarding her. "Me, I do not know what this means."

She laughed, resting her forehead on her bent knees, and thinking she was fast losing all control over her own life. "I confess I don't know what it means, either—it means very safe, I suppose."

He assured her, in all seriousness, "Me, I will keep you very safe; do not be afraid, Juno."

She turned her head to face him, her cheek on her knees. "I am fearful by nature, my friend—I was not made for adventures such as these."

"The tiger, he would not agree."

Before Juno could respond, they were joined by Aditi, incongruous in Juno's dress, her long black hair tied with a ribbon that had been purloined from Juno's drawer. The girl spoke to Jost in an Indian dialect, as she sank down beside them, her amber eyes sliding from Jost to Juno with an uneasy gleam of speculation.

"English," he commanded. "You must practice the English."

"There is nothing wrong with my English," the girl retorted. "It is much better than yours."

"You were supposed to stay where I put you—you have caused me much trouble."

Tossing her head, the girl countered, "You left; I wished to leave, also."

"No more," he warned. "Me, I will not come for you, next time."

An unrepentant Aditi addressed Juno. "You must not anger him; he will throw you into the sea." The girl then gave Jost a sly smile that seemed to indicate a shared memory, and strategically leaned over to display the upper globes of her breasts.

Heavens, thought Juno in alarm; I must speak to Horry, and soon. Hoping to distract the girl from her purpose, Juno noted in all sincerity, "You have lovely hair, Aditi."

"I thank you." Aditi played with the ends of it, her nimble fingers graceful. "What is in Madras?"

Jost nodded toward Juno. "Juno must make a visit to the judge."

Displaying a spark of interest, Aditi asked, "You will go to gaol?"

"I hope not," replied Juno gravely. "But one never knows, considering the company I keep."

"I would break you out of gaol," Jost assured her. "Me, I have done it many times."

With a smile, Juno shook her head. "I will admit that I am not one whit surprised."

Aditi's amber eyes slid from one to the other, but she made no comment, saving it instead for later that night, when the two girls had settled into their berths. "You have known Jost a long time?"

Unsure of how much should be disclosed, Juno admitted, "A few days, only."

"Ah," breathed the girl with a superior air. "He knows many girls, a few days only."

Not this one, thought Juno, but offered aloud, "He was a friend to my father."

Silently, Aditi assimilated this information, and it seemed to reassure her. "Your father will come to England with us?"

Noting that a favorable decision had apparently been made about the forthcoming journey, Juno replied, "I'm afraid my father has died."

But this revelation apparently swung Aditi back to wariness. "You must find a husband, then. You will find one in England?"

"Perhaps." Juno wondered whether Jost owned any land and where it was located—he held a title, but perhaps he had been deprived of his inheritance by the late war. Inspired, Juno offered, "Perhaps you will find a husband in England, also."

The Indian girl found this amusing, and chuckled aloud. "No—it is the husbands who find me."

"I see," Juno said, and the two settled into silence.

11

"Your father's pipe; do you wear it still?" Jost and Juno were preparing to disembark at Fort St. George in Madras, and Juno stood beside him at the stern, whilst he and one of the sailors lowered the skiff to the water below. The fort could be seen on the shore, its tall flagpole visible over the stone walls.

"Yes—I keep it with me always." Diplomatically, she did not add that with Aditi now sharing her cabin, it seemed particularly important to keep the diamonds well-hidden.

His hands on his hips, Jost observed the shoreline for a moment. "Be careful to show it to no one—we may have need of it."

"Oh; are we going to bribe the judge?" The idea made Juno a bit nervous, as she wasn't certain how one broached such a subject to an officer of the law.

"I think not," he said only, and directed the sailor to board the skiff.

Juno had noted that her brother was not in evidence. "Horry does not come with us to shore?"

Jost leapt into the skiff, and held the rope ladder steady for her. "Horry does not come. Landon and Aditi will stay here with him; you and Horry must not be both together."

"Oh, I suppose that makes sense—although Horry will be wretchedly disappointed." Juno herself had mixed emotions; although she looked forward to finally getting off the narrow confines of the schooner, she noted that the Dutchman wore his sword and brace of pistols, and that his sharp eyes were almost constantly scanning the shoreline.

Because she was slated to appear in court, Juno wore her best new-purchased frock, and carefully gathered up the skirts in one hand to make the descent. Unfortunately, the new chip bonnet she had purchased at the commissary had been left behind in their hurried flight, and—as she had dire need of a hat in this climate—Jairus had offered his own; a broad-brimmed straw hat that Juno had feminized with a ribbon, threaded across the front, and tied under her chin. The only drawback was that the large brim tended to obscure her vision, so that she was obligated to tilt her head back more often that she would like.

Jost steadied her in the small vessel, which was rocking with the rougher waves outside the breakwater, and then seated her in the stern. After a nod to the sailor--who was himself armed--the other man took up the oars, and they were underway. They began to thread their way through the ships anchored in the bay, Juno firmly holding her broad-brimmed hat on her head against the strong breeze, whilst Jost continued to keep a wary eye on the shoreline. Although she shared his concern about the coming confrontation at the court, she had other concerns as well, and ventured, "I confess that I am a little worried about leaving Horry with Aditi."

"Me, I talked to Horry," he assured her, scrutinizing the dock through narrowed eyes as they approached. "As one man speaks to another of such things."

"Thank you—I wasn't certain what to say."

He smiled. "Me, I knew what to say." But she could see he was preoccupied, and so she did not distract him with any further conversation.

After a few more tense minutes, they arrived at the fort's dock. Jost made a comment to the sailor in what sounded to Juno like Dutch, and the man responded in the same language as they stayed in place for a moment, carefully reviewing the men who were working on the wooden walkway.

"Perhaps you should have given me a pistol, instead of a kiss," Juno whispered, trying to make light of the situation.

"Me, I will give you a better nightdress, instead." Placing his hands on the dock, he vaulted easily onto it, and then stood guard whilst the sailor tied down the skiff. Jost then took Juno's hands in his, and pulled her up onto the wooden planks, setting her down and helping to replace her hat, which had blown backwards.

He then directed her to follow him down the crowded dock, his hand resting on the hilt of a pistol. In this manner, they progressed toward the sloping ramparts that surrounded the fort, with the sailor walking a few yards behind them.

Juno noted that several of the men who were engaged in various tasks on the dock stopped to stare, then tug at their caps as Jost passed. Hoping to appear less nervous than she was, she observed, "More friends of yours, I think."

"Me, I have many friends," he replied absently. "Come this way, *lieve.*"

As they approached the nearest gate, he seemed to relax his vigilance a bit, and she tilted her head back to glance at him from under the brim of her hat. "Was one of your friends Aditi's brother? What happened to him?"

"He was killed by raiders in Tripoli."

Juno nodded and returned her gaze to the path in front of her, thinking that there was undoubtedly more to this story. She was fast becoming very perceptive, when it came to the man beside her, and she realized that on those occasions when he gave a short answer, much was left unsaid; she remembered he had done the same, when she'd inquired after his family in Holland. "I am sorry for it—he was a good friend?"

His hand still resting casually on the hilt of his pistol, he studied the soldiers posted at the gate. "He was one of the *niyama*; the—" he thought about the translation "—the agreement between men."

"A pact?" suggested Juno.

He bent his head to hers. "What is this 'pact'?"

"A solemn promise—very serious," she explained.

"Yes," he agreed as he straightened up again. "A pact." He said the word slowly, trying it out.

Juno decided she may as well ask. "What were its terms, this *niyama*?"

They were now within the busy fort, and he glanced up at the turrets in an assessing way. "That the others, they would care for the family, if anyone died. There were four men, and I am the last left alive."

Juno looked up to him in surprise. "Oh—how many must you care for?"

Shrugging, he answered easily, "One, she is a widow, with a child. I gave her a bridegift, so that she will wed soon—one of the overseers from my plantation."

For a moment, Juno wondered if perhaps she hadn't heard him correctly, and lifted her brim with her hand so as to look at him. "You have overseers? And a plantation?"

"Yes." He nodded to the soldier who stood guard at the wrought iron gate that surrounded the Government House building, and then slanted her an amused look as he stepped back to allow her to pass before him. "Me, I am a rich man."

She shook her head, which caused the hat to slide off-kilter. "Someone once told me I was not to be impressed by such things."

"You must know this, for when we are wed." He paused, to help straighten her hat. "Maybe it makes you wed faster, yes?"

Bemused, Juno could only smile. "If I marry you, my rich friend, it will not be for your money. And just where are these overseers, if I may ask?"

"Tortola." He tucked her hand in his arm. "Stay close to me, now."

With a knit brow, she tried to make sense of this revelation. "But isn't Tortola held by the British?

He explained patiently, "Your king, he gives me the land when he gives me the title."

Wordlessly, she stared at him, wondering how on earth this had come about, whilst he observed her confusion with some amusement. He leaned in and added in an undertone, "He is mad, you know—your king."

"So it would seem," was her tart reply, and he chuckled in appreciation.

They stood for a moment at the entry, and it occurred to Juno that their progress was unhurried; it seemed that he was taking pains to ensure that they were well-observed, on this excursion to the Government House.

Jost continued, "I must take care of Aditi, now; she is all that is left of the *niyama*."

But another thought had occurred to Juno, and she tilted her head to peer up at him. "Did you have such a pact with my father? Is that why you came for me and Horry?"

"No," he answered as he reached to open the door. "I came, because I thought there was a danger to you. Then, when you tried to shoot me—"

"—and you saw the color of my eyes—"

He bowed his head in acknowledgment, "—and I saw the color of your eyes, I thought it would be good to have someone to take care of, for my own."

Touched, she bent her brim back to look upon him with a full measure of warmth. "Yes. It would be very good."

"Ach, Juno," he chided, gently steering her forward. "You must not look at me in such a way, or I will think of the bed sport. Me, I am trying to be decorous, so you do not shy away."

"I beg your pardon," she offered gravely. "I shall try to be less alluring."

"Me, I do not know what this means," he admitted as he held the door. "But I can make the guess."

They entered the cool confines of the stone building, and were directed toward the courtroom on the second floor. Their footsteps echoed on the wood flooring as they approached a clerk who sat in the judge's chambers, his cubbyhole desk piled high with various briefs, each rolled and bound with a red ribbon. The young man looked from Juno to Jost, and then back to Juno, apparently deciding that she was most likely to speak his language. "Might I be of assistance, miss?"

Juno lifted her brim. "I must speak to the judge, if you please. On a very important matter."

The young man nodded and lifted a pen to take a note. "He is in trial, at present, but he should be free this afternoon. What does this concern?"

She could feel her color rise. "An illegal marriage, I suppose."

After glancing at Jost with a hint of censure, the clerk nodded, pen poised, "Your name, please?"

"Miss Juno Payne. But the marriage license—the one that is illegal—apparently states that I am married to a Mr. Finch."

The clerk's astonished reaction was immediate, and he stared at her. "Why—why, how extraordinary; I have just two days since issued a death certificate for Mrs. Finch, *née* Miss Juno Payne."

12

"And who wished to file this death certificate?" Jost asked the court clerk in a soft tone. "You will tell me, yes?"

But the clerk, in the manner of all good bureaucrats, decided to pass this unprecedented tangle to a higher authority. "I'm afraid you must take this matter up with the judge, sir; I will calendar you for his first available—"

Jost took Juno's elbow, and steered her toward the courtroom door. "No need; we will see him now."

"But—but you mustn't interrupt—" The clerk cast a look of appeal toward the British soldier who was stationed at the door, but the man made no response, and indeed, reached to open the door for them. As they passed before the guard, Juno heard Jost say in an undertone, "Your help may be needed, yes?"

"Right, then," the man replied, and he entered the courtroom behind them, to close the door from the inside.

Juno--who was not at all used to barging into court-rooms, unannounced--tried to appear composed as a hush suddenly fell over the room. The judge sat on his bench, robed in black and sporting the traditional white horsehair wig in defiance of the heat and humidity. Two barristers stood before him, and an assortment of other gentlemen sat in the small gallery area, but everyone ceased whatever they were doing to turn and stare at the newcomers. Self-consciously, Juno walked down the aisle to take a seat, whilst Jost followed her, his boots sounding heavily in the silence. It was a novel experience; Juno was an attractive girl, and well-used to male scrutiny, but of all the men in the room, not a one was watching her; instead, all eyes were focused on her companion.

No one moved for a long moment, then the judge spoke into the silence. "Gentlemen, please allow me to assist this young lady."

The barristers bowed their acquiescence, and backed away, but not too far—it seemed no one had any intention of missing whatever was to come.

"You may approach," the judge invited Juno in ponderous, rolling tones. He was heavy-set, and florid of face; multiple chins appearing as he bent his head to watch her from his elevated position.

Trying without much success to conceal her nervousness, Juno duly approached the bench. "I—I must set the record straight, your honor. I believe that a marriage license and a death certificate have been filed in error."

The judge contemplated her for a long moment, and Juno was a bit surprised that he asked no questions—indeed, did not even inquire as to her name. Instead, his gaze abruptly turned to Jost, sitting negligently in the gallery with his boots crossed before him. "What concern is this of yours?"

There was a long pause, whilst the two men regarded each other, the tension in the room palpable. "Me, I take an interest." There was a hint of steel underlying Jost's tone.

The rest of the room was silent, watching. Sensing undercurrents that she did not understand, Juno stood quietly before the judge and prudently held her tongue, wishing that her hat's brim wasn't such an obstruction--she would have liked to keep track of Jost, in the event that a brawl broke out.

The judge turned his gaze to Juno, and his tone was skeptical. "Can you prove you are who you say, young lady? Have you any witnesses? I have it on unimpeachable authority that the late Mrs. Finch was drowned while returning to England—an unfortunate mishap. How can I be certain you are not an imposter, making a fraudulent claim?"

"I've not drowned," Juno insisted, and thought of the despicable faux-priest—apparently slated to murder her— whom she had comforted, and then buried at the risk of her life.

"Me, I am the witness," announced Jost, rising to his feet, with a clank of pistols and sword.

His face betraying an unbecoming flush of color, the judge looked upon him with a wary eye. "*You* can swear to her identity?"

"Assuredly. I have known her from the time she was a child."

With an effort, Juno maintained her countenance, and hoped she wouldn't be called upon to bear false witness— Sister Marie would be aghast.

"Not good enough; two witnesses are necessary," proclaimed the judge. Juno made a small sound of vexation, as it seemed evident that the judge was making up obstacles at will.

Jost casually drew his sword with a sliding, metallic sound that echoed in the quiet courtroom, and the barristers immediately drew back a few more paces. The Dutchman then approached the bench, deftly tossing the sword from hand to hand. "Here is another witness."

With some alarm, the judge glanced up at the soldier at the door, who hadn't moved.

Jost came to stand beside Juno, the tip of his sword indicating the witness box. "We will proceed, yes?"

Mottled of face, the judge conceded with poor grace, "Swear her in, then."

After Juno's testimony was taken, the clerk officially struck the marriage license and the death certificate, and then they all waited whilst the clerk made out a copy of the orders for Jost.

"I will be in my chambers," announced the judge, rising to his feet.

But apparently Jost was not yet done, and lifted his head. "This girl's father; who do I ask about his death?"

For the first time, Juno had the impression the judge was shaken, and he blustered, "You are chasing your tail, sir—the investigation has been closed. Cholera, I believe."

Watching him thoughtfully, Jost nodded. "I will speak to the coroner, then."

"Suit yourself." The judge then retreated to his chambers, as the other men in the room began to murmur to each other about these untoward events.

Taking her elbow, Jost steered Juno out of the courtroom. As they passed the wooden-faced guard, Jost said in a low tone, "Many thanks; The Bell, tonight."

As they walked down the corridor, Juno declared hotly, "Oh—oh, Jost; he was *horrid*—"

"Wait until we leave this place, *lieve*," he cautioned mildly, and kept his hand on her arm as they descended the stairway to exit the building. Juno noted that their sailor from the schooner stood outside, and upon their appearance, once again fell in to follow them at a distance.

As they approached the wrought iron gate, Juno asked in a low tone, "May I speak now?"

"As much as you like, *lieve*."

"The judge is corrupt—that much seems evident."

"Yes," her companion agreed. "There is much at stake."

"My wretched bridegift." Juno glanced back at the building, half-expecting a pursuit to be mounted. "Infamous; that someone like that is entrusted to dispense justice."

"Infamous," Jost agreed, apparently liking the sound of the word.

But Juno was distracted by a sudden thought, and bent her brim back, so as to address him in an earnest tone. "Jost--do you think it is possible that Papa is not really dead, that it was another false death certificate?"

With his other hand, he covered hers, tucked into his arm. "No, *lieve*; your father, he is dead."

But Juno had seen a ray of hope, and didn't want to relinquish it. "You cannot be certain—you said yourself you must speak with the coroner."

"I am certain." The words were gentle as he lifted her hand to kiss it. "Me, I buried him at sea."

Surprised, she stopped to face him, her hat falling down to hang at her back. "Oh; oh—I didn't know."

"I went to find him. I was too late."

Something in his tone made her clasp both her hands around his arm, and gaze up at him with all sincerity. "You did your utmost—if I know nothing else about it, I know that."

"They will pay," he promised, the expression in his eyes very serious as they looked into hers. "And today, they are made aware that they will pay."

"Assuredly," she agreed. "Who are you, exactly?"

He shook off the somber moment, and made a gesture indicating they should continue along the walkway. "Me, I am a sailor."

"Everyone seems to do whatever you say." She eyed him sidelong.

"Except you," he pointed out in a reasonable tone.

He still held her hand in the crook of his elbow, and she debated whether to allow it to stay there. Anyone observing them might leap to a certain conclusion, but she was beginning to believe that it didn't much matter what anyone else thought—he certainly didn't care, and truth to tell, there was a certain freedom in not caring. Sister Marie wouldn't recognize her former charge, but on the other hand, Sister had never met Jost.

"I am wondering," the Dutchman said thoughtfully, "if we should marry today."

"Now?" asked Juno, pausing in alarm.

"It would be best," he explained in a practical tone. "You would be safe—there are few men who would wish to cross me."

With wildly mixed emotions, Juno dropped her gaze in confusion; he had pressed her to marry him nearly from the first moment they met, and there was always the possibility—hideous to contemplate—that he was making up to her so as to seize the bridegift. She was not the best judge of such things, having been raised in a convent school; she had believed the priest, after all, and the wretched Nabob. To allow for more time to think, she stalled, "I can't imagine the judge would agree to do the ceremony."

"He would, and it would be the highest amusement." With a tender expression, he watched her for a moment. "But you are not ready, yes?"

"Not yet," she admitted. "More time is needful."

"So," he tilted his head with regret. "Always, I must try to be decorous."

She had to smile, thinking that if this was his version of decorous, then undecorous must be truly alarming. "You needn't try to be anything, you know—you can be your true self with me; I do not mind."

He paused to lift a booted foot to the border railing, and bend his head to hers. "Me, I will tell you a secret, *lieve*. I am my true self with you—I think you are the only one."

Good heavens, thought Juno, who fought a sudden inclination to cry—I believe I am going to marry this pirate. Making a mighty effort to pull herself together, she asked, "What is happening tonight at The Bell?"

He glanced around. "You must not say, *lieve*."

"Oh---I am sorry," she offered, contrite. If she was going to throw in her lot with his, she'd best work on discretion and duplicity, neither of which were her strong suits.

He relented, and replied in a low tone, "A meeting—I must discover some information."

She nodded, unwilling to ask too much, and thus make another misstep.

"I would like to know where your father's ship rests."

Juno blinked; this was unexpected, as it seemed the least of their concerns. "Hasn't it been sunk?"

"No," was all he offered, and she was reminded that the reported sinkings were false; merely a scheme to defraud the insurers.

"Come, come—we go back." With a gesture, he indicated they would make their way back to the gate. "Those who watch have seen enough."

Mildly alarmed, Juno fell into step beside him. "We are being watched?"

"Assuredly. Me, I make everyone uneasy, and the birds will begin to beat their wings."

"I see," she replied, although the allusion wasn't at all clear. "The coroner will confess?"

"No; instead, the coroner will be dead," he said matter-of-factly.

"You are going to kill him?" She was shocked, but reminded herself that she should try not to be, if she were truly contemplating the role of a pirate's bride.

"I will not need to." He set her hat on her head once again, and tugged the brim down for emphasis. "Me, I only kill someone when it is necessary."

"That is to the good," agreed Juno, abandoning twelve years of religious training without a moment's hesitation. "As long as it is truly necessary."

He sighed. "Often, it is necessary."

Juno belatedly came to the realization that he was teasing her, and said with some severity, "I never know when you are serious."

"Me, I am infamous," he agreed.

13

The landing party returned to the schooner to find Landon and Horry trying to teach Aditi how to play cards in the cramped half-galley. Horry looked up with extreme relief upon their entrance. "Thank God you're back—can I come out of hiding? Aditi can't keep her suits straight."

Juno noted that Aditi's gaze flew to Jost, and thinking to forestall the girl so as to allow Jost a chance to confer with Landon, she offered, "I'll be happy to help Aditi with her hand. What are we playing?"

"You're not much better," her brother ruthlessly pronounced.

"Boy's got a good head for it," remarked Landon with laconic approval as he closed his own hand of cards with a snap.

"I played with Papa's crew, when they were in port," Horry tossed his cards on the table, then rubbed his face. "Sometimes, we'd play for licorice drops."

Jost reached over to put a hand under Horry's chin, lifting his face. "The sickness, it comes?"

Horry pulled his head away with an impatient gesture, and Juno's heart sank; Horry had seemed so much better that she'd forgotten his health was always an issue. With a knit brow, she strove to remember the treatment administered at the Fort William infirmary—usually she was not with him when the attacks came. "Perhaps we can find an apothecary on shore—I think St. John's wort is helpful."

Unhappy with the attention, Horry said in irritation, "The ague may not come—sometimes it doesn't. And I am dying to go above decks."

"What is it? What is this sickness?" asked Aditi, looking from Horry to Jost with some alarm.

"Horry has malaria," Juno explained. "The attacks are unpredictable."

Aditi shrugged and promptly lost interest. "He needs the neem leaves, then." She turned to gaze up at Jost from under her lashes. "We should swim tonight, yes?"

But Jost bent over the girl, speaking intently in her own language. Reveling in his undivided attention, Aditi made a long explanation with a pantomime which seemed to include a mashing gesture.

"Does she speak of the chinchona bark?" asked Juno, watching them. "I think there is very little chinchona bark to be had in India." Indeed, it was the main reason they sailed to England.

"No," said Jost. "The neem is another tree, and is in many places." He retrieved his pistols. "Aditi will come with me to find what is needed."

Nothing loath, Aditi scrambled to her feet as Jost handed the court document to Landon, who pocketed it without comment. "Stay below, the two of you," Jost instructed Horry and Juno, and then he was gone, a delighted Aditi close at his heels.

Into the sudden silence Landon suggested, "Might as well deal another hand—it may be a while."

With an annoyed sigh of resignation, Horry gathered up the cards and began to deal. "What happened at the fort, Juno?"

Hesitating, Juno was trying to decide whether to give Horry an edited version of events in front of Landon, when Landon solved her dilemma by remarking, "Stirred up the hornets, I imagine."

As Jost had given Landon the document, Juno decided there was no harm in admitting, "I had been reported married and deceased, but the record is now corrected; although Sir Jost had to be—persuasive, I suppose is the best description."

"Good God, Juno," exclaimed Horry, staring at her in outrage. "To think that the Nabob would pull such a trick—"

Fearing he would bring on the ague, she soothed, "He is no match for Sir Jost."

But Horry seethed in impotent rage. "The *dastard*. If I were just a few years older. . ."

Landon reached to grasp his arm. "Steady there, Master Payne. We are on to him, and all is in train."

Subsiding, Horry looked to his cards, but their interest in the game was now desultory at best. Juno thought it an opportune moment to put her theory to the test, and remarked to Landon, "You no longer seem to believe Papa a villain; it is quite a change from when first we met."

Landon looked at her for a long moment from beneath his grizzled brows, then admitted, "No, your father was not a villain. I was bringing pressure to bear."

"You did an excellent job," said Juno in a wry tone. "If I had the first clue about the bridegift, I would have gladly handed it over."

"Ridiculous," Horry expostulated, and Juno could see he was out of sorts, due to the impending fever. "If there truly was a bridegift, we would know of it by now. At the very least, Papa would have told Juno. "

Juno ventured, "Sir Jost seems certain there is a bridegift, Horry."

"Oh, there's a bridegift," said Landon as he studied the cards in his hand. "Make no mistake."

Juno glanced up as she made a discard. "How can you be so certain, Mr. Landon?"

The man shot a look at them from under his brows. "Because your father said there was," he replied. "Your turn, Master Payne."

But the Payne siblings were staring at him, and Horry ventured, "*Papa* told you of the bridegift?"

"Not me," the man disclaimed in his laconic manner. "But he told others." He glanced up. "Can't say more, I'm afraid."

They played cards for the better part of an hour, whilst Juno lost an imaginary fortune and Horry's forehead began to display the telltale sheen of perspiration. The game concluded when Juno suggested that Horry should rest, and for once, her brother did not argue.

"Stay below," cautioned Landon.

"You can lie down on my berth," offered Juno. "I'll keep you company, if you like."

The retreated to the fore cabin, and Horry stretched out on Juno's berth as she covered him with her blanket, then sat across from him, crouched over under the low ceiling. "Is it horrid?"

"Not yet," he replied stoically. "I think this won't be a bad one."

Juno leaned forward and said in a low voice, "I wanted to ask your opinion about a theory I have formed."

"I am all attention." He offered a wan smile, and pulled the blanket up closer around his shoulders.

"I believe that Sir Jost and Mr. Landon are—employed—by the Crown in some manner."

Horry thought it over. "Because of the war? Do you think they are trying to stop Napoleon from seizing the money?"

"Yes," she nodded, relieved he hadn't laughed at her out of hand. "I think they may be—may be spies of some sort."

This did earn her a skeptical look. "Landon—perhaps; I'd believe it. But Sir Jost? He doesn't seem a likely spy."

Juno spoke with low intensity. "I know it seems implausible, but you should have seen it today, Horry. Everyone—even the judge—seemed to know him; as though he was powerful in some unexplained way. And the soldiers we've met seem to be willing to follow his direction, which doesn't make a lot of sense. And recall what Landon said tonight—that all is in train, and Papa was not a villain. There is an undercurrent—it is hard to explain, but Jost turns the subject when I question too closely."

Her brother drew his brows together, and contemplated the ceiling. "Are you worried? Do you think they can be trusted?"

"Yes, I do," she assured him. "But I wanted to ask you if you thought Papa was involved in this, himself—if he ever said anything."

Horry thought about it for a moment or two. "He never mentioned Landon, but I think he saw Sir Jost fairly often." He paused. "He never said anything to me about spying—he just went on his trade routes. But on second thought, it does seem an odd kind of friendship."

Encouraged, Juno emphasized her point. "Yes, it does—do you see? I wonder if Papa was involved in some way with this—whatever this is. Pretending to be aiding the Nabob in the insurance fraud scheme, but in actuality, trying to catch him."

"Mr. Landon does seem allied with Sir Jost in some way—even though he shouldn't be," Horry noted. "You may be right."

"There is a Rajah involved, too, although it is not clear exactly how," Juno disclosed with a small frown. "Sir Jost hinted that he is also part of the scheme."

They were silent a few moments, considering this, when Horry suddenly shuddered from head to foot.

Juno eyed her suffering brother with sympathy, and tried to keep his mind from it. "Sir Jost told me that he has a plantation in Tortola—a gift from the British king."

Horry's teeth chattered. "Does he? Well, that certainly supports your theory."

"Yes—I thought I'd tell you, just so you are aware that it's a possibility." She paused, wishing she didn't feel so helpless. "Are you thirsty? Shall I fetch some lemon water—or hot tea?"

But before he could respond, they heard the skiff bump up against the hull, and Juno rose to tuck the blanket around him. "I'll see what the foragers have found, then I'll return."

"I'll be here," Horry chattered, and Juno gently squeezed his shoulder in sympathy as she left.

Upon entering the half-galley, Juno could see at a glance that Jost and Aditi had been quarreling. Jost's mouth was pressed into a grim line, and it was clear Aditi had been weeping; now she nearly smoldered with rage and misery. Juno had a good guess as to what had transpired, and chafed at the awkwardness of having everyone at such close quarters—she almost felt sorry for Aditi, who had nowhere to retreat to have a good cry.

"Now, you will show us how to make the cure," directed Jost as he dropped a small packet of tree leaves on the galley table.

Aditi stole a resentful glance at Juno, and muttered, "Where is Horry? I think that he is not so very sick."

With an effort, Juno bit back an exasperated retort, only to find that succor came from an unexpected source as Landon crossed over to take up the packet. "You should get some sleep," he advised Jost. Then he addressed Aditi, and pulled a small pot from the shelf. "Come here, missy—no more of your foolishness."

It turned the trick; Aditi was only too happy to demonstrate how cooperative she could be with another man, and practically simpered at Landon, whilst Jost retreated to his hammock in the aft cabin. Juno watched with interest as the girl explained to Landon how the leaves needed to be ground, mashed with vinegar, and then simmered in a small quantity of water.

"How did you learn of this, Aditi?" Juno infused her voice with as much sincere admiration as she could muster, it having occurred to her that she should cultivate Aditi's friendship so as to stave off a potential attack in the dead of night.

The girl shrugged. "Where I am from, everyone knows of this."

"Where are you from?"

The girl glanced at her sidelong. "I am from many places; the last place was the *bagnio* in Algiers—I lived with a missionary, there."

"A missionary?" asked Juno, very much shocked.

Aditi gave her a superior smile. "A missionary is yet a man."

Juno quickly changed the subject. "How much of this should Horry drink?"

"All of it—while it is yet hot, otherwise it separates." The girl poked at the simmering brew with a fork. She said to Landon, "You watch and stir—I will go see if Jost is no longer angry, and then I will come back."

"No, you won't, missy," said Landon in a firm tone. "Even if I have to hold a pistol to you."

Surprised, Aditi glanced at him in alarm, and then settled in to sulk, occasionally stirring the infusion.

To break the tension, Juno asked, "I wonder how anyone discovered such a cure—how it came about."

Landon offered, "Probably a folk remedy for centuries—a shame more do not know of it."

Juno could only agree. "If only they could find a cure for yellow jack—there was an outbreak in Calcutta last year, and thousands died; we had to go to the fort, and no one was allowed to come or go for days." With a great deal of heat, she warmed to her theme. "There was never such a place for horrific diseases—honestly; it is a wonder anyone survives."

"Perhaps you will die," Aditi suggested.

"There is always that possibility," Juno agreed, and noted that Landon stifled a smile.

Aditi prodded the simmering mash one last time with the fork, and then announced, "It is done. Let it cool—but not too long."

Cradling the hot pot in a rag, Juno carefully carried it to Horry, while the other two stood in the passageway and watched from behind her, Aditi craning to see over Landon's shoulder.

Roused and made to sit up, Horry tentatively drank, then made a face. "Good God, that's bitter." He lay back again, shivering and miserable.

"How often must he take it?" Juno whispered to Aditi, watching Horry with some concern.

"Only the once," Aditi explained with a superior air. "It now stops."

This seemed too good to be true, and Juno breathed, "Thanks be to God."

"Thanks be to me," Aditi corrected her.

14

Later that evening, Juno waited patiently on deck for Jost to awaken. He had slept through dinner, and Landon decided they could all go above decks as night fell, since the threat of danger had lessened, after their visit to the court. Juno gratefully emerged to sit on the fore deck, lifting her face to enjoy the breeze that always materialized as the sun set. Aware that someone approached, she looked up and tried to contain her disappointment when she discovered that it was only Horry, still wrapped in the blanket. As Aditi had predicted, within a remarkably short space of time the ague had dissipated, and then disappeared altogether. Juno smiled as he settled beside her. "Aditi turned the trick."

"That she did." He looked out over the harbor with a grin that nearly matched his usual grin. "With the aid of a promiscuous missionary."

"She has led an unusual life, I think," Juno offered diplomatically.

He met her eye with extreme skepticism, but Juno felt a twinge of compassion. "We should give her the benefit of the doubt, Horry; I think her parents must have died when she was young, and she has had to survive as best she could."

"Well, I have the impression she's thrived, rather than survived, and has no regrets whatsoever."

"Be that as it may," Juno cautioned with some severity, "You shouldn't be speaking of such things."

But Horry was unrepentant. "It is so obvious, Juno—it would be ridiculous not to speak of it."

Reminded that Jost had warned Horry about Aditi, Juno could only be grateful to the Dutchman; her brother showed no signs of infatuation, and instead seemed inclined to mimic Jost's casual exasperation with the girl. "Well, she and Jost have quarreled—that much is evident. I'm afraid she's not one to temper her actions; it is a shame she doesn't realize that she only makes things worse."

"He is not one to temper his actions, either," Horry pointed out. "And you are in the middle, Juno—it's dashed hard on you; he shouldn't have taken her on."

"He felt an obligation," Juno decided to disclose. "Her brother was a friend of his. And don't forget that she knew about the neem leaves, Horry."

Horry rubbed his face in his hands. "Oh, Lord—I am required to be grateful, I suppose."

"We should all try to be civil," Juno advised. "We've a long journey ahead, like it or not."

"I can't be *too* civil," Horry pointed out with a gleam. "I don't want to give her the wrong idea, if you catch my meaning."

"Perish the thought; best be polite, but passive."

"Concerned, but not committed," he countered.

"Chilly, but courteous," she parried.

"Deferential, but disinterested," he declared, with the air of the winner.

"Me, I do not know what any of this means," said Jost, who'd appeared beside them. He carried his boots in his hand, and sat to pull them on. Juno found his bare feet very appealing, and wondered if he was ticklish. If Horry had not been present, she might have tested him out—she was positively longing to touch him.

"We were speaking of Aditi," Horry explained. "Whatever is to become of her?"

Jerking on his boot, Jost answered in a grim tone, "Me, I would drown her."

"Perhaps she can be taught a trade," suggested Juno. "Other than the trade she practices, that is. Can she read, or write?"

"Juno," said Jost with heavy patience. "I do not wish to speak of Aditi."

"Very well." She lowered her voice. "We were wondering what should be done with the diamonds, now that we know the Nabob must not have them."

Jost seemed to weigh his words, and kept his gaze fixed on the deck. "The diamonds, they are part of the bridegift."

"The diamonds that the priest gave me?" Juno looked to Horry, but saw that he was just as puzzled as she. "How so?"

"The insurance money, it is exchanged for diamonds, because it is easier to smuggle diamonds," Jost explained as he pulled on the other boot. "A fortune can be carried by one man—very simple."

"Oh," said Juno, her brow clearing. "Is that how the Rajah is connected to the scheme?"

Jost nodded. "The Rajah of Sattara; he trades the money for the diamonds—they come from the Deccan plateau, under his control."

"Then he should be arrested," Juno declared with some heat. "He must know that the entire enterprise is treasonous."

"He's not British, Juno," Horry pointed out.

"He should be arrested, nevertheless," she insisted. "Can't the British at least threaten him?"

"There is much money at stake, and the Rajah, he is loyal to whoever pays him the money." Jost shrugged. "It is the way of it."

"Well, it is the wrong way," Juno declared, her cheeks flushed. "To care only about material gain, with no thought of who will suffer as a result."

Horry shot her a meaningful glance, and thus reminded, Juno amended self-consciously, "Present company excepted, of course."

Horry laughed aloud at her *faux pas,* while the Dutchman only smiled, his white teeth flashing in the fading twilight. "Me, I am the honest man, now."

"Can you tell us of it? Before you were honest, I mean." Horry was apparently eager to hear tales of piracy.

With a meaningful glance toward Juno, Jost said only, "Some other time," and Horry nodded in male understanding.

Juno sighed in exasperation at the both of them, but secretly she could not help but be pleased that Jost was taking Horry under his now-honest wing. Her little brother was not yet a man, but no longer a boy, and he must miss his father acutely. Reminded, she pulled at the string around her neck and said to Jost, "I think it may be best if you carry the diamonds, after all. I was so afraid, today, that I would lose them."

His expression one of mock-surprise, Jost stared at her. "Yes? I am to be trusted, now? What of your very important promise to the priest?"

"I will no longer honor the obligation, being as he was going to murder me," she explained dryly. "And do not think I don't know that you could have taken them any time you wished."

"They stay in the pipe—it is a good hiding place." Without further comment, he stuffed the clay dragon into his pocket.

"Do not forget they are in there, and smoke the diamonds at your meeting, tonight," she teased.

"What meeting is this?" Horry asked, his expression alert.

Coloring up, Juno castigated herself for failing to learn her lesson in discretion. "Nothing," she finished lamely.

Jost took pity on her. "I go to discover information—but you must not say."

"Capital; may I go?" Horry's eyes shone.

To Juno's surprise, Jost seemed to consider this option, but he then shook his head. "Tonight, you must rest, to be sure the sickness, it does not come back. But tomorrow night, you will be needed ashore."

As Horry grinned in anticipation, Juno asked with some dismay, "Oh—how long do we stay?" She was under the impression they were slated to leave Madras with all speed, and after her experiences on shore today, this plan seemed prudent.

"As long as we must," replied Jost, and Juno could see that a more satisfactory answer would not be forthcoming. "Now," he continued, "I will speak to Horry."

Juno blinked. "I am to leave?"

"If you please." Jost gestured with his head toward the stern.

Bemused, Juno rose to her feet and curtseyed as though she was taking her leave from a drawing room. "Pray do not conspire against me, you two."

Thinking to make her way to the aft deck, she saw that Landon was attempting to teach Aditi the fine art of night fishing off the stern, and so Juno decided not to disturb the lesson—best to give Aditi a wide berth, after this tumultuous day.

The other crew members were below deck, cleaning up after dinner, and so she leaned against the gunwale, and breathed in the familiar scent of India. They were to leave soon, and sail half way across the world to England—an England she didn't remember. Juno faced the prospect unafraid, and she was honest enough to admit it was because of Jost; she would gladly follow him anywhere, down any rugged road.

Unable to suppress her happiness, she lowered her head, watching the water, and hugging the knowledge to herself. Amazing, that she hadn't know him very long, but felt she knew him very well indeed; amazing, that her allegiance could be transferred so easily, and so irrevocably. She felt as though she'd been waiting in suspended animation, until he appeared before her that night—like the answer to a prayer. Although no one could accuse him of saintliness, certainly; this being borne out by the nature of the tattoos on his fine chest—tattoos that she would very much like to trace with her fingers. Soon, she thought; it seemed he could not keep his mind from what he called the bed sport, and truth to tell, she felt the same way.

She trusted him--although perhaps she was being foolish, given his past. On the other hand, she didn't care two pins about his past, or the women he had known—and one would imagine there were more than a few. Once committed, he would be loyal--she could sense it; he was loyal to her father, and to the pact he'd made with the other men to care for the bereft—she paused, struck by a sudden thought. He wouldn't have participated in the pact unless he had family to see to, himself, but it seemed evident they were no longer alive—he had hinted as much that first night.   Perhaps if the opportunity arose, she would ask him; he seemed reluctant to speak of his past.

Horry came to join her, leaning on the rail with his elbows, and watching as the lights begin to appear, one by one, on shore. "Have you resolved all problems?" she teased. She had a good guess as to the topic of their conversation, and would have very much liked to eavesdrop.

"We were just making plans," Horry replied with his newfound maturity.

Juno wrapped her arm around his in a fond gesture, and leaned her head against his shoulder. "We are due for an adventure, it seems. It is only fair; Papa had all the adventures, up to now."

"We are going to find out what happened to him," Horry promised, "and clear his name."

"Yes; I was doing some wishful thinking, and hoping he was still alive, but Sir Jost said he buried him at sea."

Horry lifted his head, considering this news. "It is fitting—Papa loved the sea."

"As do you." Juno looked up at him. "Landon says you'll make captain, someday."

Horry placed his hand over hers and squeezed. "Be brave, worrywart."

Smiling, she shook her head. "I'm not a brave soul, I'm afraid. The family trait has skipped over me."

"Slayer of tigers," he teased, imitating Jost.

But Juno disagreed, "It's not brave when you have no choice, Horry—truly."

He let it go, and they watched the shoreline a bit longer. "Sir Jost went to his meeting. I think your theory is right—that he's some sort of spy for the Crown."

Tracing the wooden railing with a finger, Juno nodded. "He seems to have a great deal of influence. And he is careful about what he tells us—did you notice it, when he spoke of the diamonds?"

Horry nodded. "Yes; he wants us to know only so much, and no more, and he never said what was to happen to them."

Juno knit her brow. "No—he didn't, did he?"

But Horry had moved on to a more interesting subject. "He's going to give me one of his knives—he says I'll have need of a good knife."

"Wonderful," his sister replied in a dry tone, "Pray do not go about with it clenched between your teeth."

Horry let out a bark of laughter. "Don't worry—it is double-edged, and I would only hurt myself."

"And no tattoos," Juno warned.

"A small one, perhaps," Horry teased. "Your name."

She pretended to consider. "I suppose that would be acceptable."

"I imagine," said Horry with a sidelong glance, "—that mine won't be the only one."

Juno did not deign to respond.

15

"Is it the *Minerva?*" Juno asked Horry in a low tone. They were standing at the East India Company's dockyard in the Bay of Madras, Jost holding aloft a shielded lantern that cast a narrow beam of light on their surroundings. Their object was an East India Company frigate, known as an East Indiaman, to those in the trade.

"I can't tell at this distance," Horry whispered in response. "They all look so much alike, especially in the dark."

Several frigates were in dry-dock for repairs, the shadowy shapes looming darker than the surrounding darkness, and two additional ships were being stored in the floating docks. One of these was—perhaps—their father's last ship, the *Minerva.*

"We will board, then." That morning, Jost had informed them that their father's ship was reportedly berthed here, her name painted over so as to conceal the fact she did not sink. Because Horry was the one who was most familiar with the ship, Jost had brought him here, under cover of darkness, to verify its identity.

Juno, to her pleased surprise, was asked to come along, also. "Me, I will keep you close by," Jost had explained, and she wasn't certain whether he wished to keep her safe, or to take the opportunity to kiss her—hopefully both. Landon stayed behind to keep an eye on Aditi, who in her current state could not be trusted not to run away again.

"Keep the lantern shielded," Jost directed Horry, and then bent to slide the wooden board that served as a make-shift gangplank onto the vessel. Juno had been aboard her father's ships only on rare occasions, as females were not welcome. Horry was, by contrast, a frequent guest, and would occasionally accompany their father on one of his short but profitable spice runs.

Once on the deck, Horry stood for a moment, assess-ing the shadowy vessel. "I think this is her; it is hard to tell, since she's so stripped-down. Perhaps if I could go below, and see the main deck."

Jost led them toward the companionway stairs, so that they could descend to the lower deck, and cautioned Horry, "The lantern, it will show for miles on the water; be careful."

Horry adjusted the shield, and they stood in the main cabin as he circled its perimeter, the tiny beam dancing on the walls. As the ship was in storage, there was little to see; only the bare walls, and those items which were affixed to the floor. "This was where the binnacle stood, I think. If I see the captain's cabin, I'll know for certain."

"Go then, we will wait, and keep watch."

Juno watched Horry sweep the beam of light systematically back and forth as he slowly walked the length of the main cabin to the stern, leaving them in darkness. With an unhurried movement, Jost took Juno gently by the waist and pulled her against him, wrapping his arms around her and pressing his cheek against hers. "*Lieve,*" he whispered. "*Ik houd u.*"

Juno didn't recognize the words, but she recognized their tenor, and sighed with delight as she melted into his chest, relishing the feel of the muscular arms around her, and the stubble of his beard against her face. They stood thus, for a small space of time, and it seemed—rather surprisingly—that he was content to remain in this chaste embrace during this rare opportunity to be alone and unobserved. She, however, was not so content, and raised herself on tiptoe to tentatively press a kiss against his throat. He made a quiet sound in response and bent his head to find her lips. The kiss deepened, his mouth opening upon hers and Juno instinctively responding in kind as she caressed his broad chest and shoulders. A warm hand came round her ribcage, then slowly stroked downward over the contours of her hips as he pulled her closer in an intimate way. Adrift in mindless pleasure, Juno hadn't even noticed that Horry had re-entered the deck until Jost reluctantly set her from him.

"It's her, it's the *Minerva,*" Horry whispered in excitement, the beam of light bouncing with his approach "I am certain."

"Very good," said Juno, her voice a bit thick, and Jost gently ran a hand down her arm.

"What now?" asked Horry, coming to a halt before them.

"We look to see what we can see." Jost took the lantern from Horry, and they began a painstaking circuit of the ship's interior space, scrutinizing the hold, and in particular the captain's cabin. In was necessarily a slow progress, as the lantern's small beam cast only limited illumination, and the cargo hold in particular was pitch dark.

"Are we looking for clues?" Juno followed along, privately thinking there was little of interest to observe.

"We look for anything," explained Jost. "We have no clues."

After a careful perusal which turned up nothing, they emerged back on deck, Juno grateful to breathe in the sea breezes after the stale, still air in the hold. She speculated on the chances of arranging for another embrace, and reluctantly concluded that the odds did not favor her. Taking hold of herself, she remembered that she needed to set an example for Horry, then almost immediately wished Horry were elsewhere.

They took a cursory perusal around the empty forecastle deck, but nothing of interest was revealed. "She looks so different," Horry observed in a somber tone, uncharacteristic for him. "Like a ghost ship."

"Then the ghost, we must bring her back to life," said Jost. "She is sound, and we need a bigger ship."

Juno stared at him in the dim light. "Surely we cannot just—just commandeer the ship, and sail it to England?"

"Not me," replied the Dutchman. "Landon, he will seize her for his investigation."

"Will he? He's a trump, then," proclaimed Horry with enthusiasm. "It will be like it used to be—" his eyes slid toward Jost "—Papa would allow me to take the helm, sometimes."

"Your father, he was a very foolish man," Jost replied, and Horry chuckled in appreciation. They continued their inspection toward the stern, where the lifeboat was stowed on the quarter deck, the davits which normally supported it turned inward for storage. Juno noted that a small skiff was strapped, bottom-up, in the lifeboat's interior.

"The *Juno*," breathed Horry in wonder. "Why—there she is."

"What?" asked Juno.

But Horry was already standing next to the lifeboat, allowing the light to shine upon the skiff that rested inside. His voice was gruff, and it was clear he was moved by a strong emotion. "Papa's skiff—the *Juno*. It's the one we would take fishing." He indicated the nameplate on the stern. "He carved it himself."

Juno reached in to place a hand on the wooden plate bearing her name, tracing the furrows with her fingertips. She began to cry, the loss as agonizing as the day she had heard the terrible news from Landon. As she sobbed, Jost moved to hold her against his chest, and put his other arm around Horry, who was struggling to control his own tears. The three of them stood in a tight circle, heads bent, while Juno wept, and a man was mourned.

Juno subsided into sniffles, wiping her cheeks with a palm while Horry ran his hand in a comforting gesture over her head. Into the silence Jost said, "Me, I boarded his ship, and held him with my sword, back when I would seize cargo for the Dutch West India Company. He said, 'Your talents are wasted, come with me,' and he took me to his cabin to drink rum."

"That sounds very like him," Horry noted, his voice thick.

Jost continued, "The both of us, we got very drunk, and then I came with him and left my old life." He paused. "There will never be another like him."

"He was larger than life," Juno agreed with a watery smile.

Jost tilted his head. "Yes? What does this mean?"

"It means that you are right—there will never be another like him."

Jost took her hand and raised it to kiss the palm, even though Horry stood beside them. "Me, I never saw him angry with anyone."

"No," Horry agreed. "Everyone was a potential friend."

Juno remembered, "He used to flirt with Sister Marie, much to her amusement."

"When he had too much of the drink, he thought he could sing," Jost revealed. "But he could not sing."

Horry gave a bark of laughter. "He used to sing at the top of his lungs, just to embarrass me."

Juno smiled. "And now you have his skiff, Horry—it is like providence." She saw Jost lean in, and forestalled him, "It means as though it was meant to be."

"Assuredly. Now—how many sailors will we need, Horry?"

Juno watched them as they moved amidships to discuss the preparations needed to launch. There was no question Jost knew down to the last barrel of salted cod what was needed for the journey, but Juno surmised he was training Horry for his future role. They had said goodbye to the past, and were moving toward the future; Juno felt immeasurably better as she paused to gaze out over the stern, toward the shadowy ships on the scaffolds in the dockyard. Horry was right—the scene was ghostly; she should catch up to the men, being as she was not a brave soul.

A smaller shadow moved among the larger ones, and she gasped in surprise. There was a man watching her, she had the quick impression that he was a native, but she did not see his face, only his quick movement of retreat back into the shadows.

"Jost," she called in an urgent, low voice as she hurried toward them. "Come quickly."

Motioning to Horry to stay back, the Dutchman drew a pistol and deftly pulled her behind him, next to the mizzen mast as he scanned the area. "Tell me."

"There was a man, watching from the shadows."

"Describe," he commanded, and she did, as best she could.

"Do you want me to stay with Juno while you look?" asked Horry.

Jost was peering into the darkness with narrowed eyes. "No—we will wait."

And they did, Juno straining to listen, but she heard nothing except the occasional call of a loon, echoing on the water. One would think the dockyard was secure; it was enclosed by a stout wooden palisade, and the entrance gate was guarded by a rough-looking individual, who was apparently another friend of Jost, as he'd made no protest when they'd entered. Another watchman patrolled the docks—it seemed unlikely that an intruder had been allowed in, but there was no doubt in Juno's mind that he was real, and had been watching her as she looked out over the dockyard.

After a few long minutes of silence, Jost indicated they would leave. They made a slow progress back to the gate, Jost instructing Juno to stay behind him, with her hand holding the back of his coat. Occasionally, he would have them pause so that he could listen. When they finally arrived at the gate, he stepped aside to confer with the guard in a low tone, and Juno could tell by the other man's gestures that he had seen nothing untoward. Nevertheless, she could see that Jost was wary, as he shepherded them back to the skiff to return to the schooner. They arrived without further mishap, however, and Juno began to wonder if she had mistaken a harmless dockworker for something more sinister.

Once on board, Jost asked Juno to recite what she had seen to Landon, who listened without comment, then cast Jost a long look. "We can assume the ship has been searched—perhaps they think we know something they don't."

"Perhaps," Jost agreed, his black brows drawn together. "You and me, we will go to see the ship fitted tomorrow; we will speak to those who know."

Landon nodded, then as Juno excused herself to go below, the older man warned her, "Aditi's in a state—I told her some home truths."

With some trepidation, Juno entered her cabin, but it appeared Aditi was already asleep--or was pretending to be asleep. Juno changed into her plain and unacceptable nightdress, wondering exactly what Landon had said to Aditi. It was an uncomfortable situation, what with Jost unable to conceal his partiality, and Aditi an unhappy witness. As for Juno, she could still feel his warm hands on her body, and chafed at the lack of opportunity to seek more of the same. I am no better than I should be, she thought with no real contrition, and hoped they could find the occasional private corner on the *Minerva*; otherwise it was going to be a long and frustrating journey to England.

16

J uno sat on the stern of the schooner, her chin resting on her knees, drowsy in the morning sun. Last night's adventure had deprived her of sleep, but it was impossible to stay abed in the morning, due to the brilliant sunlight that shone through the cabin's porthole. So instead, she had asked for a sliced mango from the good-natured Jairus, and had come up to sit in the sun, and eat her breakfast.

How extraordinary that they had found Papa's ship—it was symmetrical, she decided. That was the word to describe it; it was symmetrical that they would sail to England on Papa's ship, with the enemy unaware that they were going to avenge his death, once they got there. Circumstances had seemed so bleak such a short time ago, and now all dire events were behind them; indeed, her future—and Horry's—were looking very bright indeed.

Even though it was morning, the Madras sun was hot, and she decided she should fetch Jairus' straw hat from down below. In a moment—she didn't have the energy, just yet. Jost and Landon had left to arrange for the fitting-out of the *Minerva*, leaving Horry and Jairus armed, and with strict instructions to keep a weather eye out for any sign of trouble—although it seemed clear they felt they'd discover the identity of the night watcher once they were at the dockyard. They both seemed convinced that it was an enemy spy, watching to see if they discovered anything of interest on the abandoned *Minerva*.

Horry was hugely disappointed to be left behind—it was his father's ship, he'd insisted, and argued that he had every right to accompany them.

"You will follow orders, and stay with your sister," Jost had commanded in a tone that brooked no argument. "I must take Landon to seize the ship, and Juno must be guarded."

"Jairus can simply sail away, if anyone approaches," Horry argued. "It's not fair."

"On the ship, the 'fair' does not matter; only the orders matter. You must learn this."

Horry had subsided with poor grace, a mulish cast to his mouth. "Yes, sir."

I wonder if we can set sail soon, Juno thought. The sooner we embark on the long journey, the sooner Horry will accept his secondary role; here in India, there was too much excitement that he was loath to miss. And he did feel that it was his obligation, as a son, to clear their father's name, which--while a laudatory goal—was not a practical one, for a boy of sixteen.

Juno realized she had dozed off, when her head fell from her knees, waking her up. Thinking that she may as well lay down below, Juno opened her eyes to see Aditi, seated at a small distance on the deck, and regarding her with simmering hostility. As Juno met her gaze, the other girl declared with some spite, "He will tire of you. You do not know how to please him."

Aware that she hadn't had any trouble in that respect, thus far, Juno turned a mild reply. "Have done, Aditi; I will not discuss such a topic with you."

With an abrupt gesture, Aditi turned her head and looked to the shoreline, sulking. Juno decided that she should not go down below just yet, or Aditi would believe she'd been routed, so instead, she sidled over to the stern, and dangled her legs over the edge, thinking it would be nice to swim in the cool water and perhaps—one fine day—she would swim with Jost in some private place where they would be unobserved. Leaning her cheek on her folded arms, she imagined such an idyll for a very pleasurable few moments.

Suddenly, her legs were grasped and yanked, hard, from down below the hull. Juno gasped, and instinctively turned to her stomach, scrambling to cling to a nearby stay, and drawing a breath to scream. No sound emerged, however, because a hand came over her mouth, jerking back on her head, and pulling her backwards toward the water. Her fingers began to lose their grip on the stay, and frantically, she managed to wrap her other arm around a line that was secured to a cleat on the deck, hanging on desperately, even though the rope burned into her arm. A grunt of frustration could be heard from behind her, and her assailant hoisted himself atop her, to claw at the rope over her shoulder, knocking the breath out of her body in the process.

Struggling and in a panic, Juno looked up to Aditi, who had sprung up, and now backed away in amazement. The girl's eyes met Juno's, and Aditi watched, unmoving, as the rope was forcibly unwound from Juno's arm, and she was dragged down toward the water, her screams muffled by the hand over her mouth.

As Juno kicked and twisted, she felt her legs grabbed by another pair of hands, and, with a yank, she was forcibly pulled over the edge of the schooner, and down into a waiting *teppa*—one of the small, log catamarans used by fishermen. Whilst the second man quickly dragged her under the canvas tent cover, the first man lifted his hand for a moment to press a wet cloth to her nose and mouth. In horror, Juno tried to twist her head from side to side so as to avoid the sickly, sweet smell, but her assailant held her in a grip of iron. Unable to draw an adequate breath, she panted in a panic, as the world gradually went dark.

17

J uno didn't know how much time had passed when she awoke again; she had experienced a variety of disturbing dreams, and so when she opened her eyes, it was with a certain amount of relief. Struggling to gather her scattered wits, she became aware that she was lying on a soft bed in a quiet place, and her blinking gaze beheld a sumptuous silk canopy overhead, colored a deep, columbine blue. When she closed her eyes for a moment, she discovered that she had to work to open them again, as though there was a disconnect between her will, and the response. Her head ached, her arm hurt where the rope had burned it, and her mouth felt like cotton wool, but other than that, she seemed to be uninjured. Blinking in an attempt to focus, she turned her head on the silken pillow to observe a woman, dressed in a luxurious *sari*, and seated beside her bed, watching her. The woman was slim and very beautiful, with a *ghungat* veil covering her long, unbound hair.

"You are awake," the woman said in careful English. "Good."

"Where am I?" Juno croaked, through dry lips.

The woman turned to convey a silent message to a hovering maidservant, who brought water, and assisted Juno to sit up and drink. Juno drank thirstily, then fought a wave of nausea, and had to lay back again, her fingertips pressed against her temples whilst the room spun.

"These are your rooms," the woman said with her soft, cultured voice. "Do you like them?"

Juno wondered for a moment if this was another dream, and wished her head didn't hurt, so that she could assess the situation. She thought she could hear a fountain gurgling outside somewhere, and was cautiously optimistic; perhaps she'd been rescued by a wealthy Good Samaritan. Gingerly, taking care not to jar her poor head, she propped herself up on an elbow only to realize she was dressed in her own luxurious *sari,* in the same blue color as the bed canopy. The diaphanous trousers she wore were embroidered with silver flowers, and the blouse, which exposed her midriff, was a silk brocade, shot with silver thread, and trimmed with pearls. Matching silk slippers--also trimmed with pearls--completed the outfit.

Blinking, she studied her raiment in bemusement, and tried to pull her wooly thoughts together. Judging from the light, it was late afternoon. Jost, she thought suddenly—Jost and Horry must be frantic. "I must go," she announced to the woman. "To whom should I speak?"

"This is your home," the woman explained kindly, making a gesture toward the well-appointed suite. "These are your rooms."

Juno decided that perhaps this beautiful woman was a bit simple, and smiled at her in a non-threatening manner. "Is there anyone from the British Consul, nearby?"

Showing her white, even teeth, the woman smiled. "You are no longer British." She made a graceful gesture with a slender hand. "Hassid is your maidservant."

The maidservant humbly bowed her head.

Juno decided she should simply start over. "I am Miss Juno Payne, of Calcutta. Who are you, if you please?"

"I am Najeera." The woman steepled her graceful hands and bowed her head. "I speak English."

"And very well," Juno complimented her. "Is this your home, Najeera?"

"Yes." The woman seemed pleased that Juno was now making sense. "With the other wives."

Juno raised her brows. "Oh, I see. Are there many other wives?"

"Only four are allowed by the law," the woman answered with her precise diction. "One had to be removed to make way for you—she is now a concubine."

A faint alarm sounded in Juno's mind. "Who is your husband, Najeera?"

"The Rajah of Sattara," the woman pronounced proudly.

Juno stared at her, thinking furiously--or at least as furiously as her wits would currently allow. The surreal scenario was no longer surreal, but instead had taken on a disturbing reality; the Rajah was obviously aware that a fortune in diamonds was secreted somewhere—none knew better than he, after all---and apparently, he wanted to have his cake and eat it too. Unfortunately, she was slated to be the cake.

"I will marry no one," she said firmly. "I must speak with this Rajah."

The woman allowed an expression of faint alarm to furrow her serene brow. "You must not disrespect your husband."

"I mean no disrespect," Juno assured her. "But he will not be my husband."

Looking a bit doubtful, the other replied, "I am to call when you have awakened. Shall I call?"

Swinging her legs over the side of the bed, Juno nodded. "If you please." She stood up, tested her equilibrium, and then decided she would stay seated on the edge of the bed for a short time longer. Straightening her spine, she took a breath, and folded her hands on her lap. *People are not allowed to abduct brides nowadays,* she assured herself. *I need only be firm, and demand to be returned.*

Najeera opened the carved mahogany entry doors, and gestured to a servant in the hallway, whilst Juno waited, and tried to calm her nerves. After a short space of time, four men entered the room, and which one was the Rajah was immediately apparent; he was an older man-- perhaps fifty--with a neatly trimmed grey beard, and an arrogant manner that proclaimed the hereditary leader. She noted with some misgiving that he was accompanied by a Hindu priest, carrying a brazier, and two men who appeared to be servants, of some sort.

The Rajah spoke to Najeera, and his gaze briefly rested on Juno, who was given pause—the expression in the man's eyes was cold and calculating, not someone given to persuasion. Turning to one of the servants, he gave an instruction, and the man reverently took the brazier from the priest, and set it on the floor.

Juno said in a steady voice, "Sir, I must advise you there is no bridegift; you are laboring under a misapprehension."

The Rajah turned to her in surprise. "You will stay silent," he commanded in English.

One of the servants indicated that Juno was to step forward, next to the Rajah, and Najeera smoothed Juno's *ghungat* back over her shoulders, in preparation.

Feeling as though she was still dreaming nightmares, Juno protested, "No," although there was a slight quaver to her voice. She then addressed the Hindu priest, thinking that a man of God would surely listen to her. "Sir, I will not marry him—I do *not* give my consent."

Behind her, Najeera made a faint sound of distress at Juno's effrontery, and with a curt gesture, the Rajah made an order to the two menservants. One on each side, they seized her arms, and pulled her upright. Still weak from being drugged, Juno had not the wherewithal to fight, and tried to assure herself that a forced marriage could be easily annulled.

Pinioned between the two men, Juno stood with the Rajah before the burning brazier as the officiate chanted in a language she did not understand, and the Rajah leaned to place a necklace around her neck. Apparently her spoken consent was not required, as it was never sought.

At a gesture from the Rajah, the men allowed her to sit on the edge of the bed again, which was just as well, because standing near the fragrant brazier had made Juno feel a bit dizzy. She bowed her head for a moment, trying to gather herself, while Najeera moved forward and, with the help of the maidservant, began to remove her veil and her slippers.

Horrified, Juno realized what was to come—the marriage must be consummated, and as quickly as possible, so as to preclude potential challenges. With murmuring voices, the servants assisted the Rajah in removing his outer garments while the priest gathered up his brazier and departed; clearly, there was no aid to be sought from anyone in the room.

Her mouth dry, Juno tried to calm herself. Think, Juno; think. Wait until you are alone with him, and then remember what Jost taught you—don't panic. She kept her head bowed, and tried to appear wan, and faint. Tamping down an almost overwhelming panic, Juno bided her time.

Najeera unwound the silken *sari* Juno wore over her clothes, and mentioned with just a hint of malice, "Your children will not be heirs, of course."

The thought that she may be forced to have the Rajah's child, only added to Juno's resolve; wait, Juno—steady—

She held a hand to her head, and swayed, quietly marshaling her strength while she watched the others leave the room, steepling their hands, and bowing to the Rajah. When he approached the bed, she gathered her legs beneath her, and stood with all appearance of docility.

"Good. You will obey me," he directed in a harsh tone, and pulled her to him, as he brought his mouth to her shoulder.

With all her strength, Juno drove her knee into his groin, and with an anguished grunt, the Rajah dropped like a stone to the floor.

18

Juno didn't hesitate, but darted for the doors that opened onto the balcony, frantically unlatching the latch as the Rajah managed to call for help from his position on the floor behind her. Just as she swung the door open, and catapulted through, she was grasped from behind, an arm snaking around her throat. Striking as hard as she could behind her head, she attempted to gouge her attacker's eyes, and was rewarded with a howl of pain, as the servant loosened his hold upon her. Tearing free, she ran out onto the open balcony, but her ankle was grasped from behind, and she fell forward to land on the stone floor, hard.

Juno twisted over, so as to kick at the man's face with her free foot, and managed to scuttle backwards on her hands. Her attacker then launched himself atop her, tackling her so that she fell back, frantically beating at his head with both fists, and crying out. Scratched and bleeding, the man cursed her fluently, as he grasped her hands, and wrestled her into submission.

After being hoisted to her feet, Juno was half-dragged back into the bedchamber, trying to resist with what remaining strength she had left. The Rajah had staggered to his feet, and was bent over in residual pain, leaning against the bed and watching her recapture with malevolent eyes. He issued a command, and the servant forced her onto the bed with little difficulty, as she was fast running out of stamina. The man then sat at her head to pin down her arms, while the Rajah clambered atop her, spreading her legs apart with his knees and cursing at her as he fumbled with the opening at the front of his *dholi*.

Gasping, Juno found she had little strength left, and could not even muster a scream. Twisting her head aside, she closed her eyes tightly, but then heard the manservant make an exclamation of surprise just before she felt the Rajah's weight suddenly lifted from her. She looked up in amazement as Jost, his face a mask of rage, pulled her new husband from her, and swung his sword at the servant, severing the man's head with a single blow.

The headless corpse collapsed on the silk coverlet in a bright fountain of blood, and Juno watched, agape, as Jost grasped the Rajah's throat in one hand and threw him bodily against the wall. Clutching at the Dutchman's hand, the Rajah's face turned purple as Jost very deliberately took the bloody sword and emasculated him, thrusting the weapon into his groin, and carving, whilst the

Rajah's screams of agony were strangled by Jost's grip on his throat. Juno looked away, unable to watch.

She heard the mutilated man drop to the floor as Jost said to her, "Up, Juno. We go, now."

Willing herself to move, Juno slid off the bed, and stood rather stupidly, glancing at the Rajah, who writhed and bled on the floor, making gurgling sounds through severed vocal cords. Jost removed a coiled grappling rope from his shoulder, and then re-coiled it with deliberate movements.

"Someone--someone will come," Juno warned, when she managed to find her voice.

"Not soon." Jost stepped over to the balcony doors to peer out, surveying the immediate area in the fading light. He then seized her slippers from the floor and secured them in his belt. "On my back, now. Come, come."

On stiff legs, she walked to him, and began trembling from head to toe as he crouched to hoist her onto his back. He paused to stroke her arm, clutched around his neck. "Be easy, *lieve*. Me, I will not drop you."

"I—I cannot seem to stop shaking," she faltered, her teeth chattering uncontrollably. "I—I am so—so sorry."

"No," he replied in a grim tone. "I am the one who is sorry."

With Juno clinging to his back, Jost slipped through the doors, then sidled along the wall of the building, leaping up to stand on the balcony railing, where it joined to the wall. Bracing himself with one arm, he swung the rope with the grappling hook on its end back and forth, and then threw it toward the roof overhead. Juno was afraid to lean her head back to look, but she could hear a metallic scraping sound as hook clattered, and the rope fell down beside them. Patiently, Jost looped it once again, and heaved it upward for the second time, Juno feeling her weight shift with his effort. This time, the rope did not fall, and he tugged on it, grunting in satisfaction.

Still violently shivering, Juno voiced her main concern. "I—I don't think he is—is dead."

"He will be, soon," Jost soothed in a whisper. "You must not speak, *lieve*."

"He—he made me marry him—I had to walk around the brazier—I—I could not stop it, Jost."

"Hush, my heart; try to stay silent."

She buried her face in the back of his neck and shut her eyes tightly, striving not to gabble as she clung to him, arms and legs, whilst he held on to the rope, and walked up the wall with a remarkably quick series of movements.

Once at the roof's edge, he grasped the ornate stucco façade that decorated its border, and then heaved them over the top, unhooking the grappling hook from where it had lodged, and pulling the rope up after them. Setting Juno down, he then took one of her shoes, stepped quickly over to the far corner of the roof, and threw it as far as he could, so that it cleared the outer wall of the garden.

He returned to where she sat behind the façade, still trembling uncontrollably, and dropped beside her, gathering her in his arms. "Now we wait for darkness," he whispered. With a tender hand, he pulled her head against his shoulder and stroked her hair, trying to soothe her.

Embarrassed by her inability to control herself, she took a shuddering breath and replied, "Good—that is good."

"Ach, Juno," he said softly into her ear. "I am so sorry."

Her hands clutching his shirt, she stuttered, "No—no—please, Jost; it was not your fault—how could you know? And—and you did kill him. He—he is dead—are you certain?"

"Yes, he is dead," he assured her with quiet emphasis, his arms tightening around her. "Me, I am sure."

Bending her head, she broke down and sobbed against his chest, twining her fingers in his braid whilst he held her tightly against him, murmuring in unintelligible Dutch. Stop it, she ordered herself—you are making him so upset. With a monumental effort, she wiped her face and tried to control her trembling, with only limited success.

After holding her gently in his arms for a few minutes, he whispered against her temple, "Juno, *lieve*—I am sorry for it, but I must lie with you this night. If there is a child to be born, we will then know that it is my child, and not the other's."

Her cheek against his shoulder, she took a shuddering breath. "No—no, Jost. He did not—"

He gently drew her away to look into her eyes. "No? There is blood on your legs, *lieve*. You can say to me—do not be afraid."

"No," she said again, wiping her eyes. "It is the servant's blood—I scratched at his eyes, just as you showed me—I--I didn't let him know ahead of time—it worked wonderfully—I almost got away—" With a deliberate movement, she pressed her lips together, so as to halt the torrent of words.

He pulled her close again, and she could feel the relief emanating from him. "*God zij dank.*"

She started to cry again, thinking of his selfless offer. "I love you—I should have said, when we were aboard the *Minerva,* but I was too shy. I love you."

He made a sound in his throat and pulled her closer against him. "*Lieve,*" he whispered, his voice thick.

Still sobbing, she lifted her face and found his mouth with hers, kissing him passionately as she slid her hand between the buttons of his shirt, to caress his chest with her fingers. He broke off the kiss, and gently pulled her hand from his shirt, lifting it to kiss it. "Not now—we must take you to the ship, where you will be safe."

"Now," she insisted, pulling up at his shirt, her teeth chattering all the while. "Please, Jost."

He began to kiss her throat and neck, even as he voiced his hesitation, his actions contradicting his words. "You are upset, *lieve.*"

"Please." She raised her chin so as to grant him greater access. "Hurry, please."

He made no further protest, and wrapped an arm around her so as to gently lay her back on the tiled roof, still warm from the heat of the day. What followed was a wrestling match, as she arched against him, pulling his hips to hers whilst he resisted, trying to gentle her fevered movements. "Juno," he murmured into her ear, "You must listen, yes?"

"Hurry," she breathed. "They will come."

"No." He held her head by the sides and looked into her eyes. "No one will come—and if we hurry, it will not be as easy for you, *lieve*."

"Jost," she bit out in frustration, raising her head for emphasis. "Do not argue with me."

And he didn't, instead positioning his heavy body so as to carefully do the deed, which was—truth to tell—a bit painful, but had the immediate benefit of putting a stop to her trembling hysterics. Once she could anticipate his rhythm, she did her best to countermove, relishing his reaction to her actions. It seemed evident he was nearly mindless with pleasure, and in turn, her own pleasure was compounded, in the knowledge that she had such an effect on him.

When he had stilled, he lay atop her, spent and silent. "Thank you," she offered, her fingers tracing his back. "I feel much better."

Raising himself on his elbows, he kissed each of her eyelids in turn, then dropped a lingering kiss on her mouth.

"I should have married you at Fort St. George—even with that despicable judge."

"You were not ready. But me, I think you are ready, now." He casually bent to kiss an exposed breast.

She smoothed back his hair, which was falling out of the braid and around his dear face. "All I could think about was how frantic you must be. Oh, Jost—it was terrible."

"It was terrible," he agreed. "We will not speak of it, yes?"

But she needed to speak of it. "How did you come to be here? How did you know?"

He rolled beside her, and carefully tucked her in the crook of his arm as they gazed up at the sky, where stars were beginning to appear, one by one. "There are many watchers, here, where so many seek an advantage. Me, I had only to ask the right questions, and jingle the coins."

"I see. They drugged me, you know—I don't know where we are."

"We are a few miles from Madras, only." He kissed her head. "It was the luck that you ran outside, *lieve*. I saw you, and did not need to search."

"Thank God for you." She kissed his neck, breathing in the scent of him, and feeling the last vestiges of anxiety melt away.

Loud voices could be heard, raising an alarm from below, and Jost put a cautionary finger to her lips, instructing her to stay silent. It was evident that the bodies had been discovered, and a contingent of men could be heard speaking on the balcony below, their voices dismayed and incredulous, as the sound carried up to the roof. The voices retreated inside, and Jost crawled on his elbows toward the façade, listening, as he gestured to her to stay low, and be silent. It was nearly dark now, and Juno put her cheek against the warm tile and lay quietly, feeling the heat seep into her aching body. It will never occur to them that we are still here, on the roof, she thought. And they will find my shoe, and think the garden gate was our escape route. He is clever, this man of mine—I cannot wait to see what life holds next.

19

It was no surprise that Juno dozed, on and off, whilst they waited for the cover of night; it was warm on the palace roof, and she was exhausted, mentally and physically. After they heard the searchers return, dispirited and empty-handed, Jost indicated they would leave, and unrolled his rope yet again.

Now that Juno had the hang of it, it was a simple matter to descend from the roof—or at least simple as compared to their ascent. As they made their quiet way through the ornate garden and out to the road, it seemed to Juno that security was rather lax, considering the undeniable breach earlier in the evening. In response to her observation, Jost explained that the guards had other matters on their minds. "They will be thinking of the transfer of power; much is at stake."

"Didn't the Rajah have an heir?" As she had no shoes, once again Juno was hoisted onto his back, for the long walk back to the dockyard.

"The heir, he is a child. Such a situation, it is trouble—especially here."

As they trudged along, Juno entertained a spiteful desire that Najeera would be handed over to marry some man she didn't much like. She then observed, "Napoleon will be unhappy, if there is no Rajah to send him diamonds." She laid her cheek against his shoulder, watching their progress along the tree line, where he kept to the shadows.

The Dutchman cocked his head in agreement. "Napoleon, he will not sleep well. There is no war without the money."

As they wound their way back to the ship, they had to hide amongst the trees only once, when a messenger came flying by on a lathered horse. Other than that, the journey was quiet— save for the night insects making their rasping noises in the undergrowth—and Juno experienced a profound sense of well-being. She squeezed her arms around Jost's neck. "I am well and truly ruined."

This comment inspired her mode of transport to swing her down, and kiss her very thoroughly for a few minutes. "Me," he claimed as he mounted her on his back once more, "I will not let you out of my sight again."

"I have no objection to such a plan." She pulled his braid to the side to kiss the nape of his neck.

When they finally came to the palisade that surrounded the dockyard, Jost stood in the shadows for a few minutes, listening, then lowered Juno to the ground. Putting his fingers to his mouth, he blew two short whistles.

Whilst they waited for whatever response Jost expected, Juno asked in a low voice, "Do we set sail with all speed? They must know it was you who killed the Rajah."

Watching the entrance gate, Jost shook his head. "No, we do not run—no one will come after me. The wrong, it was done to me, and so it is understood that I—" he struggled with the translation.

"Avenged the wrong—made it right?" Juno suggested.

"Assuredly. I am the strong horse, now, and not to be crossed. It is the way of the men who fight."

Juno nodded, thinking it unlikely that anyone who saw the mangled heap of flesh that had been the Rajah would want to invite Jost's displeasure; small wonder the judge had been uneasy when the Dutchman's sword was unsheathed. Juno suppressed another spiteful wish that the judge would hear of what had happened, and sleep with one eye open for a while. Heavens, she thought; I am a vengeful creature all of a sudden—or perhaps I was always vengeful, but never had so many opportunities for it.

The gate opened, and she sighted a man approaching, plodding along with his hands in his coat pockets, as though heading toward the saloons in the high street. Jost whistled twice again, more softly, and the man changed course slightly without breaking stride, to head straight toward them.

Taking her arm, Jost positioned Juno so that she stood behind him, and called out, "Here."

Seeing his location, the other man approached and tugged on his cap. He was sandy haired and stolid-looking, of moderate size and unremarkable, except for a scar that graced his temple. "Cap'n," he said in greeting.

"She will need your coat." Jost indicated Juno.

"Miss." The man nodded respectfully, and doffed his frieze coat without a qualm, handing it to Jost.

Juno slipped her arms into the sleeves with gratitude; she had been trying not to think about making a reappearance in her blood-spattered, diaphanous clothing.

"Report," directed Jost.

The sandy-haired man obliged. "No sign of trouble, sir. The ship should be fitted by late tomorrow; the crew has been vetted—Mr. Landon felt a few soldiers would be needful."

Jost nodded. "You will escort us to the ship."

"Yes, sir." The man unsheathed a pistol, and turned to lead them toward the gate. As had happened on the last occasion, Jost had Juno walk behind him, holding on to his coat, as she tried to avoid stepping on any debris with her bare feet. The guard at the gate could not resist giving her a sidelong glance as they passed through, and Juno could hardly blame him; she must be a strange sight, with her tangled hair unbound, and wearing a man's coat.

Once through the gate, it seemed to her that Jost was less vigilant, as they approached the dock where the *Minerva* was berthed. Their escort said over his shoulder, "Do not be alarmed if you hear gunfire—Mr. Landon and the boy are shooting."

Juno stared at him, bemused. "Shooting? At this time of night?"

The man replied in a neutral tone, "They've been shooting at targets since noon."

Poor Horry, thought Juno, her heart aching for him. She hastened her step.

They could hear the target practice well before they made the *Minerva*, and Jost gave his distinctive whistle as soon as they were within earshot. Within seconds, Juno could see Landon and Horry appear at the rail, their faces showing pale in the lantern light. Smiling, she raised an arm over her head and waved as she walked. "Horry," she shouted. "I am returned, safe and sound."

Her brother met her halfway down the gangplank and enveloped her in a bear hug, lifting her from her feet. "Juno," he said into her temple, his voice breaking. "Oh, Juno—I am so sorry."

She placed her hands on each side of his head, and shook it slightly. "Take hold of yourself, Horry--there was no harm done. Sir Jost rescued me nearly upon my arrival." She turned to board the ship, carefully wrapping the coat even closer around her disheveled clothes. "Where is Aditi?"

Horry looked over at Jost, stricken. "Thank you, sir—I promise I will never let you down again."

"No one has let anyone down," Juno insisted. "How could any of us have known, for heaven's sake? Is Aditi still awake?"

Landon stood at the railing, and nodded as she came aboard. "Miss. Glad you're back."

"Thank you." She paused, as she realized she wasn't certain where to go, on the newly outfitted ship.

"This way," Landon offered, and indicated the companionway as he escorted her down the steps, Jost and Horry following. "You are with Aditi again, only in an officer's cabin, this time."

"No," replied Juno grimly. "I am not with Aditi again."

Hearing her tone, Landon slanted her a speculative glance, but any further questions were forestalled when Aditi herself emerged from the cabin in the narrow passageway, sleepy but undoubtedly eager to greet Jost's return.

Juno advanced on her in two strides, and slapped her face, as hard as she was able. The Indian girl cried out, backing away with her hands to her face.

"I *say*, Juno," Horry protested in surprise, but Juno had decided, many hours ago, that she was going to do violence to Aditi. She had never done violence to anyone before, but this was a day of many firsts.

Determined not to revert to hysteria again, Juno said in an even tone, "She watched them take me. She watched them, and didn't help, and didn't sound the alarm."

Before the incredulous stares of the others, Aditi shrank back against the bulwark. "Put her in the brig," ordered Jost in a curt voice. "Me, I will decide what is to be done."

"This way, missy." Landon took Aditi's arm in a firm grip as she began to weep and plead with Jost in her own language. Jost made an abrupt gesture to Landon, and the man tightened his grip and wrestled her down the passageway, the girl trying to drag her feet and calling to Jost in alarm.

"*Infamous*," breathed an outraged Horry. "And to think she pretended to be concerned about you—she acted as though she was very upset."

"Nothing more than crocodile tears." Juno saw Jost cock his head at her, and so she explained, "It means she pretended to be sorry but was not, like the crocodile, who cries when it eats."

"Yes," he nodded. "Like your nabob."

"He is *not* my nabob," Juno corrected him with some heat.

"And my physician," added Horry. "Another villain, pretending to be an ally."

"Me, I prefer the honest enemy." Jost rubbed a hand over his eyes. "Not the crocodiles."

"You must be exhausted," Juno touched his arm. "Shall we retire for the night, and discuss our many false friends in the morning?"

"I have performed the many tasks today," Jost agreed in a mild tone, and Juno hoped Horry didn't notice the color rising in her cheeks.

She turned to her brother, "As part of your penance, you may fetch me as much hot water as you can lay hands on—I desperately need a bath, and I hope there's a fire going, somewhere."

"If there isn't, I'll start one—back in a trice." Horry threw her a look indicating he was aware that he was being sent away, and departed.

Alone in the narrow passageway, Juno looked up at Jost, and smoothed the end of his braid—she had earned the right, certainly. "I haven't thanked you, but I don't know how anything I could say would be enough."

He took her hand in his, and pressed it flat against his chest. "I save you, and I save myself. It is the same thing."

It was so simple, and yet so true. She nodded in agreement, and asked a bit shyly, "Are you too tired to come wish me goodnight, once I am in my paltry nightdress?"

He ducked his chin and regarded her. "On a ship, nothing is private, *lieve.*"

"All right," she conceded. "I shall behave, then—-and you are asleep on your feet, anyway."

He lifted her hand and kissed it. "Me, I will be decorous—but only like the crocodile."

Laughing, she allowed him to push her through her cabin door.

20

When she awoke the next morning, it took Juno a few moments to regain her bearings; she'd slept heavily through the remainder of the night, and hadn't yet seen her cabin in the daylight. The memories from the day before came flooding back; she was on the *Minerva*, getting ready to set sail for England to confront the Nabob, find her bridegift, and presumably thwart Napoleon. She had been abducted, married and widowed in a single day, and had made wonderful love to a wonderful man to top it off, although at the time she had been admittedly a bit crazed. I am not at all steady in a crisis, she conceded—it is a miracle the man wants to take me on.

She smiled at the timbered ceiling because if she'd learned nothing else during that tumultuous day, she'd learned that he truly loved her, and did seek to take her on—indeed, if he had his way, they would be already married. Her concerns that he was only after her mythical bridegift—as were apparently half the men in India—had been laid to rest. It seemed evident he was some sort of agent for the Crown, and did not have a personal stake in the matter, other than a very personal interest in herself, of course.

Tentatively, she sat up and swung her legs over the edge of her berth to assess her condition. Her arms ached from hanging onto Jost, and her rope burn still hurt, but other than that, she seemed to be in one piece. Sliding to her feet, she gingerly stretched her aching arms, then reviewed the meager offerings in her wardrobe. A dress had been lost in the Rajah's palace, and since she had given another to Aditi, she was left with only the one. Perhaps I can request that several yards of material be purchased, she thought; it seemed evident that Jost would not allow her to set foot off the ship, and so she would have to be grateful for whatever she was given. Juno might not be expert in the use of firearms, or in bloody hand-to-hand combat, but at least she could sew.

Reluctantly, she turned her mind to Aditi, who would also need another dress, if she was still to accompany them to England. It was a terrible dilemma for Jost, who wanted to honor his *niyama;* but the girl had betrayed them in the most heinous way imaginable. If I had never returned, Aditi would have thought it all well-done of her, thought Juno in disbelief; it was incomprehensible to her that one human being could treat another in such a fashion. Hard on such a thought, Juno came to the reluctant realization that she could not do unto Aditi what Aditi had done unto her—Sister Marie would be relieved to hear of it.

Shaking out her sole remaining frock, Juno dressed, and made her way above-decks to observe the flurry of activity, as final preparations were made to set sail—sailors climbing the ratlines above, or painting the shrouds with tar. Now that it was daylight, the *Minerva* seemed much larger; the three huge masts sporting furled sails, with sailors clinging to the booms, their legs crossed beneath them as they worked on the rigging. Gazing about her, Juno became aware she was the focus of many a covert glance, and she could feel the color rise in her cheeks. She spied Jost in conversation with the sandy-haired man from the night before, and with Horry, who looked up and saw her.

"Juno," her brother called out. "I came by to check on you earlier, but you were asleep."

Juno could see that he continued contrite, and so she approached the group with a smile. "I'm fully recovered, and more than ready to shake the dust of this place from my sandals."

But Jost interrupted any further conversation, his smile softening the words. "Juno, you must go below. The men, they must work."

"Yes—but I wondered if you have decided what is to be done with Aditi."

The smile disappeared. "Aditi stays in Madras."

Unsure how to broach her idea in the face of such implacability, Juno lost her nerve, and only nodded. "Yes; I will see you both later, then."

As she turned, Jost took her elbow to stay her. "Ach, Juno; you wish to speak of Aditi?"

Juno hesitated. "Only if you do not mind—you must do as you think right."

"Me, I will come." He turned to give a brief instruction to the other man, and then accompanied her below.

"Who is he?" she asked as they descended to the captain's cabin. Jost has never told her the sandy-haired man's name.

"Peyton," was the only response. Juno gave him a speculative look, but he did not expand on the topic. Another one like Landon, she surmised; answerable to Jost, and given mysterious duties that would not withstand the light of day.

"Did you sleep well?" He slid open the captain's cabin door.

"I did, did you?"

He cocked his head, his gaze warm upon hers. "Me, I would have slept better if I came back to tell you goodnight."

She returned his look in equal measure, unable to suppress a thrill of hopeful anticipation. I am shameless, she thought; but surely we cannot be expected to remain celibate all the way to England—that horse has already left the barn. Or opened the barn—I cannot think of the right metaphor, when he looks upon me in such a way.

As she took a seat at the map table, there was a knock on the door, and Landon joined them, slipping in to lean against the wall. Jost said to him, "I sent for you because we speak of Aditi, and what is to be done." Crossing his arms, Landon nodded.

Jost met Juno's eyes in all seriousness. "Me, I cannot forget what she did, Juno. Her brother would not want me to."

"Yes," Juno agreed. "That is what I thought too, at first—but then I decided I cannot make who she is change who I am."

Thinking over her words, the two men made no comment, and Juno continued, "You have an obligation, Jost. If she stays here, we know what will become of her. If she sails to England, there's little enough trouble she can cause on the way." She paused, because the two men exchanged a glance, obviously thinking this pronouncement naïve. Juno hurried on, "And I can teach her to sew, and at least give her the opportunity to make an honest living. Then--if she continues down the path she is on—well, it would be her choice, and not out of necessity."

Jost bent his head to consider the table top, the braid falling forward. I would like to see his hair unbound, Juno thought, then tried to pull her thoughts back to the matter at hand.

"You can forget this? Forget what happened to you?" There was a hint of incredulity in Jost's voice.

"Of course not," Juno replied in all honesty. "But I am called to forgive."

Jost was silent, and Juno glanced at Landon, only to see he was watching Jost closely. The Dutchman looked to the other man. "You will answer for her? She must stay out of my sight."

"I will," Landon nodded.

"She comes, then."

Juno sincerely hoped she was not going to regret championing this particular cause. Reminded, she asked him, "Would you mind sending someone to buy fabric for me, before we sail? I can have her start on a dress, as we will both have need of another."

"Tell me what is needed," offered Landon. "I will see to it." There was a pause before he added gruffly, "You have a good heart, miss."

"She is like her father," Jost observed.

Thinking this a fine compliment, Juno smiled in appreciation, as Landon nodded to her and then left, presumably to speak to Aditi. Watching him go, Juno turned to Jost. "Why would Landon take on such a task? It does not seem in keeping."

The Dutchman grimaced and leaned back in his chair. "Me, I am afraid to tell you."

Juno laughed and raised her brows. "Oh? Is he being punished, poor man?"

"No—if she behaves, he will marry her."

Agog, Juno stared at him, completely shocked. "*Truly?*"

He nodded, amused by her reaction. "Truly."

After staring at him in utter dismay for a moment, she observed in bewilderment, "He may as well take a viper to his bosom."

Jost cocked his head, still smiling. "I thought Aditi, she was the crocodile."

"She is both," Juno pronounced with some severity.

He shrugged his broad shoulders. "Speaking the English—it is very confusing."

But Juno would not be distracted. "Jost—why on earth would Landon be mad enough to marry Aditi?"

Jost met her eye in amusement, and she had to smile, and shake her head. "That is not enough—*surely*—upon which to base a marriage."

He spread his hands in mock-apology. "The men, they like the bed sport, Juno."

"I am aware of this—" she assured him, "—being as how I am ruined."

Throwing back his head, he laughed loudly, and then reached across the table to grasp her hand. "No longer— me, I will marry you this day."

Suddenly breathless, Juno stared at him. "Today?"

"Yes. I will have the chaplain from the fort come this afternoon—if you agree?"

Delighted, she said, "I do," and wished she had sent Landon to find a better nightdress, too.

21

The chaplain from Fort St. George peered over his spectacles at the proposed bride with little enthusiasm. To compensate for her ordinary frock, Juno had carefully arranged her hair and threaded ribbons through it, but the result seemed to have little influence on the chaplain's cheerless disposition, as he eyed her with misgiving. A scold, surmised Juno, and he probably found his congregation wanting in every respect—she had known others of his ilk, and it always astounded her that such men claimed to have heard the call to serve.

The *Minerva* was ready to set sail on the evening tide, and since Juno would not be allowed to leave the ship, the clergyman had been persuaded to perform his office on board, rather than at the church within the fort. Because the man appeared to be a stickler for the proprieties, Juno surmised that filthy lucre—and plenty of it—had crossed his palm in order to persuade him to make such a visit.

She was also vaguely aware that a special license was required to marry on such short notice, but the arrangements had been made, nonetheless. She hoped Jost hadn't spent a fortune arranging for this wedding, but on the other hand, a fortune would be presumably saved because once she was safely married, she need no longer fear abduction by anyone with an eye to the bridegift.

"Popish?" the sharp question interrupted her train of thought.

Juno had just informed him of her former address at the convent school in Calcutta. "I am Roman Catholic, yes," she responded. She could feel Jost bristle at the man's attitude, and hoped this particular Anglican Catholic was not going to antagonize her husband-to-be; she had seen first-hand the result of such tactics, and she didn't want to ruin her only remaining dress with even more bloodshed.

The chaplain turned from Juno after conveying the unspoken conclusion that any further discussion with her would be unavailing. Addressing Jost, he poised his quill and asked, "Last residence address?"

"Cutler Street, London."

The chaplain raised his brows, impressed. "Company man, eh?"

"Assuredly."

Juno could hear the thread of steel in Jost's voice, and knew he was unhappy with the man's condescending attitude. To calm him, she gently placed her fingers on his arm and he responded by covering her hand with his. We need only to marry, she thought; we can discuss how much we disliked the officiate later, at our leisure.

The chaplain's pen scratched across the parchment. "Bachelor?"

There was a pause. Juno leaned toward Jost and explained, "It means a man who has never married."

"Yes," said Jost. "Bachelor."

The chaplain turned to Juno. "Spinster?"

Knitting her brow, Juno had to consider the question fairly. "More correctly, I suppose I am a widow."

The man glanced at her with raised brows, and poised his pen. "Husband's name and date of death?"

There was a pause whilst Juno realized she'd made a tactical error, and tried to retrench as quickly as she was able. "In all honesty, sir, I am not certain there was a wedding ceremony to begin with; I believe I misspoke, and the comment should be disregarded."

Frowning, the chaplain sat back in his chair and contemplated her with the air of a man whose worst suspicions have been confirmed. "Please explain."

As this task was beyond her powers, she looked to Jost, who said in a firm tone, "Me, I can swear to you that she is not married."

"So—you were living with this other man without benefit of clergy?" He sounded unsurprised.

"Of course not," Juno retorted hotly. "I was abducted, and he was killed."

After considering this bald statement with his brows raised in incredulity, the clergyman returned to safer waters. "Were you at any point married to this man, Miss Payne? If so, I must see his death certificate; I cannot sanction a bigamous relationship."

Conceding defeat, Juno admitted, "I—I am not certain whether the marriage was legal." She could sense Jost winding up to make an argument, but she turned to him and said, "We must postpone, I think."

Without comment, Jost stood and opened the door for the departing chaplain, who did not hesitate to leave with all speed, probably in the hope that no one would demand a refund. After shutting the door, the Dutchman walked over to Juno and took her into his embrace, running his hands down her back and resting his chin on her shoulder. "*Verdomme.*"

"My fault," Juno admitted, returning his embrace with a sigh. "I was caught unawares, and spoke without thinking."

"Next time," he suggested with a tilt of his head, "It would be best not to mention."

"When is the next time?" she teased, tugging on the braid hanging down his back. "I had so looked forward to your goodnight wishes."

Bending his head to kiss her shoulder he said with regret, "Me, I cannot risk waiting another day—we must sail."

"Aye, Captain," she replied lightly. "I'll accept a postponement, as long as you promise you won't change your mind."

"Assuredly not." He gently kissed her mouth. "The wedding, it is already done for me."

Touched by the sentiment, she lifted her face to his with all sincerity. "And for me, too."

He kissed her again lingeringly, his hands cradling her face, then laid a palm against her cheek. "I must give the orders to cast off."

"I know—go, then." She watched him leave, thinking that there was such a thing as being too *ridiculously* honest and she needed to work on this failing, if she was to pass muster as a pirate's wife. Trying to quash her disappointment, she made her way above decks to look for Horry, who had been awaiting his cue to stand up with her, once the ceremony was underway. She found him hovering near the mizzenmast, intensely interested in the activity surrounding the unfurling of the mainsail.

"False alarm," she announced as she came to stand beside him. "You are free to join the sailors, Horry."

With some surprise, her brother searched her face. "What happened? Never say he backed out?"

"No, nothing like that," she assured him. "Further documentation was needed, and there wasn't enough time to fetch it." The last thing she wanted was for Horry to discover the details about her harrowing adventure at the Rajah's palace.

The sailors behind them shouted in unison, and to his credit, Horry did not turn to watch the mainsail come cascading down, but instead kept his sympathetic gaze on his sister. "So what happens next?"

"We'll wait for England—since there is little chance of abduction, between here and there. And I didn't much like the chaplain, in any event—I confess I was afraid Jost would leap across the table, and do him injury."

Horry grinned. "Now, that would have been something like."

"No," Juno disagreed forcefully. "It would not have been."

Horry threw back his head and laughed. "You never know with him, do you? Although I knew right from the beginning he fancied you—remember? Lord, he wouldn't stop talking about you; he said I looked like Papa, and that you had his heart."

Juno found her throat had closed so that she could not respond for a moment, and her brother clasped her shoulders with a casual arm, touching his head to hers. "Let's sail to England, shall we?"

"Yes—let's sail to England. Now, go off with you; I know you are dying to help."

Needing no further encouragement, Horry bounded off to assist with the topsail, and Juno stayed on the deck for a moment, watching the flurry of activity as men leapt on board, after casting off from the dock. The sails began to fill out, and soon she could sense the movement of the ship as it listed to one side, catching the wind that blew with the changing tide. It is so very exhilarating, she thought, breathing in the scent of the sea; small wonder Jost and Horry love it so much.

Sensing a presence beside her, she brought her gaze down to observe Peyton, who nodded at her in greeting and cautioned, "It may be best if you stay behind the mizzen, miss, so as to avoid injury." He steadied her arm as she stepped over coiled ropes, and then he lingered as they both watched the ship's progress out of the harbor. From what little contact she'd had with the man, he seemed quiet and rather thoughtful—a sharp contrast to her father and Jost. Perhaps his job had been to keep them in check; he seemed like someone who would look before he leapt.

In a rather abrupt manner, he addressed her again. "Am I to wish you happy, miss?"

Disconcerted, she turned to face him; he must have observed the chaplain's visit, and drawn his own conclusions. "No," she disclaimed, blushing, and decided she'd rather not make an explanation.

His own color high, he nodded but did not leave, and instead appeared to be trying to decide whether to tell her something. With some surprise, she waited politely, but he only bowed and wished her good day before rather abruptly walking away. How odd, she thought; I wonder what that was about.

Shouted directions were exchanged between the sailors on the foredeck, as the genoas were hoisted, billowing outward as the ship made the open sea. She looked for Aditi, but the girl was nowhere in sight, and Juno wondered if Landon was keeping her out of sight somewhere. Earlier in the day he'd delivered the fabric yardage, together with the appropriate notions and thread in his usual understated manner. To Juno's relief, the patterns were very pretty, and she expressed her appreciation.

"Nothing to it," he admitted. "My mother was a seam-stress, in her day."

Juno silently hoped Landon's mother, if she still lived, had a strong constitution—she was going to need it, when she met her new daughter-in-law.

22

"**J**uno—*lieve.*"

Startled, Juno blinked sleepily in the darkness, feeling Jost's fingers gently touching her face. She opened her mouth to ask what was amiss, but he touched her lips. "Be very quiet," he whispered.

As she nodded he ran his hand gently over her forehead, stroking her hair with his callused fingers. "If you want me to go, I will go."

"Oh," she breathed, as the purpose of the visit became clear. She turned her head on the pillow to meet his gaze, although in the dark she could not see his face very well; he smelled faintly of soap, as though he had recently washed.

"Me, I thought we would be wed tonight."

"Yes," she commiserated. "So did I." Sit up, Juno, she thought—if you don't sit up, you are lost. She propped herself up on an elbow and sat up, facing him as he crouched beside her berth. From this angle, his face was dimly illuminated by the moonlight that filtered in through the porthole, and his dark, liquid eyes were fixed upon hers. She thought; here is a man who wears his emotions on his sleeve—there is never any doubt as to how he feels at any particular moment.

Almost without conscious volition, she put a hand to his face, and he pressed it to his cheek and turned his head to kiss her palm. "Me, I think of you and I do not sleep."

"I love you," she whispered, the words filled with longing. "What are we to do?"

He held her hands in his and looked up into her face. "To me, we are wed."

The nuns never explain to you that temptation is so very tempting, Juno thought. Truly, it makes all the difference. "Perhaps once in a while, then," she suggested, her pulse beginning to accelerate, "—but not every night." She wasn't certain why an occasional sin seemed forgivable, but she was past logic at this point, since her hands seemed to be caressing his shoulders, even though she wasn't directing them to do so.

"I will see to it there is no child," he assured her, his gaze steady upon hers.

"Unless there already is." This thought had already crossed her mind more than once, as she tried not to contemplate her arrival in England with a blossoming belly, and a man not yet her husband.

But he, as always, had a plan. "If there is a child, we will say we were married today in secret, and the license will say this, too."

Except Horry would know the truth, she thought as she nodded in agreement, but decided there was nothing for it—they may have anticipated their vows, but the vows would definitely be said, so there was no real harm done.

Rising up on his knees, he began to gently work her nightdress over her head. "This time, you must try to stay silent," he teased in a tender tone, kissing her as her head emerged from the folds of fabric.

"I was not myself," she defended, her fingers on his buttons. "I can be as silent as a stone—you will see."

This, as it turned out, was not exactly true, but any involuntary sounds were muffled by his mouth on hers as she clung to him, and relished every sensation. "May I see your hair?" She felt for the leather string that secured his braid, her hands damp upon his back.

"No, *lieve*—if I am seen, it will tell the tale."

"When we marry—" she gasped as his mouth worked its magic "I will see your hair—and your tattoos."

"Assuredly," he breathed, and then all verbal communication ceased.

Afterward, she lay in the crook of his arm, adrift in bliss, with his lips in her hair. The ship tilted and creaked; Juno felt as though it would take an enormous effort to move, and so decided not to make the attempt.

"*Ik houd u*," he whispered, his fingers moving gently on her arm.

"Teach me, please." He said the words again, slowly so that she could repeat them. "Will you tell me of your life in Haarlem?"

"Some time," he whispered, and despite her best efforts to savor every moment, she fell asleep.

Juno awoke the next morning with the feeling one has when there is a residual euphoria, but the memory is not yet in place. Breathing in, she remembered, and imagined she could still catch his scent on her pillow. This time, their lovemaking had been unhurried, the emotion intense. He craved her—she could sense it, and she was fast developing cravings of her own, now that she was becoming accustomed. I don't know if I could raise much of a resistance if he seeks a repeat performance every night, she admitted to herself. But I should—we should not live as man and wife, when such is technically not the case.

Stretching, she contemplated her day, and wondered what her routine should be during the lengthy voyage— aside from trying not to dwell on the pleasures of the flesh. Aditi's sewing lessons were to commence, there was that; and perhaps she could convince Jost to teach her to shoot. Her misadventures at the palace and at the school had convinced her that she should at least make the effort, although it may be too little too late; it seemed unlikely she would be required yet again to defend herself, once they were in England. On the other hand, she was as yet unmarried, and the bridegift beckoned, so it would be best to look lively.

After she'd dressed, she came into the quarter-galley, which served meals to the captain and the officers. Horry was already there, eating eggs and bacon without pause, and speaking in an excited manner to Landon, who listened without comment. Juno watched them for a moment with a full heart—a few short weeks ago her brother had been thin and weak; now his sunburnt cheeks glowed with health, and he'd gained at least a stone. *We were slated to die at the hands of evil men*, she thought, *and my wonderful pirate rescued the both of us. If I weren't already in love with him I should be, out of sheer gratitude.*

"Hallo, Horry," she greeted him. "I haven't kept track of you—are you sleeping with the crew?"

"No, I'm bunking with Jost." Her brother picked up the crumbs on his plate with a finger. "He wants me to learn how to do the hour of 'turn to' with him in the mornings."

Juno smiled and privately thought that it was just as well; here was another reason Jost should not come to her bunk very often—if he kept slipping out in the dead of night, Horry may guess what he was about, and she should *try* to set an better example, although thus far she'd not made much of an effort.

Juno spoke to Jairus—who had resigned himself to frying an additional rasher of bacon, as Horry showed no signs of slowing down—and requested toast and jam for herself. With a practiced movement, the cook sliced a slab from the loaf, and placed it in the toasting rack, all whilst turning the bacon without a pause.

"Landon is teaching me the sextant, and the chronometer." Horry broke a biscuit as his sister sat beside him. "He says I can chart a course soon, if I practice."

Juno turned to Landon, trying without success to imagine the man offering marriage to Aditi. "That is excellent news, Mr. Landon—and I am willing to commence the sewing lessons this morning, if you'd like."

Landon shot her an assessing glance. "No hurry, miss; it can wait till she's learned some manners."

"Ridiculous," pronounced Horry with some heat, as he paused in his meal. "Aditi should have been left behind, Juno, and a good riddance."

Juno knew that Horry was still stung by his own guilt, and so she teased, "I shall push her overboard if she so much as looks at me cross-eyed, Horry; my word of honor."

With a skeptical glance, Horry returned to his meal without comment, and so Juno said to Landon, "I can bear her today as well as any other; I suppose it is best to begin the rehabilitation process immediately." She paused. "And since everyone seems to be giving lessons, perhaps someone will teach me how to shoot."

"Oh, Lord." Her brother shook his head. "Not me—I haven't the patience."

"What? I can certainly learn the fundamentals, one would think."

"I imagine Jost will teach you, if you ask him nicely," Horry glanced at her sidelong as he continued to eat. "He is that brave—or that besotted."

"Jost will what?" asked Jost, doffing his hat as he made a signal to the busy cook.

"Teach Juno to shoot," Horry explained. "Promise you won't use live ammunition without giving everyone on board a warning."

Jost turned to Juno, his teeth flashing. "Me, I am not afraid."

"Unfair," laughed Juno. "How difficult can it be?"

"Shooting is not difficult," Horry observed. "It's the being shot that is difficult."

Even Jairus joined in the general laughter, but Landon came to her rescue, "I think it a fine idea; it gives a female a fighting chance—evens the odds, so to speak."

Jost put a boot on the bench, and rested an arm on his leg as he contemplated Juno. "Me, I would like to teach you to shoot a blunderbuss, I think."

Horry stopped eating long enough to lift his head and stare at him. "You are daft if you think she can heft a blunderbuss; is there even one on board?"

Struggling not to laugh, Juno said only, "I believe Sir Jost is teasing, Horry."

"As long as you don't forget my knife-throwing lesson," Horry reminded him, trying to pick up the hot bacon with quick fingertips. "I asked first."

In response, Jost made a quick movement into his boot, and Juno gasped as a knife was suddenly embedded in the bulwark, a foot from Jairus' head. The cook only sighed, and shook his head as he continued to turn the breakfast meats.

With an admiring exclamation, Horry jumped up and removed the knife from the wall, turning it over in his hands as he brought it back to Jost. "Here's a wicked blade, sir. Where did you come by it?"

"Me, I had a disagreement with a man in Algiers," Jost related in a mild tone. "And then he no longer needed it."

Horry practiced a throwing motion, until Jost snatched it away and--with a deft flick of his wrist--embedded it in the bulwark again.

"'ere now," the cook protested. "I'm makin' the young lady 'er toast."

"Hold the toast in your hand like so—I will spear it," Jost suggested, making a throwing motion. Jairus only gave him an admonitory look, as he served up the toast and bacon. Jost slid onto the bench next to Juno, and she was very pleased that she could greet him with polite friendliness, considering that she had plied her tongue in his ear only a few hours earlier.

"What was it like, in Algiers? Is it as lawless as they say?"

While Jost considered Horry's question, Juno caught Landon giving him a quick glance from under his brows. Here's a story, she thought with interest; and whatever it is, Landon doesn't think Jost wishes to speak of it.

"Algiers, it is a dangerous place—you must not visit."

Horry agreed, shoveling eggs into his mouth. "Not likely—they'd make me a slave within a minute."

"You'd not fetch a good price, Horry—not with your malaria," Juno teased. For hundreds of years, the Barbary pirates had captured slaves from other countries, either holding them for ransom, or putting them to work. She cast a thoughtful glance at Landon, whose gaze now remained fixed on the table, and decided to change the subject. 'Would it be acceptable if I hold my sewing lesson on deck?"

"On the aft deck," Jost directed. "So that I can watch you."

"Yes, sir." No doubt he was worried she'd disappear again; and truth to tell, she was more than happy to stay under his watchful eye—it would be a long time before she would dangle her legs over the side of a boat again.

23

"I am very sorry," offered Aditi, the words stilted, and carefully rehearsed. "I was wrong not to call for help." The girl was doing her atonement, her hands folded before her, as the sea breeze lifted her hair off her forehead.

Deciding that the occasion called for it, Juno bowed her head and replied formally, "I accept your apology, Aditi," and noted that the girl's amber eyes moved to watch for Landon's reaction. The investigator had escorted her to the aft deck, and now stood at a small distance to listen. There was nothing remotely lover-like in his manner, and Juno could only continue amazed at his alleged interest. I'm not sure I believe it, she thought; he seems far too sensible for such a course of action.

To prepare for the sewing lesson, Juno had set up two stools in an area of the deck that was sheltered from the wind. Aditi took her seat, and Juno pulled up close to her, so as to demonstrate how to thread a needle, which seemed the appropriate place to start. Apparently satisfied that fisticuffs were not about to erupt, Landon bowed, and left.

Aditi lifted her gaze from Juno's hands, and watched the man's back as he walked away. "Aditi," prompted Juno. "Please pay attention."

But Aditi was preoccupied, and turned to say to Juno in an intense undertone. "He says he will wed me."

Nonplussed, Juno fell back upon protocol. "My best wishes."

Incredulous, Aditi indicated her left hand to Juno. "He says I will wear a ring, and everyone will see."

"He is a very fine man," Juno equivocated—a very fine man who had lost his senses, it would seem. Although to be fair, Jost was right about the bed sport—it did preoccupy one's mind.

"Everyone will see," Aditi repeated in wonder, and held her left hand out before her, the fingers tilted up—clearly imagining it adorned with a wedding band.

Juno watched her, oddly touched--it was clear that such an event had never been considered within the realm of possibility. Hitting upon a strategy, she observed, "As a married lady, you will need to know how to sew."

Aditi raised her head, thinking this over with narrowed eyes. She then leaned forward, intent. "Show me."

And so the lesson commenced, and Juno took hope. She had already noted that the Indian girl had nimble fingers—which had given her the idea in the first place—and so progress was rapid. There was little conversation other than instruction, but on occasion, Aditi would elevate the fingers of her left hand and glance at them, dwelling on the promised ring.

Juno demonstrated the merits of an overcast stitch. "Do you see? It is useful if there is a tear in the fabric."

"Yes," agreed Aditi, watching carefully. "Preya would sew up the men's clothes in this way." Pausing, she looked toward the distant horizon, a slow smile on her lips. "I cannot wait to tell Preya," she declared with a note of triumph. "She will not believe it."

Indulging the girl, Juno asked, "Who is Preya, Aditi? Is she your sister?"

"My brother's woman," the girl answered matter-of-factly. "We were taken together."

"Oh? Taken where?" Juno absently bit off the thread.

"To Algiers." Aditi took up her needle again. "To the Dey's prison—the *bagnio*."

Juno looked up in shocked dismay. "Never say you were captured by Barbary pirates?"

"I have already said it," Aditi retorted with an impatient frown. "Sometimes, you are very stupid." Catching herself, she retreated. "I should not have said that—do not tell him."

But Juno was more interested in the disclosure than in the insult, and dropped the sewing to her lap. "Heavens, Aditi; what happened—were you ransomed?"

The other girl shrugged, as though it mattered little to her. "No. I was tired of waiting for Jost to come, so the missionary sent me to India." The memory did not seem a fond one, and she tossed her head. "I had grown tired of him, anyway."

Having recently had a brush with slavery, Juno decided perhaps there was something to be said about Aditi's lack of sensibility—she certainly didn't seem scarred by her experience. She thought of Aditi's brother, now dead, and Jost's obligations to him. "What happened to Preya—did Jost rescue her, also?"

But this was another sore point, apparently, and the girl said with some heat, "Jost took her somewhere, but I was not told—as though I was a child—and so I left, to show I was not a child." It seemed clear this memory stung, and was the main reason Aditi had taken up with the smitten missionary. Stilling her hands, Aditi paused to contemplate Juno with a faint frown between her brows. "I thought Jost took Preya away to be his woman again, but Mr. Landon says no—he wants you, not Preya."

But Juno was not following this confused recounting, and knit her own brow. "I thought you said Preya was your brother's woman."

Aditi smiled in a superior manner at Juno's ignorance. "First she was for Jost; then they played dice for her, and my brother took her."

"I see," said Juno, a bit taken aback. "And yet they were friends—your brother and Jost?"

"Yes—the best friends." Aditi reverted to the original topic. "Preya will not believe it, when I tell her I am wed."

"It is a wonder," agreed Juno wholeheartedly. Then, guessing that Jost's preference for the absent Preya must have raised some bitter feelings in the girl's breast, she added, "I imagine she will be very jealous of you."

Aditi bestowed upon Juno her rare, brilliant smile. "Yes."

Juno bent her head once again over the sample cloth, thinking Aditi a font of very interesting information. It was encouraging that it appeared Aditi was resigned to losing Jost to Juno, now that the dazzling prospect of marriage had been raised. "You have done well today, Aditi; I believe we can start cutting material for a new dress tomorrow. Would you like a new dress?"

Aditi nodded, and indicated the dress she wore. "Mr. Landon says this one is very pretty. Will the next one be as pretty?"

Juno tried to imagine the laconic Landon giving Aditi such a compliment, and fell short. "We will copy the same pattern, then, so that it is similar. We'll cut two, and one will be for me."

This plan met with the other girl's approval, and she nodded her agreement. "Yes—Mr. Landon says I must watch you, and behave like you do."

But Juno had to demur, and replied in all honesty, "You are I are different creatures, Aditi—I believe he only wishes you to learn some manners, not to change completely. After all, he has no interest in marrying me."

"Yes—he says he likes my fire, but I must control my temper."

"Exactly," Juno hastily agreed, deciding she'd rather not be privy to any intimate conversations between this unlikely pair.

Her wishes were not to be fulfilled, however; imitating Juno, Aditi bit off a thread, and then sighed with resignation. "He says no more men."

Juno could only concur. "Gentlemen do not like to share—except Jost and your brother, apparently."

But the corners of Aditi's beautiful mouth turned downward. "How do I know I will be pleased with him? He will not let me into his bed—not until we are wed."

Here's irony, thought Juno—the virtuous concubine, speaking to the debauched maiden. Tentatively, she suggested, "Perhaps you should seek to please *him*, instead. After all, he will give you a ring, so that everyone can see."

The girl thought this over. "I can please him—I know many things."

Thinking she'd best change the subject before she was tempted to ask about particulars, Juno inquired, "Where are you sleeping, Aditi?"

"The brig," the girl responded calmly. "I am to stay away from you, from Jost, and from the crew."

"I'm sorry for it," said Juno diplomatically, thinking this was, in fact, a very good plan.

Tracing her rudimentary stitching with an idle finger, Aditi bent her head. "I do not mind. He comes to talk to me. Usually, the men do not talk to me."

I hate it, thought Juno, when my preconceptions are questioned—it makes me think I should do a little less judging, and a little more judging not.

Gazing at her left hand once more, Aditi pronounced with some spite, "I will have a ring, but you will not."

Ah, thought Juno. Back to normal.

24

After the sewing lesson concluded, Juno could only marvel at the hold Landon had established over the willful girl, and felt compelled to broach the subject later, when he approached Juno to thank her. "Truly, it was not as much of a trial as I had expected—you have worked wonders."

"Best to keep her busy," he explained in a practical manner. "Idle hands, and all."

"I understand I am to wish you happy." Juno smiled, to show she would not berate him as a fool; they were leaning on the pin rail, watching the ocean hiss and churn in the ship's wake.

"You must think me mad," he conceded bluntly. "Small blame to you; but I think she would benefit from a firm hand on the tiller, so to speak. She's run wild."

As this seemed an understatement, Juno could make no encouraging reply. Watching her reaction, Landon shifted his feet. "It was your brother, miss; he was the one who brought it to my mind."

"Horry?" Juno gazed at him in puzzlement.

"A fine boy," Landon pronounced, his lean cheeks a bit reddened. "Never thought to marry—nor have any children, but now I think I would like to have a son or two, and the girl's young enough to do the deed."

"Oh—oh, I see. Then I wish you all the best, Mr. Landon."

"The best of luck, you mean," he responded dryly.

"You do have a ring?" Juno held the brim of her hat up so that she could meet his eyes in all seriousness. "I think it is important."

"I do." He smiled. "Knew it would be."

Juno nodded, and then turned to watch the waves again. "Will you tell me what happened in Algiers? Aditi spoke of being captured with Preya."

She had hoped to catch him off guard, with this change in topic, but he did not seem discomfited, and said only, "Not my tale to tell." He then seemed to weigh what to say, and added, "Don't know as I would ask."

Juno wasn't certain she would take the advice—she was willing to share Jost's burdens, support him in any troubles. On the other hand, it may have something to do with the work for the Crown that he shared with Landon. With some delicacy, she asked, "Would it be that he *cannot* tell me, or he would choose not to?"

Landon pursed his lips, deliberating. "A bit of both."

Her brow knit, Juno was winding up to ask another question, but Landon was too wily to await one, and bowed, thanking her again for her generosity to Aditi.

He was replaced almost immediately by Jost, who stood at her elbow and pretended to be jealous. "You must not smile at Landon—me, I need him to take Aditi away from me."

"It is the eighth wonder of the world that he wishes to," she agreed. "Perhaps I should make a push to beguile him, just to save him from his fate."

"I do not know what this means—" he placed his hand on hers even though it would be in plain view for anyone who happened to look "—but I forbid it."

"Fine, then; I shall beguile you, instead." She smiled up into his eyes, very pleased by this public show of affection. Truly, when he looked upon her in such a way, the bed sport was brought very much to mind.

As though reading her mind, he asked, "Tonight?"

The giddy feeling dissipated as she reluctantly remembered the strictures of society. "Jost," she replied in all seriousness. "I love you—you know I do; but we mustn't—you must help me to be strong, and to resist you."

"Yes." He ducked his chin, and withdrew his hand. "If you have the unhappiness, we will wait until we are wed."

She hastened to assure him, "It is not that I don't wish to be with you, or that I regret it—not for a single moment—" Aware that she was talking herself out of her resolution, she firmly closed her lips.

"Last night, it will be our secret," he concluded philosophically.

Juno was a bit surprised that he would so readily concede—she expected at least an attempt at persuasion. Firmly reminding herself that she shouldn't be disappointed, she shook her head. "It is just as well—I have had my fill of secrets, this day."

Playfully, he tugged on the brim of her straw hat. "Me, I have no secrets from you, *lieve*. Only things I cannot tell you—not yet."

With a quirked mouth, she prompted, "For example, how you threw dice for Preya."

"Assuredly," he agreed without missing a beat. "You must not be told of this."

She laughed aloud, and he joined in with her. "It does seem a bit callous—heartless," she corrected for his benefit. "If you tried such a trick with me, I would take the blunderbuss to you."

But he cocked his head, and shrugged. "Me, I was tired of her; but he desired her—it was the easy way for men to speak of it."

"I imagine there was a prodigious amount of drinking involved," she observed.

He chuckled softly, and glanced behind her on the deck. "Back then, there was always the drinking—but not now. Now, I am the decorous man."

Thinking of the definitely un-decorous things she had learned from him the night before, she diplomatically refrained from comment. "Where is Preya now? Is she part of your *niyama*?"

But he hesitated, and appeared to weigh what he would say for a moment. "She is. But I could not find her—and your father, he needed my help, so I could not stay to look for her."

Aditi must have been mistaken, then, in thinking Jost had rescued Preya, and taken her away without telling the other girl where they went. Juno touched his arm in sympathy. "You will find her; I have the utmost confidence in you."

"She had a little girl." He met her eyes, and the manner in which he said it told her that it was a confession of sorts.

"Your daughter?" Juno asked, guessing this was the case.

He shrugged his broad shoulders. "Perhaps—mine, or the other's."

So then, thought Juno, careful to maintain her poise; if I accept the man, I accept him as he comes. "Is she safe, the little girl?"

"She is dead."

Her heart aching for him, she said quietly, "Jost, I am so sorry."

"It was the yellow jack. In the Dey's *bagnios*, it spreads very fast."

"How terrible," she whispered, placing a gentle hand on his forearm.

"I came too late for her. I came too late for your father."

His disappointment was palpable—he was not one to accept defeat in any form, and she longed to console him. "But you did not come too late for me." She emphasized the words, as she pressed both her hands around his arm. "And not for Horry—you came in the nick of time for us, Jost."

"The nick of time," he repeated, trying out the phrase.

Earnestly, she gazed into his eyes. "Without a doubt— we would have both been dead by now. And you rescued me from the Rajah, too—that would have been worse than being dead."

"No," he corrected, his gaze serious upon hers. "Dead would have been worse."

"If you say," she agreed, deciding not to argue. "So you have prevailed more often than you have not, Jost."

"They will pay," he assured her, a hint of steel in his voice. "For everything."

They stood together, looking out to the sea, whilst she thought over what he had said. "What was her name, the little girl?"

"Bala."

"Perhaps we shall have a daughter," she ventured. "Not to replace Bala—but so that her loss is lessened."

"Yes," he agreed, the glint of humor returning. "But you must have the sons, too—do not forget this."

"If you insist," she teased, pleased that she had apparently said the right thing to lighten his mood. Turning to view the ship, she noted with surprise that Peyton stood at a small distance, awaiting a chance to speak to Jost. Juno colored up, hoping he hadn't overheard their intimate conversation. She indicated the other man with a tilt of her head. "I will go below."

Jost nodded. "If you will find Horry, I will teach him the chart."

"I will send him." She then hesitated, self-conscious. Now that she knew of his loss, it did not seem the best time to withhold such comfort as only she could give him. Trying to convince herself that she was not fishing for an excuse, she offered in a low voice, "Perhaps I shall leave my door unlocked tonight." She met his eyes, a question contained in hers.

"The lock, it would not stop me," he replied, just as softly. "But your words, they would stop me."

So—he was not going to allow her to give the choice back to him. She looked into his eyes for a long moment and decided there was nothing for it. "Come, then—please."

25

"What are you two laughing about?" Juno approached Jost and Horry, who were seated on the forecastle deck, splicing together a broken fishing line and chuckling, their heads close together.

Horry, his eyes alight, looked to Jost to give the explanation, which he did with his usual forthrightness. "We think, how long before Landon needs to eat?"

Juno blushed and laughed along with them. After a month at sea, it was determined that Aditi's wedding would go forward, and so the previous day Jost had performed the ceremony as captain.

Rather than radiant, the girl had looked anxious, as though she expected at any moment to be told it was all a cruel joke. In the end, the ring was firmly on her finger, and the couple withdrew to the first mate's cabin, not to emerge again for twenty hours running. It appeared that Aditi did indeed know some things—or perhaps it was Landon who did. Juno was fast learning some things herself, what with her own betrothed visiting nearly every night. She had decided to assuage her conscience by referring to Jost as her betrothed, so as to grant a fig leaf to her transgressions—which were many, and unrepented. If there was a priest aboard, she thought with some ruefulness, she would be so often in confession that her knees would ache. It was beyond all bearing that Aditi was wed before she was, and could explore such matters at leisure, whilst Juno had to be content with a mere hour of managing it quietly in the dark--and with a guilty conscience, besides. Although—and here she drifted into a blissful reverie—last night it had been a magical hour, indeed. The memory made her feel a bit warm, and she glanced at Jost, only to find his amused gaze upon her.

"What are you thinking, *lieve*?"

"I am thinking about how I would like some fresh fish for dinner," she replied in a tart tone, giving him a look. He shouldn't tease her in front of Horry.

With a sigh, Jost held up the broken fishing line. "Your brother, he breaks the line, again and again." He tilted his head toward Horry. "Fetch Landon, and tell him to stop whatever he is doing—he must fish for Juno."

"Pray do no such thing," Juno protested, laughing.

"I could check to see if he is still alive," Horry offered with a grin.

Jost observed, "If he is dead, he died a happy man, and me, I will not mourn him." He then flashed his smile at Horry. "You will see, when it is your turn."

Juno quickly turned the subject. "How long do you think we will be becalmed?" The wind had died for two days running, and Jost and the crew were chafing at the enforced idleness. To pass the time, the crew was engaged in a contest to catch the most fish, with a day of leisure as the prize.

Jost glanced up at the cirrus clouds overhead and opined, "Not long, I think." He turned to Horry. "We can take the skiff out, if you wish."

"Can we, sir?"

Horry seemed to think this an excellent idea, whilst Juno could not hide her alarm. "Out on the open water? Do you think it wise?"

"We will spear a whale, maybe." Jost glanced out over the smooth sea, as though he fully expected to view such a creature. "Then Juno, she would eat for weeks."

Juno defended herself from his teasing, "You can hardly blame me for having some anxiety, for heaven's sake—it is not as though we have avoided all dangers, lately."

"Nothing can happen in the middle of the ocean, Juno." Horry pointed out. "And the water is like glass—there is no danger whatsoever."

Reminding herself that she mustn't cosset her brother, Juno conceded, "I am cautious by nature, I'm afraid."

Turning to Horry, Jost shook his head. "Do not believe her, Horry. Some time I will tell you how I met your sister--when I think of it, my heart, it stops."

While appreciating the accolade, Juno disclaimed, "It's not brave when you have no choice."

"That's exactly what makes it brave, Juno," her brother explained as though speaking to a simpleton. But he was not interested in extolling Juno's virtues, and wanted to get on with the fishing expedition. "Shall I have them lower the skiff?"

"Knock on Landon's door, first." Jost began to roll up the line on the creel.

Surprised, Horry asked, "Truly?"

"Truly—it is time he was on deck. Tell him I said this."

Horry nodded and left without further protest, apparently having been given the same impression as Juno, namely that Jost wanted Landon to be present, if he was to leave the ship. It must be some sort of chain of command protocol, thought Juno—it is not as though Jost cannot trust the crew.

Jost interrupted her thoughts, and leaned toward her with some amusement. "Juno—your face, it is like glass; you must not think of the bed sport, or your brother, he will guess."

"Oh," said Juno, blushing furiously. "Is it that obvious?"

"To me, yes." He reached to take her hand in his, to soften the rebuke. "You are the same when you play the cards."

"How mortifying—do you suppose Horry has guessed?"

"He knows I will marry you," Jost equivocated. "He is nearly a man, and understands such things."

Juno buried her face in her bent knees, wholly embarrassed. "Oh Jost—I do not set a very good example."

"Me, I think you set a very good example." Jost gently ran a finger along her arm. "It fills my head, it is such a good example."

Juno raised her eyes to his, unable to resist a smile at this fine compliment. "But you, my friend, were not raised in a convent school."

"Me, I do not know the watercolors," he conceded, "—but I do know some things, yes?"

"I thought we are not to speak of it—because my face is like glass," she teased.

He rose to his feet, and gave her a hand to haul her up. "We will speak of it later, yes?"

"After you have caught me my whale," she countered, brushing off her skirts. "Then we shall see."

His hands on his hips, he shook his head. "Ach, Juno. Now you are the callous one."

Amused that he remembered the word, she assured him, "I can be as callous as the occasion calls for—perhaps I will throw dice with some female, to take you off my hands."

"There is no female on the ship, except Aditi," he pointed out reasonably. "And she is tired."

Later, Juno smiled as she remembered the conversation, leaning on the rail and watching Jost and Horry fishing in the skiff. The air was still and heavy, and members of the crew were arrayed along the rail, fishing to while away the time. Landon had made his reappearance, self-contained and expressionless, so that none would imagine he had an exhausted new bride stowed below in his berth. Horry had made some comment with the result that Landon gave him an affectionate cuff, but otherwise, matters appeared back to normal—or as normal as they could be, considering the dire events that awaited in London.

Juno leaned to look toward the bow, watching the water lap against the hull, and reviewing what she had pieced together from Jost's comments, and from her own observations. The Nabob was a few days ahead of them, hoping to find and claim the bridegift in London, but the forces aligned with Jost and Landon were in close pursuit, and matters would presumably come to a head once they arrived. Jost told her they would apply to the Court of Chancery immediately upon their arrival, so as to unravel the scheme that had pronounced her married, and then dead—the treasonous scheme, which her father had infiltrated. Her father had been exposed as a double agent, and then murdered, but not before securing the fortune in diamonds, and depositing it somewhere, disguised as a bridegift. With any luck, they'd arrive in London before the Nabob found the diamonds—Jost felt it was unbelievable that her father would have hidden them somewhere that would make them vulnerable to the enemy, and he seemed to have known her father very well.

Juno squinted up at the sails, which were still slack, and then glanced down to see that Peyton now stood beside her, bowing his head, and holding his leather hat in his hand. "A good day, Miss Payne."

"Not a good day for sailors, Mr. Peyton," she replied with a smile.

"I don't believe it will last long, though. In this area it usually doesn't—another day at most."

I hope I shall not be called upon to speak at length about the weather, thought Juno when the man did not move away, but instead hovered to finger his hat in a self-conscious manner. Conversation with Peyton was never very easy, and she would much rather watch Jost cast a line. Instead, her companion broached a different subject, and one more amenable to her. "I knew your father, miss—a finer man never lived."

Touched by the sincere accolade, she regretted her impatience. "Thank you. I shall miss him very much."

He met her eye with a determined air. "You should take these things that have been said against him with a grain of salt, if I may say."

Wondering how much he knew, she nodded. "Yes—the accusations make little sense, to those who knew him."

Dropping his gaze for a moment, the man seemed to marshal his resolve, choosing his words carefully. "On account of your father—and how he is no longer with us, miss—I feel I must give you some information that you will not thank me for."

This disclosure seemed very unlike him, and she exclaimed in surprise, "Why, what is it, Mr. Peyton?"

He gathered himself, and met her eyes. "It's about the Captain, miss."

I am not going to want to hear this, thought Juno, her heart sinking as she gauged the seriousness of the expression in his eyes; I am a coward, and I don't want to know.

"I believe he is a married man."

The tenor of his voice betrayed the man's deep unhappiness at being the bearer of such unwanted news, and it gave her pause, because her immediate reaction was to not believe it for a moment. "Why do you say this, Mr. Peyton?"

The man shifted his weight, and seemed to gain confidence, now that the subject had been broached. "I cannot give you the particulars, miss, as the business is not something that can be spoken of. But I will tell you—upon my oath—that I heard it from his own lips. He has a wife he left behind in Algiers, and a small daughter, besides. I have not heard that his wife has died, or that the marriage has been dissolved—indeed, he mentioned her in passing, just a few weeks ago."

Juno stared at him, reluctantly remembering how Jost did not like to speak of his family, and had avoided any inquiries on the subject. Or perhaps Peyton referred to the woman Preya, and her child Bala, who had died. But that made little sense; it seemed unlikely that Jost would marry such a woman, when there was no need. And he had certainly intended to marry Juno the day they sailed—he hadn't planned on the recalcitrant chaplain, or Juno's mistake in speaking of her wedding with the Rajah. Unbidden, the memory of Jost's hesitation when the chaplain asked if he was a bachelor came to mind; Juno had assumed he hadn't understood the word, but perhaps he had, after all. Would he involve her in a bigamous relationship? With some horror, she realized it was entirely possible—Jost was a law unto himself.

As if reading her thoughts, Peyton offered awkwardly, "If it's any comfort, miss, I believe his affections are deep and sincere. It is only—" he paused, trying to find the right words, "—he is not one to care for the conventions."

This was undisputable, and Juno wished she didn't feel as though her chest was suddenly frozen. I should not believe the worst of him so easily, she rallied herself; he deserves the benefit of the doubt—if only this news weren't so plausible. Trying to right her reeling emotions, she bent her head to stare at the still, unmoving water, forcing herself to stay calm. But there were more shocks to come.

His cheeks reddening, Peyton added, "If I may ask, miss; is a husband needful?"

Raising her head, she considered him blankly for a moment, and then realized he was delicately trying to ask if she was already with child. Jost was right—there were no secrets on board a ship.

Blushing hotly, she shook her head, even though she truly wasn't certain. There had been an occasional lapse in the precautions taken—last night numbering among them. Oh God, she thought in acute dismay; what have I done?

Her companion began to finger his hat again. "You are a good, fine girl, miss, and if you have need of someone—under the circumstances—I would be honored to assist your father's daughter."

There could be no mistaking his sincerity. "I thank you," she said through stiff lips. "I shall have to think about what you have told me."

"Of course, of course; I'm that sorry, miss, and I will say no more." He then bowed and walked away.

26

Juno's immediate impulse was to hear the truth from Jost, come what may. She felt she could speak to him with complete honesty on any topic, and in the end, she simply couldn't believe it of him. Of course, if she confronted him, he may guess it was Peyton who had told her, but that could not be helped and indeed, it seemed rather ominous; if Peyton had made up the tale out of whole cloth, he must know he would face Jost's formidable displeasure. Instead, it spoke to the tale's being true.

She gazed out over the ocean, unseeing. On the other hand, here was yet another man who had asked for her hand--could Peyton be after her bridegift? She didn't believe so—one of the reasons the story rang true was Peyton's stolid manner. If it was true—if Jost was lawfully wed to another—she had committed an even more grievous sin than the one she had willingly committed. With growing horror, she realized she could not have anything

213

to do with him henceforth—what would she tell Horry? And if she escaped the burden of bearing an illegitimate child, she would nonetheless be ruined. It was hard even to contemplate so complete a disaster, and the fact that she had brought the disaster upon herself, only made it all the worse.

I must speak with him, she realized, and as soon as possible. I should not be surprised if he attempts to convince me that the story is false, but it is past time that I began thinking without the distraction of lust.

No, she corrected herself immediately; not lust, but love. If I know nothing else, I know I love him and he loves me. Taking a steadying breath, she focused on this. I shall hear what he has to say and assess what is to be done—and I definitely need to put a stop to our trysts, until I can verify his status. I can't imagine Peyton would have gathered his courage to speak of it, unless he sincerely believed it was true.

Walking to the rope ladder, she positioned herself in plain sight, willing Jost to return and hoping that the sight of her waiting would encourage him to curtail the fishing trip. The *Juno* rocked a bit as Horry stood to cast his line, and Juno felt a sudden pang, watching Horry on their father's skiff, and thinking of the catastrophes that had been visited upon them, one after another in a seemingly endless series. Let us have an end to it, she pleaded, trying not to give in to despair—I am truly, truly not this brave.

Watching them, she realized that Horry had yet again broken his line, and Jost was laughing at him. They returned to the ship, Horry made to row the skiff, as a penance. As they came to, Jost looked up to give Juno his flashing grin. "Your brother, he is a *schaapskop*." He stretched out a hand to tie the skiff to the rope ladder.

"He is indeed," she agreed, looking down at him, and although she tried to keep her voice level, he gave her a sharp look, and began climbing up the ropes, his movements graceful and quick.

"What is it?" he asked softly, watching her as he ascended. "Tell me."

I forgot that my face is like glass, she thought. "There is no emergency," she assured him as he came to eye level, and then hoisted himself on deck. "I need to speak with you, is all."

"Horry," said Jost, who did not take his eyes off Juno. "Your sister, she wishes to fish."

"She does?" asked the skeptical Horry, who was starting his ascent. "But the line is broken."

Jost turned around to give him a look, and her brother responded by scrambling up the ladder without further demur.

"Come, Juno." Jost held out a hand out to assist her down the ladder.

"Oh," said Juno with some doubt, as she looked down the length of the knotted ropes. "I don't know, Jost—perhaps we could speak in your cabin."

"Me, I will go first," he assured her. "But come you must."

And so she went down the rope ladder, her back against his chest, and stepping when he directed her to because when it came down to it, she would always do as he asked, even when it went against her better judgment, and even when she was more afraid than she had ever been in her life.

He seated her in the stern of the skiff, and took up the oars, facing her. "Now then," he said as he began to pull on the oars, "—you will tell me what Peyton said."

"I am worried you are already married," she blurted out, unable to think of a way to spare Peyton, nor of a more diplomatic way to divulge her fears.

He met her eyes, considering, and she felt another wave of misery—there was no be no angry refutation as she had half-hoped; he was a serial bigamist, and she was only the latest bride to catch his fancy. Like Bluebeard, she thought, but then remembered that Bluebeard had murdered his wives, and so, technically, was not a bigamist.

Don't cry, she instructed herself. Not here, where everyone can see. The Dutchman continued rowing until the small vessel was stopped at a distance from the ship. Out of earshot, she realized; he wants to be certain we are not overheard—perhaps he wishes to ensure no one will refute what he says to me.

"I wish you had mentioned it," she ventured in a small voice, and tried without success to control a quaver.

He made no immediate response, but picked up the fishing rod, and made as if to prepare the line. "It is broken," she reminded him.

"Watch—you will see." He bit off the line, just above the hook and sinker, and tied it with a deft movement directly to the twine on the creel, without using the pole. He then dropped the hook into the water beside the boat, and handed her the creel. "If the fish bites, do not drop the creel."

Juno found she had to steady her shaking hands against the gunwale whilst Jost moved beside her, his broad shoulder touching hers as he spoke in an even tone. "Me, I say to the Dey in Algiers that I am married to Preya. I have the English title; they will put Preya and Bala in a safe place, so that I will be made to pay a fine ransom."

"Yes—if you said such a thing, it would keep them alive." She perceived a glimmer of hope. "I see."

"It was not true," he said with heavy emphasis. "Me, I have never married anyone. Me, I have never wanted to marry anyone until you." He paused, then added, "If it becomes known I am not married to Preya, she will suffer for it. But it is more important that you know the truth."

"Preya is still a captive?" Juno knit her brow, remembering the conflicting story she had heard from Aditi.

Again, he weighed what he would say to her, his gaze on the line where it disappeared into the ocean. "If anyone asks you of Preya, you must say you do not know anything."

"I don't make a very good liar," she reminded him in a small voice.

"It is a problem," he agreed in all seriousness. "Me, I hope no one asks you the questions."

"Do you still love her—Preya, I mean?" Juno found she was not dismayed by this thought—despite everything, she was certain of him.

He turned to meet her eyes. "No; Preya and Aditi's brother—they loved each other. But she is in the *niyama*, and I have made the promise." He watched her, and she could see the anxiety in his dark eyes, so expressive. "You believe this, yes?"

Juno nodded, and the frozen feeling in her breast begin to ease. "I should have married you in Fort St. George. You should have held your sword to me, until I agreed."

"Juno, *lieve*," he said quietly, the smooth, vast ocean surrounding them. "I belong to you and you belong to me. It is simple."

This was inarguable. If she were honest, she would admit she had already been turning over ideas in her mind to stay with him—somehow—despite the disgrace. She took a breath. "I was so frightened for a moment, Jost, about—well, what would become of me if the tale was true. Please—no more bed sport until we are truly married."

"No," he agreed immediately. "You must not be made unhappy."

She gasped, because the creel was suddenly tugged so hard that she nearly dropped it. "A fish," she exclaimed in astonishment. Turning the creel in her hands, she fumbled with the winding mechanism, but the Dutchman grasped the line and pulled it up, hand over hand, until the wriggling bass was hauled aboard, flopping about on the floorboard.

"That is a good fish," he laughed. "Horry, he will not be happy."

"Jost." She looked at him, then wasn't certain what she wanted to say.

"Juno—it will all be well. My promise to you."

"No more secrets," she implored. Then, imitating him, "My heart, it stops."

"There are more secrets," he admitted, "—but none that will take you away from me."

As he rowed back to the ship, she reflected that the convent school truly didn't prepare you for the complexities of life—or for unconventional men. They climbed aboard, Jost with a finger hooked through the fish's gills and brandishing it like a trophy, to the amusement of the crew. Among the watchers at the rail stood Aditi, and as the sailors hauled the skiff back aboard, Juno approached and greeted the girl, thinking that a bit of gentle teasing may be in order. "Mrs. Landon; you are well?"

"I must learn the English curtsey," the girl said without preamble. "You are to teach me." Thinking for a moment, she added, "Please."

"I shall be happy to demonstrate," Juno offered, thinking it surprising this was deemed a necessary skill. "Only not just now, perhaps."

"Before we land, I must know the English curtsey—already, I know how to make the English tea."

Ah, thought Juno; the light dawns. "You are to meet Mr. Landon's mother."

Aditi nodded, her expression a bit anxious. "He says it will not matter that I am not English—that she will be very happy." The girl sounded as though she very much doubted this would be the case.

Privately thinking that having a foreign daughter-in-law would be the least of the concerns, Juno assured her, "I imagine she thought he would never marry; you will be a very pleasant surprise."

"I am not to speak of many things," the girl added philosophically, watching as the sailors stowed the skiff. "I must not speak the truth."

"It is probably the better tack," Juno admitted. "All things considered."

The men then raised a signal flag on the mainmast, pulling on the sheet until the small banner fluttered in the awakening breeze.

"What does that one mean?" asked Juno, shielding her eyes to consider it.

Aditi shrugged impatiently, unhappy to be off-topic. "Mr. Landon—my husband—will teach me to read. He says when he is away, I must be able to read to the children."

It appeared Landon had many and sundry require-ments for his new bride, and Juno could only admire his strategy. "I can help," Juno offered. After all, if she partici-pated in good works it may take her mind off how much she was missing the pleasures of the flesh.

"I am to have children," Aditi repeated, making it clear that Juno had not appreciated this aspect of the story to the extent she should have.

"How wonderful, for both of you," Juno offered with appropriate fervor. "I imagine it was a terrible loss to you when Bala died."

Aditi turned to meet her eyes, startled, and there was a long pause. "I am not to speak of it," she said self-consciously. "I should not have said about Preya, before."

"To Mr. Landon's mother," Juno corrected gently. "You may speak of it to me, if you'd like."

"To no one," she insisted, "No one at all," and in the words Juno could hear the echo of Landon's instruction. So—it appeared there was indeed some concern about Preya's safety, and the less said, the better.

Horry came to congratulate Juno on her catch, and express his shock and amazement that his sister was capable of such a feat.

"Pure chance," Juno assured him, laughing. "The poor fish was begging to be caught, and it happened so quickly that even I could not muff it."

"Fish for dinner," pronounced Horry with some satisfaction. "And the breeze has started up again—our luck has turned." He nodded toward the sails, which were beginning to luff with life.

"What does the signal flag mean?" asked Juno.

Horry squinted at it. "It is a request for provisions from another ship."

Surprised, Juno asked, "Are we so desperate for provisions?"

"Apparently," said her brother, "—if we're going to have to rely on you to catch more fish."

27

A few days later, Juno was reading with Aditi when she felt the ship begin to come about. Lifting an arm to brace herself against the cabin's wall, she exclaimed, "Heavens—we're turning out of the wind. I wonder what's happened?"

"I am not finished," Aditi complained.

Because Juno's Bible served as the only available reading material, the reading lessons had been painstakingly slow. Aditi was not overly familiar with current English--let alone seventeenth-century English--and the close-set type only added to the girl's extreme frustration.

Then, Juno happened upon the story of Judith, the Old Testament heroine who seduced Holofernes, and then cut off the enemy general's head whilst he slept. Enrapt, Aditi heard the story again and again with bloodthirsty relish, and was now determined to learn the words so that she could read them herself. It was not exactly an appropriate bedtime story for potential children, but it was a start, and the girl was rapidly making progress.

"Let me go investigate, Aditi—perhaps something is amiss." Juno stood, and made her way above-decks to investigate the ship's sudden cessation of movement. As she emerged from the companionway, she could hear raucous laughter and voices, and could see that another ship had pulled alongside, the crews from both ships swinging grappling hooks so as to pull them together.

Oh—I suppose they saw our request for provisions, she thought. Shading her eyes, she saw that Jost stood on the forecastle, shouting in a language Juno guessed was Dutch, as his counterpart on the other ship roared back with equal gusto. The other captain was a huge bear of a man, with a full red beard, and a smile that revealed missing teeth.

"*Klootzak!*" the other shouted, "*Zoon van een hoer!*"

Jost leapt across just as the two ships were brought together to be lashed, and it seemed evident that the two captains were well-acquainted, particularly because their greeting involved socking each other in the chest with a great deal of force.

After spying Juno in the companionway, Horry came over to stand beside her, and she asked, "Who is the other captain? Do you know?"

"I haven't a clue. He must be Dutch, too."

"Evidently," Juno agreed, and then watched as the red-bearded man threw back his head to laugh uproariously at something Jost had said. To her surprise, the man turned to scrutinize the *Minerva*'s deck, then pointed and shouted something unintelligible upon spying Juno in the stairwell.

"Oh, dear," she exclaimed, as color flooded her cheeks.

"Better go below," said Horry, taking her arm. "I hope Sir Jost hasn't offered to trade you for the provisions; I don't think I could best either of them in a fight."

But their retreat back to her cabin was interrupted by Jost himself, who bounded down the steps after them, two at a time. "Juno—Juno, wait. You will marry me, yes?"

After a startled moment, Horry laughed aloud, whilst Juno gazed at Jost in bemusement. "Oh—oh; is that what this is all about?"

"Captain Spoor, he says he will marry us."

Unable to suppress a delighted smile, Juno curtseyed to Jost in form. "You do me great honor, sir."

Jost tilted his head. "This is 'yes'?"

"Of course it means yes," interjected Horry. "Give over, Juno."

"Now?" Juno looked from one to the other, finding that she could not contain the effervescing happiness that bubbled within her breast. "This moment?"

"In the time of nick." Jost held out an impatient hand to her. "Make haste—you come too, Horry."

Blushing before the interested scrutiny of both crews, Juno followed him to the gunwale, and hoped her petticoat was not on display as he lifted her from her feet and handed her over to the other captain, who did not hesitate to run his gaze over her body with approval, as he set her on his deck. "*Sappig*," he declared, and smacked his lips in a manner that required no translation.

Horry and Jost followed her over the gunwale, and the wedding party assembled on the forecastle deck of the Dutch ship, whilst both crews gathered to watch, exchanging rough but good-natured raillery in both languages. Captain Spoor grinned, the spaces between his teeth prominently on display as he directed a question to Juno, which Jost translated as he took her hand. "You are ready, Juno?"

"I am," she replied, because indeed she was. "Are you here, Horry?"

"Right here," her brother assured her. "In Papa's place."

The captain said something to Jost, and Jost translated for them. "He does not know the English so well, so I will tell you what he says."

And so in the midst of a crowd of sailors who stood with their hats in their hands, Juno said her vows to Jost, after he first translated them from the Dutch. Her bridegroom then held her hands in his and made his own promises, his sincere devotion unmistakable. I believe I am going to burst with happiness, thought Juno, who kept blinking away tears so that she could see his dear face. And for once, I am completely unafraid; I willingly bind my life to his, and with a whole heart, I accept whatever is to come.

At the conclusion of the ceremony, Jost put his ring upon her finger, then took her in his arms and kissed her soundly--to the cheers of the assembled men, who shouted suggestions which Juno pretended not to hear. They thanked Captain Spoor, and a sailor from the *Minerva* tossed Jost a bottle of rum, which was then presented to the officiate with a flourish. Juno was given to understand that the man invited them to share it with him, but Jost disclaimed, and the other, eyeing Juno in a lascivious manner, conceded with a knowing grin.

All it wants is for Jost to heave me over his shoulder, thought Juno, mortified, but fortunately, she was spared this humiliation, and instead she was handed over the adjacent gunwales once again, and returned to the *Minerva*.

As they waved goodbye, she said to Jost, "If you wish to stay and become reacquainted, I do not mind."

"Assuredly not," he responded under his breath. "The bottle, if it is opened he will drink for the whole day, and we have no time to lose."

Juno regarded the gold band on her finger and had to resist an impulse to extend her fingers upward and stare at it, Aditi-fashion. "What a wonderful surprise."

He leaned in to admire her ring, then lifted her hand to kiss it. "Me, I did not want to tell you, in case it went wrong again."

Horry interrupted them to kiss Juno's cheek, and shake Jost's hand in a formal fashion that made Juno hide a smile. "My congratulations. You are a lucky man."

"Horry, you are out of my cabin."

"Understood," her brother laughed. "First things first."

"First things first," Jost agreed, liking the phrase, and saying it slowly. "Now, second things; you will help Landon reset the course—the sun, it is in the wrong place."

Jost signaled to Landon, who had stood at a respectful distance, reluctant to intrude. "Make haste; Horry will help you set the course."

"Such a hurry to make England," Juno observed, teasing him. "It might cause one to believe you are eager to lay hands on my bridegift."

"Me, I am eager to lay hands on your bridegift," Jost agreed, in such a suggestive tone that Juno didn't know where to look. To spare her blushes, Landon bowed, "My best wishes, Lady Van der Haar."

"Oh," said Juno, much struck. "I suppose that is me; how strange."

Horry offered, "Papa said they gave you a title because they couldn't let you work for the other side."

"Which other side is that?" asked Juno in surprise. "The Mughals?"

"Valuable services were performed," Landon interrupted, giving Horry a look. "Enough said."

"Then where is your title, for valuable services performed, Mr. Landon?" Juno teased him.

"Don't know as I deserve one, my lady," the man responded, deadpan. "Being as how I am merely an investigator for Lloyd's of London."

Peyton joined them, offering his congratulations and bowing with the appearance of perfect complacency to Juno, who was reminded she should make an explanation to the man, given as he had been good enough to give her a warning—not to mention an offer of marriage to save her from ruination. To this end, when the others were busy adjusting the sails to suit the new course, she approached him. "May I speak with you for a moment, Mr. Peyton?"

"Of course, my lady," he said immediately, and came to stand aside with her.

"So that you do not think me mad, I must explain that I have discovered you were mistaken." She smiled, so that he wouldn't believe she held any grudge over the confusion.

Bowing his head in acknowledgement, he responded, "I didn't doubt it for a moment, my lady, and I so I was very happy to see you wed."

His manner was sincere and forthright, but to be certain he didn't think her a fool, she added, "He had to claim that he was married in an effort to protect—" here she paused, uncertain as to whether she should broach the particulars "—others who were dear to him. But now the subterfuge is no longer needed."

She thought his gaze sharpened on hers for a moment. "I am sorry for the confusion, then, my lady, and I am glad there was no harm done." He shook his head in a rueful manner. "It would have been better to hold my peace, so to speak."

But Juno disclaimed, and assured him with all sincerity, "No—your intentions were honorable, and you had my best interests at heart. Pray do not vex yourself over it."

As she watched him walk away, she reflected that Peyton must have been involved in the Algerian matter—he'd made reference to it, after all—so it made sense he would know of Jost's subterfuge about his marriage to Preya; apparently he had not been aware that it was only a subterfuge.

She glanced at her ring again, and admired it, moving it around her finger with her thumb. Everything has turned out perfectly, she thought; Horry is right, our luck has changed. Feeling as though she was floating down the companionway steps, Juno went to pack her things, and prepare for her wedding night.

28

J uno and Jost shared a wedding dinner in the captain's cabin, Jairus serving up an excellent fish filet, which grew cold on the table as the newlyweds discovered they had more of an appetite for each other. In a frenzy of mouths and hands, they retired to Jost's berth, which allowed for more freedom of movement than Juno's berth and as a result, Juno finished the evening lying beneath her spent husband, as the candles guttered on the table. The cook hadn't bothered to bring in the second course, and Juno suspected he may have put an ear to the door and then retreated. She was past being embarrassed, and instead drew her hands through Jost's hair, which fell about his shoulders and back. "Are you asleep?" she asked softly.

"No," he answered, his mouth in her neck. "But my strength, I think it is gone."

She tugged on his ear lobe with her teeth. "You may rest; you have done well."

"Give me a few minutes, only," came the muffled reply. "And then we will see."

Giggling, she clasped her arms around his neck, and nuzzled the side of his face, planting soft kisses. "Your eyelashes are so long—I noticed them straight away."

"You were too frightened, *lieve*."

"I was not," she protested. "I knew from the start that you were not going to hurt me."

He made a skeptical sound, and she giggled again. "You *are* fearsome, but I was not afraid—not truly."

With an effort, he managed to lift himself, and prop up on his elbows. "I think to myself, 'I must be very decorous, or this girl, she will not marry me.'"

Remembering the occasion, she made a wry mouth as she smoothed a lock of his hair away from his face. "Yes; it was decorous of you to offer to take me to bed."

He kissed her nose. "Me, I make the joke, so you do not think I am serious."

"An excellent joke," she agreed. "And I confess I was ready to reconsider the whole taking-to-bed idea, when I saw you without your shirt, the morning next."

"Ah." His mouth moved to kiss the corner of hers. "I think to myself, 'she will fall into the well, this girl.'"

Laughing, she agreed. "You are so beautiful, I nearly did." With a gentle hand, she pushed against him so that he rolled onto his back, and she ran her hands over his chest, and placed her mouth against a large tattoo depicting a dragon. "Do you like dragons? The pipe you gave Papa is a dragon."

"It is my ship—the *Dragon*."

This was of interest, and Juno lifted her head to look at him. "The one in Algiers? Is it an Indiaman?"

"No, *lieve*. Me, I smuggled the opium for Rochon."

He said it in a casual tone, his fingers rolling a tendril of her hair, but Juno was aware the statement was significant—she was very sensitive to his emotions, now. Tracing the dragon, she asked, "And who is Rochon?"

"Me, I will kill him," said Juno's husband. "Very slow."

"Oh. He deserves it, I suppose?" Juno was not certain how supportive she should be of such a stated goal.

"Yes." He paused, and Juno knew he was debating what to tell her. "He gathers the money for Napoleon."

She assimilated this. "Like the diamonds?"

"Like the diamonds. But sometimes the money, it passes through the opium traders, instead of the Rajah."

Feeling that she was doing an admirable job of hiding her shock, Juno continued to trace the markings on his chest, and said in a neutral tone, "You were—you were aiding Napoleon."

He smoothed the tendril of hair behind her ear. "Me, I was aiding whoever pays me the most money. I was not the honest man, then."

So—his was a redemption tale; thanks, apparently, to Papa. "Why are you so angry at Rochon? I would think instead that he would be angry at you, for turning coat."

"What does this mean?" With an idle finger, he traced hers, spread out on his chest.

"It is when you change which side you are loyal to. You turn your coat inside out, so it is not the same color as before."

He shifted his head on the pillow, and kept his gaze on his fingers, still stroking hers. "The English, it is very confusing."

Sensing his reluctance, she told him gently, "If you'd rather not tell me, I truly don't mind—you are the best judge of such things."

"The men who fight—" he paused, gathering his thoughts. "Everyone understands together."

"There are rules," she guessed, trying to help him out. "A code."

His gaze remaining on her hand, he continued, "No one hurts the women; no one hurts the children."

This seemed indisputable, and Juno hid her growing horror. "But Rochon did?"

His eyes met hers. "He does not want me to work with the British. He takes my mother, he takes my sister. My half-sister," he corrected. "She was ten."

"Despicable," she breathed.

"Despicable," he repeated slowly. "Yes."

Juno waited, afraid to ask.

"He cannot make me change my mind—so they die."

Laying her cheek on his chest, she said softly, "Oh, Jost—I am so, so very sorry."

"So now he will die."

"It does seem justified." She turned her head to kiss the hard muscles beneath her cheek. She had surmised he had no family left—small wonder he didn't like to speak of it.

But he was not yet finished with the tale. "My mother, her life was not easy."

Her head still on his chest, Juno could sense this was important, and not a random remark. "Poor woman," she offered, waiting for whatever was to come.

"She worked on the docks. I did not know my father."

So—his mother was a prostitute. Juno lifted her head to meet his eyes. "It does not matter, Jost."

He watched her, and nodded. "But I think I must tell you."

She said with complete sincerity, "You are the finest man I have ever known."

There was a pause, as those dark eyes rested on hers in the flickering candlelight. "Except for your father."

"No," she disagreed. "Papa would disregard his obligations if they were inconvenient—you are indeed the finest man I have ever known."

He sighed, and gathered her to him, squeezing tenderly. "Me, I send her the money so she has a better life—so she can buy a house. Then she marries a good man—a merchant, and has the daughter. But he was forced to fight for the French, and was killed at Stralssund."

I must never complain about anything—ever again, thought Juno. "I wish I could have met her."

There was a pause for a few moments. "You are the finest woman," he said softly.

She smiled into the dark cabin. "Then we are well-matched."

Placing his hands gently under her arms, he pulled her so that she slid up to his mouth, and then kissed her until he rolled her beneath him for another session of lovemaking. Juno was more than willing, and knew that he was relieved to have gotten over the heavy ground as lightly as possible. I imagine there are more revelations to come, she thought--whilst she could still put two thoughts together—but these must be the most worrisome, because he felt he had to confess them as soon as we were safely married. As if I would back out, foolish man.

Still later, she lay dozing against him, when she felt him slowly slide away from her. "Where are you going?" she murmured sleepily.

He leaned to kiss her. "Me, I am hungry."

"Landon wasn't hungry, on his wedding night," she pointed out.

Chuckling, he stood up. "So—Landon is the finest man?"

"No." She reached out to clasp his hand. "You are—go eat."

Tugging on her hand, he said, "Come with me."

"Bring me something," she replied, rolling over. "I cannot face Jairus."

29

"It's nothing like Calcutta, is it?"

"No," Juno agreed, and pulled her coat closer around her. "Mainly, it's cold."

Horry stood with her at the rail, as they watched the port of Southwark come into view through the dense blanket of fog, the lights from the shore barely visible, and glowing in diffuse halos. The fog blunted all sound, as the *Minerva* pulled slowly into the harbor, the bells on the buoys echoing eerily. Juno exhaled, watching with interest as her breath formed a cloud in the cold air—a novel experience. It had been a long journey, and they were both eager to make port, so eager that they had stood thus during the past hour, straining to catch the first sight of England. Horry had no memory of it at all, and Juno could only remember vignettes—the sound of horses' hooves on cobblestones, or tiptoeing up the stairs with her nurse, whilst her mother lay sick.

Juno shivered, and curled her toes in her half boots. A week ago, when the weather had turned colder, Jost had procured a sailor's frieze coat for her, and she had worn it nearly without pause, the sleeves rolled up to fit her arms. Jost also told her he'd buy her a pair of boots lined with sheep's wool, which sounded a bit strange, at the time, but which now seemed very sensible. He also wanted to buy her a fur-lined cloak, along with other items too numerous to mention, but which he'd rattled off with great relish, as she lay in his arms one night. She smiled at the memory—having worn a simple uniform most of her life, she could only shake her head and tease him about saving his money.

"Me, I am a rich man," he had reminded her. "You will have these things—and many more things."

"I think I would trade it all for a roast chicken." She was heartily sick of the shipboard fare of hardtack, bacon and molasses, which was all that was left, now.

Reminded, she now said to Horry, "I can't wait to eat a piece of fruit—or anything fresh, for that matter."

"Meat," her brother replied succinctly. "I don't care what kind—even mutton sounds delicious."

The spires of tall masts began to appear in the ghostly panorama before them, and they were silent for a few moments as the ship glided into the harbor, the lapping of the water on the hull sounding louder than usual in the fog.

"It is enormous." With wonder, Juno viewed the huge port—larger even than the one at Madras. "How does anyone keep track of it all?"

"It's the Blackwall Yard," Horry explained. "Papa said it can handle two hundred fifty Indiaman frigates, all at the same time."

They watched the dockyard come into view, and Juno confessed, "I have mixed emotions, Horry. I'm glad the journey is over, but I don't look forward to another brangle over the bridegift. I don't know how I am supposed to face the Nabob, knowing what I now know."

But Horry only smiled in anticipation. "I hope I can come to court, this time. I'd give anything to watch Sir Jost knock a few heads together."

"Let's hope it doesn't come to that," Juno replied in a dry tone. "It's not like Madras, after all, where the judge was corrupt. This is England; I've no doubt that the court will award the bridegift to Sir Jost, and Napoleon's people will be thwarted."

"Assuming they can find the bridegift in the first place," Horry reminded her. "Let's hope someone knows something."

They watched the activity on deck, as the mainsail and foresail were stowed, leaving only the smaller sails aloft to propel the ship forward. The sailors lined the railing, as eager as the Payne siblings to view the port, and the general mood was celebratory, the murmuring voices making plans for shore leave.

"There's the entrance lock, do you see?" Horry indicated a huge walled enclosure, with multiple ships berthed within. "We'll have to register, and be inspected."

"I hope it doesn't take too long—I can't wait to walk for more than twenty paces in one direction." Juno then saw Jost, striding toward them as he spoke to Peyton and another sailor. After a final word, the two other men nodded, then left toward the bow, whilst Jost continued toward Juno and Horry.

"Good morning," Juno called to him. He had left their berth in the pre-dawn, before she was awake, because he'd much to arrange before the entry into port.

"Good morning. Come, come; we go this way." He indicated they were to follow him down the stairs to the main deck.

"Are we going with you to register?" asked Horry, clearly hoping this was the case.

"No, Peyton will register." He then kept up a rapid pace toward the opposite side of the ship, with Horry and Juno in tow. "Horry, you will follow orders, yes?"

"Yes, sir; of course," Horry replied, a bit surprised.

"Good. Me, I take Juno to the court. Instead of the court, you will go to a safe place, where you will do what you are told."

Horry nodded without comment, but Juno found this speech ominous, and could not help but ask, "Why is Horry going to a safe place? And where is it?"

"Me, I do not know where." Jost came to the port side of the ship, away from the docking activity going forward on the other side. Looking up, he signaled, and Jairus approached them, holding a sailor's knit cap. "Juno, you must hide your hair."

"We are leaving now? Before we dock?" asked Juno in some confusion as she donned the hat.

"Yes, *lieve;* we go now."

Jost took her elbow, and they approached a rope ladder that had been lowered down the port side, away from the dockyard. Looking over the side, Juno could see the skiff already in the water, rocking in the waves below. Dismayed, she was girding her loins to make the climb down the swinging rope ladder, when Landon suddenly appeared beside them at the rail.

Jost's mouth became a grim line, and he did not look up at Landon. "Enough; we go."

It was clear that Landon wanted to reopen a subject of disagreement, and that Jost was less than pleased by the attempt. His gaze intent, Landon indicated Juno with a tilt of his head. "I am not as recognizable, and you will draw the wrong kind of attention. She would be safer if I take her."

"Me, I will not leave her again," Jost replied in a tone that brooked no argument, and Juno could feel Horry flinch beside her.

Landon tried to reason with him. "You cannot bull your way in; not here."

"We will see." Jost indicated that Jairus was to descend the ladder.

"Then I will come, also."

Jost paused to think about it "Yes; come," he decided.

Landon added, "And Mrs. Landon goes with Horry."

"No," said Jost immediately, and lifted Juno over the gunwale, so that she stood on the top rung of the ropes, positioned within Jairus' waiting arms.

Landon continued stubbornly, "I have her ready; she will do as she is told."

241

But Jost stood firm. "No."

There was a tense moment as Landon's jaw worked. "I believe---I believe she is increasing."

Juno looked up at him in surprise—this was quick work, although it was hard to imagine Aditi as a mother. Landon would be hard-pressed to have her rehabilitation complete in a mere nine months.

At this revelation, Jost turned to look upon the other man. "He will not thank us."

"I cannot be easy," Landon admitted. "I will accept all consequences."

Relenting, Jost nodded. "Fetch her, then; make haste."

The Indian girl must have been waiting in the wings, because she appeared almost immediately, her hair bound up, and her slim figure wrapped tightly in her own sailor's coat. Juno met her eyes, and saw that she was frightened, and so she smiled reassuringly, which in turn helped to settle her own nerves as she descended the ropes to the rocking skiff. With all aboard, they cast off, Aditi uncharacteristically silent, and Juno hanging on as the small vessel bucked against the waves until they entered the calmer water within the river banks. Juno noted the men were all armed and alert, and thinking over Landon's concern for his wife and child, she asked Jost in a low voice, "Do we fear Rochon?"

Landon shot her a look from under his bushy brows, and Jost rebuked her in a mild tone, "You must not speak of these things, Juno."

"Oh; oh, I beg your pardon." She castigated herself for idiocy—he would never tell her anything, if she nervously gabbled what he'd told her in confidence. I must be a better wife, and not a liability, she thought with remorse—he deserves better.

"Wot's toward, Cap'n?" asked Jairus, who was handling the oars.

"Me, I will buy Juno a chicken." Jost's easy reply was nevertheless belied by his alert posture. "Head toward the pier—there—and we will see what there is to see." He directed Jairus as they approached the riverbank, and the men tied the skiff to a large pier that was lined with ramshackle taverns.

"Keep your head down," Jost instructed Juno in a low voice, and the group walked across the boardwalk, and then ducked into a small tavern, nearly deserted at this time in the mid-morning.

Once inside, Jost kept one hand on Juno's arm, and the other on his pistol hilt as he paused to survey the room. "Go."

Jairus disappeared outside, apparently to keep watch. Jost then steered Juno to the rear of the establishment, indicating she should sit with Horry at a crude table in the back corner. Landon paused to give some low-voiced instructions to Aditi, then seated her near the door before he came over to join them. After sliding in on the wooden bench between her brother and Jost, Juno dared to raise her eyes and take a glance around, trying to quell her nervousness. The place was dilapidated, and bore a sign above the bar that proclaimed "The Nob's Fancy," but the conceit did indeed seem a bit fanciful, as the tavern could have never aspired to serve the quality. The tavern keeper polished the bar with his dishtowel, and appeared supremely uninterested in them—which was rather odd, considering they were the only patrons in the place.

"Do we eat?" asked a hopeful Horry, who seemed impervious to the grim mood of his companions.

"We do." Jost called to the tavern keeper, and they ordered a meal while Juno sat, bemused and trying to decide why they had come—disguised, heavily armed, and in such haste—to eat a roast chicken in a low tavern on the dock.

30

The meal was duly served, and Juno was surprised how delicious it was, although it may have been only compared to what the passengers on the *Minerva* had been eating for the past few weeks. There was little conversation as the food was consumed, and Juno had the impression that Jost and Landon were warily watching the door.

"Are you going to eat that, Juno?" Horry referred to a roast potato, and Juno willingly relinquished it, watching in bemusement as he devoured it, and then began to eye her bread pudding.

Suddenly reminded, she asked, "Oh—oh, Horry; did you remember to bring any neem leaves?"

"I'll be fine," her brother answered with some impatience. "And remember, we can find chinchona bark, here."

Juno looked up in surprise as a tall, lean sailor with grey eyes suddenly slid onto the bench next to Jost, his coat collar pulled up, and a cap pulled low over his eyes. As Juno hadn't seen him enter through the front door, she decided he must have come in through the back; she also concluded that he must be an acquaintance, as no chance stranger would have the audacity to sidle up next to Jost.

The newcomer ignored the rest of them, and addressed Jost in a low voice. "Who has malaria?"

"The boy," the Dutchman replied, continuing to eat with no show of surprise or discomfiture.

"Who is the other girl, by the door?"

"My wife," answered Landon. "I was loath to leave her; she will do as she is told."

The grey-eyed man lifted his head to regard Landon with a keen gaze. "My congratulations."

"She is not to be trusted," Jost revealed in an even tone.

"Wonderful," replied the man. His gaze then flicked for an instant to Juno, and he asked Jost, "Well?"

"She knows nothing. He must not have said."

The man made a soft, incredulous sound. "Not even to the boy?"

Jost raised his gaze to meet the other's, and shook his head, and Juno could see that both men were made grave by this news. With some reluctance, Jost added, "And Juno, she was given the planted diamonds by the priest, so now, I have them."

Planted diamonds? thought Juno in surprise; whatever did he mean?

There was a pause, whilst the grey-eyed man stared at Jost. "You astonish me; this entire enterprise must be cursed."

Jost shrugged. "The Frenchman, he was killed by the Rajah's men. Before he died, he gave them to her, to take to the Nabob."

The other drew his hand over his face for a moment, thinking. "We shall retrench, then, and turn this to our advantage."

"It is the bad luck," Jost observed.

"Perhaps not—we shall see," said the other, studying the table with a frown. "The players are all in place, after all."

Finished with his meal, Jost leaned back, and crossed his arms. "Me, I take Juno to the court. Me, and no one else."

"Certainly," the grey-eyed man nodded. "And while you are there, make a public show of depositing her diamonds with the court, until title is established—we will bait a new trap."

Jost raised his brows, and nodded in understanding, whilst the other man allowed his gaze to rest on Juno for a speculative moment. "Perhaps she hasn't told you anything, because she doesn't trust you—I hope you haven't terrified her."

"Me, I have married her."

This was evidently not what the other wanted to hear, and his sharp gaze flew to Jost's, who met the scrutiny steadily, and with a touch of defiance. Juno thought perhaps she should interject some comment at this juncture, but as both men were behaving as though neither she nor Horry were present, she held her peace.

"I see. Again, my congratulations."

Jost bowed his head in ironic acknowledgement.

The grey-eyed man allowed his gaze to drift to Horry. "And you—have you married, also?"

"No, sir," answered Horry with a grin.

"Good man," declared the other. "Give me the truth; did your sister wish to marry this reprobate?"

Horry rallied from his surprise, and responded, "She did; I will put my oath on it."

Apparently satisfied, the man turned back to Jost. "Judge Moore will handle the matter, and is already aware of the particulars. I suggest you make haste, and call as little attention as possible—until you are there, of course—and then the more attention, the better. If you run into trouble, others stand ready."

"Very good," agreed Jost.

Their visitor rose from the table. "I would ask that you temper your actions, but I don't think it would serve."

Jost tilted his head toward Juno, and she translated, "He thinks you won't mind his cautions, so there is no point in asking."

"Assuredly not," agreed Jost.

Watching them, the grey eyes held a gleam of amusement. "There are rooms for you in Cutler Street." He turned to Horry. "You will come with me."

"Yes, sir," said Horry, who seemed to have come to the same conclusion as Juno—that this was not a man to be trifled with.

"And Mrs. Landon," interjected Landon firmly.

"And Mrs. Landon," the other sighed in acknowledgment. "God in heaven, you are an unpredictable group." Thinking on this, he leaned in toward Jost, and gave one last instruction in a grave tone. "I know you would seek your vengeance, but I ask you to consider my interests as well as your own—there is information I would very much like to have."

Jost nodded, but Juno noted he gave no assurances. The other man straightened, and lifted a biscuit from Juno's plate to put in his pocket. "Come," he said, and Horry rose to slip through the back door, whilst Landon directed a startled Aditi to join them.

"We shouldn't tarry," said Landon into the sudden silence.

"Juno, she can finish her chicken."

But--given the recent conversation--Juno had lost her appetite, and offered in a small voice, "I am finished, Jost; truly."

After watching her for a moment, her husband laid a hand against her cheek, and drew his own face close to hers. "We are larger than life, yes?"

Gazing into his eyes with as much assurance as she could muster, she nodded.

"And Horry, he is as safe as a house."

Hiding a smile, she agreed, "Safe as a house."

Jost brushed his thumb over her lips. "If any man dares to speak to you, I will slit his throat."

"Thank you," she said gravely. "I would appreciate it."

"We go, yes?"

"We do. Do you know where the court is?"

"Assuredly." He rose to his feet. "Me, I have broken from the prison, here."

"Ah," said Juno, unsurprised.

They emerged upon the dock, as the weak sunshine was beginning to penetrate the fog, and Juno noted that she still felt the movement of the ship, even though they were now on land. Their steps echoed on the timber underfoot, the wary men in a tight circle around her, as the group proceeded toward the busy frontage street. Having gone through a similar experience at Fort St. George, she didn't attempt to distract Jost, as he carefully scrutinized everyone in the area, a hand on his pistol.

"Wot's happ'ned to Horry?" asked Jairus in an undertone. "Has he gone back t' the ship?"

"He is with Mrs. Landon; they went to a different location," Landon explained.

Nothing more was said, and although Juno was eager to gaze about her at the bustling street scene, she kept her head lowered, and the sailor's knit hat pulled down low over her brow. Landon hailed a hackney, and as they settled inside the vehicle, Juno took the opportunity to take a glimpse out the window. The view revealed a scene very similar to the market place in Calcutta, only noisier and even more chaotic, with wagons transporting goods, and vendors shouting out their wares from stalls along the street. "Oh--it is so *busy*," she noted in wonder. "Where is Cutler Street? Is it nearby?"

"First things first, *lieve*," said Jost. "You will go to the court, to tell the judge your story."

Something in his tone made her eye him sidelong; she had the impression there was more here that remained unsaid, but she did not want to quiz him in front of the others. "I hope your sword will not be needed as a witness, this time."

He teased, "Ach, Juno; it would be the highest amusement."

Juno held out a forlorn hope that he would indeed temper his actions. "Remember, it's not like India, Jost. Promise me you won't wind up in prison."

For some reason, he seemed to find this remark amusing. "My promise, *lieve*."

Eying him again, she refrained from further comment, and hoped he knew what he was about—subtlety was not his strong suit, and it seemed evident that there was a plot afoot. With some trepidation, she turned to the window again, to take in the sights of London, whilst the men around her kept a close watch on their surroundings.

31

Juno stood with Jost on the steps of Westminster Hall, as he dismissed the other men who had accompanied them from the ship, the Hall being the venerable building that housed the Royal Courts of Justice.

"Good luck," offered Landon, with a meaningful glance at Jost. He then bowed to Juno. "My lady."

I don't know if I will ever become accustomed to being "my lady," thought Juno, as she bowed her head in return. "Shall we see you tonight in Cutler Street, Mr. Landon?"

"We shall see," was all the other man offered, and he then strode away.

Trying to quash her nervousness, Juno turned to accompany Jost up the broad steps, and then once inside, tried not to gape up at the high, hammer beam ceiling—she'd never been inside a room so large. The Hall's interior was one massive space, with judge's benches set up along the walls, and a variety of advocates and other supplicants standing in groups and speaking in hushed voices, making for a solemn and softly echoing atmosphere.

Jost inquired after Judge Moore, and Juno felt a strong sense of déjà vu as yet again, she was escorted to settle her marital status before a judge, whilst the man at her side served as an object of open curiosity. The self-important clerk instructed them to await their turn on a bench along the wall, but he made it clear that Juno was expected, and that she wouldn't be kept waiting for very long. Seated beside Jost on the bench, Juno tucked her hand into his elbow, nervously contemplating the interview to come.

"All will be well, *lieve*." Jost squeezed her hand between his arm and his side. "You will see."

"I do not doubt it—although it is a shame the guards are not friends, this time."

"The friends, they are here," Jost corrected her, taking a glance around. "I do not know which ones, only."

"Oh." Juno reviewed the bailiffs who were stationed along the hall, none of whom seemed remotely interested in them—although on second thought, any bailiff worth his salt certainly *should* be interested, upon sighting Jost, so this was perhaps a good sign. "Are they the grey-eyed gentleman's friends?"

Jost nodded. "That one, he has many friends."

She lifted her face to him, and quirked her mouth. "But you do not number among them, I think."

He tilted his head, as his eyes continued to scrutinize those around them. "Me and him, we do not wish to take the orders from the other."

This seemed to accurately describe the situation, and Juno nodded with understanding. "No—and I don't think he likes women, very much."

"He has no time to like the women. And he has the many problems because of a woman—a woman who gave her husband's secrets to the enemy."

"A traitoress?" Juno could scarcely credit such a thing, and frowned in disbelief. "Unfathomable."

"She has no fathoms, she is dead, now." Jost's gaze continued to survey their surroundings. "But not before she gave to Rochon the names of those who worked in secret, against him."

Startled, Juno lifted her face to his. "Papa's name?"

Placing a comforting hand over hers, he neither confirmed nor denied this leap of logic, but instead repeated, "The woman, she is dead, now."

But Juno found that the conversation had only added to her general level of anxiety, and so she asked with some alarm, "Is Rochon here, in London?"

"No, *lieve*; Rochon, he is in France—he would not dare come here."

Her brow knit, Juno thought this over. "Then why was the grey-eyed gentleman so worried that you would take your vengeance without his say-so? Who in England would be the object of your vengeance?"

Jost sat for a moment, gazing into the distance as the muted sounds in the ancient Hall echoed off the ceiling. "Me, I cannot tell you. Not yet, yes?"

She subsided into silence for a moment, wishing there were no secrets between them. "What am I to say to the judge?"

"You tell him whatever he wishes to know, *lieve*."

This seemed rather rash, all things considered, and Juno eyed him doubtfully. "Even though my face is like glass?"

With a smile, the Dutchman nodded. "Yes, *lieve*."

Remembering what the grey-eyed gentleman said, she ventured, "And there is another trap to be set? Because the one with the priest and the diamonds didn't work?"

But he shook the hand he held in his with gentle admonition. "You must not ask, *lieve*. Me, I will tell you one day, but not this day."

She subsided, knowing it would do no good to pursue the topic. "I would love to go out walking. Do you think this will take a very long time?"

"Assuredly."

She gazed at him in surprise. "Truly? I should think we need only show the judge the documents from Fort St. George."

"The court, it moves very slow here; we must wait—a long time, maybe."

As this did not at all sound like her husband, Juno scrutinized him with deep suspicion. "I was under the very strong impression that we were in a raging hurry."

His guileless eyes met hers. "Ach, Juno," he chided her gently. "You must learn the patience."

Before she could make a tart response, the clerk approached and indicated they were to follow him. They rose, and were escorted to a heavy mahogany table, where the elderly judge rose to greet them. Juno noted that a sleeve was pinned to his chest; the man must have lost an arm, somewhere along his life's journey.

The judge's gentle smile was disarming. "How do you do, Miss Payne; please have a seat—it appears that reports of your death have been greatly exaggerated."

Juno smiled at the remark, but explained, "It is more properly Lady Van der Haar, sir, as this gentleman is my husband, Sir Jost Van der Haar."

The judge regarded Jost thoughtfully. "I see. Would you mind if I speak to your wife privately, Sir Jost?"

Juno felt a jolt of annoyance that everyone's first assumption was that she was under the malign influence of her better half, and so she interjected firmly, "I have no secrets from my husband, my lord."

"But I am afraid I do." He smiled apologetically, and with his good hand, made a gesture toward the waiting area bench.

Juno braced herself, preparing for the re-appearance of Jost's sword, but to her surprise, her normally-volatile husband seemed disinclined to lay waste to the place. Instead--much to the alarm of the watching bailiff--he reached into his waistcoat to remove first, her father's pipe, and then the Fort St. George documents, which he handed to Juno. With a final glance at the judge, he cautioned, "You will be good to my Juno, yes?"

"Without fail." The judge bowed his head, and the Dutchman retreated back to the waiting bench.

As they were seated across from one another at the table, the judge regarded Juno with a benign gaze. "Would you like tea, my lady? I can call for it."

"No, thank you, sir—I have recently breakfasted." A bit nervously, she unfolded the documents, and pushed them toward him, wanting to get to the heart of the matter without delay. "These documents are from the court at Fort St. George, Madras. They show that I never married Mr. Finch, and that I never died—although I suppose that much is obvious."

The other regarded her with a kindly expression and then glanced over the papers. "Thank you, my dear. How can I know you are whom you claim to be?"

Juno stared at him, nonplussed. "Oh. I have no idea."

"Do you have relatives in England?" he asked gently.

"My mother had relatives in Suffolk, but I never met them." She clasped and unclasped her hands. "I left England as a little girl to live in Bengal when my mother died—my brother and I. My brother can tell you that I am Juno Payne—or I was, before I married."

He nodded slowly, thinking this over. "Are there any independent witnesses in Bengal who could vouch for your identity—persons who are not relatives?"

Relieved, Juno nodded. "Oh yes—clouds of witnesses. I lived at a convent school for nearly fifteen years outside of Fort William, and I was known to nearly everyone stationed at the fort." Juno didn't mention the obvious, that it would take months to sail the aforementioned witnesses from Calcutta to London—surely the judge wouldn't go to such lengths, so as to await the testimony of witnesses from across the world.

Her companion regarded her thoughtfully, his mild gaze resting on her face. "Tell me, my lady—what do you understand is afoot here?"

Her brow knit, Juno took a moment to gather her thoughts, aware that—surely—she shouldn't be too honest; although Jost had said to tell the judge everything that she knew. With this in mind, she began, "I think my father was murdered, although it was made to look as though he died of the cholera. I think there are those— Mr. Finch—who wish to make it appear that my father was defrauding the Lloyd's insurers, by pretending his ships had sunk, when they had not." She met his gaze with her own level one. "He would never do such a thing—he'd never be so dishonest."

"You are an admirable daughter," the judge noted with approval. "Pray continue."

Thinking that she may as well tell him the whole, Juno added, "I think my father was instead working to uncover a scheme whereby the money from the insurers was transformed into diamonds, and then smuggled to Napoleon— apparently he is planning another conquest."

"Yes, that is what I have heard also." The gentleman tapped a forefinger thoughtfully on the table. "And England's Treasury is in financial trouble, because the wealthy men who fund Lloyd's of London are spending their money paying out insurance claims, instead of buying English war bonds."

Juno frowned, thinking this through. "Oh—why, that is *outrageous;* it means Mr. Finch is using English money to fund Napoleon's war against England."

The judge nodded. "In theory, that is correct. But why would he do such a thing—do you know?"

"I can't imagine," confessed Juno, "but my husband believes he was secretly trading with the French, and he now must do as they ask—even if it is treason."

"Yes; if true, it would be treason." The judge rendered his gentle smile. "It is difficult for someone like you or I to understand such a thing, isn't it?"

"Yes—it is incomprehensible."

"Incomprehensible, indeed." With his good hand, the judge adjusted the inkstand on the table so that it was more squarely aligned. "Tell me about your husband, my lady—how did you make his acquaintance?"

Oh, dear, thought Juno.

32

J uno was not certain how honest she should be. "He saved my life," she compromised. "Mine and my brother's."

The judge nodded. "He is a heroic figure to you."

Juno thought she could see where this was headed, and wanted to make it clear, "I assure you that I have not been beguiled, my lord—I love him, and he loves me."

"I meant no insult." He met her eyes, a grave expression in his own. "But there is a very valuable bridegift at issue, and you must admit the two of you are—are an unusual pairing."

"It is not easy to explain," she admitted fairly. "But it is as though we were aware right from the first that we belonged to each other." She paused and tried to put it into words understandable to another. "He is good for me—and in turn, I am good for him; together we are the better for it."

The shrewd gaze rested on her for a moment, and then the judge made a gesture toward the documents before him. "I do not see your marriage lines, my lady."

"Oh—I'm not certain they have been prepared, as yet. We were married at sea by another captain—a fellow Dutchman, named Captain Spoor. Sir Jost will know the particulars."

The other nodded as though this was a perfectly reasonable explanation. "Were there witnesses to the ceremony?"

Juno had to smile. "The entire crew from both ships. And my brother, Horry."

With a returning smile, the judge pronounced, "A festive occasion."

"And a surprise, also—I had not known it was planned." She realized as soon as she said the words that they did not convey the impression she wished, and so she corrected, "We had tried to marry before, you see—" suddenly aware she was not helping matters, she concluded, "—but we were forced to leave Madras on short notice." Mentally congratulating herself for avoiding mention of the Rajah's murder, she smiled serenely at him.

The judge leaned forward, his expression apologetic. "Forgive me, my lady, but I must ask—has the marriage been consummated?"

"Oh yes—many times," she told him with some emphasis, and then blushed.

Nodding, the man leaned back, and gazed into the distance for a few moments. "If he were anyone else, I would not be as concerned; but you must agree that a suspicion is raised. A notorious pirate marries you—quite unexpectedly—and is entitled to a fortune, as a result."

Juno could not like the tack the conversation had taken, and hastened to assure him, "I am aware that his past may not bear close scrutiny, but he is an honest man, now, and means to abide by the tenets of civilization."

As though sharing a joke, the other smiled slightly. "I confess I am glad to hear it—I wouldn't want to meet him in a back mews, in the dark of night."

Juno was honest enough to know exactly what he meant, but she assured him, "I have complete trust in my husband." To prove this point, she produced her father's pipe. "It is he who suggested that I deliver these to you, to determine what is best to do." She carefully dislodged the bowl from the stem of the clay pipe and gently shook the diamonds from it, scattering them onto the mahogany table where they lay, glimmering dimly.

Juno could hear the clerk and the bailiff stifle a gasp from where they stood, observing the proceedings. The judge touched one with a tentative finger and asked in astonishment, "The bridegift?"

"No—apparently only a small portion. They were given me by a man who is now dead, hoping I would smuggle them to Napoleon, via Mr. Finch." She decided not to mention that Jost and the grey-eyed man had referred to them as the "planted diamonds," since she wasn't certain what was meant.

The judge's expression became very grave as he sank back into his chair, staring at the gems. "You are certain of this, my lady?"

"Completely. There was no mistaking; the dead man told me himself—before he died, of course." She paused, and decided there was no time like the present. "I was hoping they would be given to the Lloyd's underwriters, so as to clear my father's name."

His chin to his chest, the judge let out a long breath. "Lady Van der Haar, you must understand that I am in a difficult position. On one hand is Mr. Finch—who is a powerful man within the East India Trading Company. He seeks title to your bridegift, and claims it is for the good of England. If I accuse such a man of treason, it will cause quite a stir--trading is based on trust, after all. On the other hand, there is a counter-group of men who cannot come forward, but nevertheless urge me to resist Mr. Finch's requests, with very little evidence of direct malfeasance—Mr. Finch can simply deny any knowledge of these diamonds, and then, where are we? This second group also claims they must have the bridegift for the good of England. However, with your advent upon the scene—and if your marriage can be authenticated--it now appears that the bridegift lawfully belongs to Sir Jost, who—you must admit—may not be the best candidate to hold title."

"Yes," Juno agreed reluctantly, seeing the fairness of this. "It is indeed a quandary."

He leaned forward, and teased, "If you would renounce your marriage, I could simply declare that the bridegift is yours, and be home in time for tea."

"I will not renounce my marriage," Juno declared firmly. "And I wouldn't want the bridegift, in any event—there have been abductions and attempts upon my life because of it; it is all very distressing."

The other nodded in sympathy. "I can see that it would be."

"And I must say that I am not certain the bridegift even exists," Juno confessed. "My father never mentioned it to me or to my brother, and one would think he would have—if it is such a fortune as they say."

"Is that so?" asked the judge with some surprise. "That does seem odd. And it appears no one is certain of its whereabouts?"

"No—but one would think my father would not have left it where no one could find it; it all makes little sense."

"You are absolutely correct; it does not make sense." The judge drew his brows together. "How very strange."

Juno asked almost hopefully, "Do you suppose they are all mistaken, and all this fuss is for naught?"

The judicial officer sighed with real regret. "No. I think everyone involved is in deadly earnest, and it seems unlikely that they are all mistaken—which brings me back to my quandary."

But Juno had no quandary, and no qualms. "It is simple, my lord; you must thwart the Nabob, save England, and restore my father's good name."

With an apologetic gesture, the judge spoke to her in a reasonable tone. "My dear, you are a credit to your father and to your husband, but you must understand my position. Apparently there is a great deal of money at stake, and that money has a direct impact on the security of England."

He looked to her, and Juno nodded, as this seemed to be expected. Satisfied, the man continued, "However, you are a bit too trusting and—may I even suggest—naïve. I must take this factor into consideration."

Juno blushed hotly and waited, unable to disagree with him, when he laid it out like this.

"I shall hold a hearing, as soon as possible, and we will take evidence from all sides, including, I'm afraid, your husband. I need to explore the validity of your marriage, with so much at stake."

Dismayed, Juno protested, "But, I assure you—"

"I understand," he interrupted in a gentle tone. "But I must be certain. Surely you can see this? My sole aim must be to do justice."

This appeared inarguable, and Juno could only concede with a nod.

He continued with resignation, "I'm afraid you will not thank me for it, but I must put you in protective custody. I have heard from your own lips that you are in danger, and until I have sorted out this matter, I cannot countenance the possibility that I may inadvertently compound that danger."

Juno stared in bewilderment. "What does this mean, sir—protective custody? Where would I go?"

"There are some very comfortable quarters on the Master's side of the Fleet for just this sort of situation. Every comfort will be afforded to you, but most importantly, you will remain safe."

"I don't know what this means, my lord," Juno confessed, "What is the Fleet?"

"The prison," he explained kindly. "You are going to prison."

Astonished, Juno stared at him. "Surely I should not have to abide in prison—why, none of this is my fault."

"Oh, it would not be for punishment—there are rooms at the Fleet for persons such as yourself; persons who need to be protected, pending further court proceedings. I assure you that you will be kept separate from the other prisoners, and treated with every courtesy."

"I cannot think this a good idea," cautioned Juno, worried that she had been too honest, despite Jost's urgings. "There must be another avenue."

In his gentle manner, the judge nonetheless confirmed, "I'm afraid it will be my order."

Juno swallowed. "Please allow me to tell my husband of this—he may need some persuasion."

"Better you than me," the judge agreed.

But to Juno's surprise, when Jost was informed of the judge's order, he did not slay him on the spot, but instead ducked his chin, thinking. "Me, I will visit her when I wish, yes?"

The other nodded. "You may; I'm afraid you cannot have direct contact, however, as that would defeat the purpose."

Jost agreed after a show of reluctance, and it occurred to his suddenly suspicious wife that this outcome had been his intent all along—she remembered his reaction in the hackney, when she had asked him to avoid prison. Whilst the men discussed the particulars, she contemplated the stone floor, and tried to puzzle out why this would be; if their marriage was valid—as indeed it was—then she was no longer in danger, because the bridegift belonged to Jost. Unless, of course, Jost was killed, and then she was back in the same situation as when she started. Her brow cleared—that must be it, then; he was making sure that the enemy was not inspired to make her a widow, and thus eligible for abduction again. She rather wished he had informed her of this plan, but then remembered that her face was like glass, and he probably didn't want her to queer the pitch by confessing it all to the judge.

"Did you give him the diamonds?" Jost asked in a negligent tone, as though he spoke of trifles.

The judge answered for her, "Indeed, I have them, and the court will keep them on deposit until it determines to whom they belong." He then turned and gave instruction to his clerk, who appeared suitably surprised with the nature of his trust.

Whilst the others were conferring, Juno took the occasion to whisper to Jost in an urgent undertone, "What is it you are plotting, husband?"

He didn't attempt to disclaim, but said only, "All will be well, slayer of tigers; my promise to you."

"I'd rather not be held in prison," she retorted, with what she considered admirable restraint. Hopefully, word would not get back to Sister Marie.

"This one, it is better than most," Jost assured her with the air of one who knows. "And you will draw the visitors, yes?"

"What sort of visitors?" she asked with suspicion, but the judge was reclaiming her attention, and gesturing to the bailiffs, who were to escort her to her new quarters.

The elderly man bade her farewell, and bowed in a courtly manner. "I shall see to it that you are made comfortable, my dear, and that an evidentiary hearing is held between the competing parties as soon as possible."

"Thank you, my lord," said Juno without much conviction. "I would like to say it has been a pleasure, but that remains to be seen."

"Precisely," he agreed with a small, dry smile.

33

And so a short while later, Juno arrived at her new quarters in the Fleet Prison, after having been transported up the Strand from Westminster. Jost was allowed to accompany her in the prisoner's coach, and he kept her spirits up by extolling the ferocity of the eunuchs who guarded the Dey's prison in Algiers.

"No more, I beg of you," she exclaimed, laughing. "I shall have nightmares."

"This place, it is nothing," he assured her, as they rattled along the cobblestones.

Trying to maintain a light tone, she teased, "Have you been held here at the Fleet, also? Perhaps you should write a guidebook about all the prisons you have known."

He disclaimed, "No—this one, it is for the men who cannot pay their debts. Me, I pay my debts, but the English, they were not happy with where the money came from.

They put me in Newgate Prison, but I did not want to stay there, so I broke out, and stole a ship."

"Well, you shouldn't break me out, Jost, but will you stay close at hand?" She was trying to suppress her extreme dismay at this latest turn of events, but thus far, had been only partially successful.

He held her hand in his, and bent his head to hers. "Me, I must be very busy, *lieve*. But I will come whenever I can."

Aware that some sort of plan was afoot, she nodded, trying to remember that her concerns were not nearly as important as his concerns in this matter—what with blood vengeance, and the fate of the world at stake. "Where will you go—can you say?"

"Me, I go to find the diamonds," he answered easily.

As the guards who were escorting them could overhear, she knew he would say nothing more specific, and so she only cautioned him to be careful. "You have a tendency to be reckless, I think—it comes from wresting things from people at will."

But he would not agree, and met her eyes in all seriousness. "Me, I am very careful, *lieve*. It is why I am alive, still."

This seemed inarguable, and did offer her some relief as she resolutely looked out the grated window at the passing scene. "I will not worry, then."

"You will worry," he corrected, lifting her hand to kiss its back. "But you will be safe, and so me, I will not worry."

"That is true; and apparently, to while away the time I shall have visitors." She threw him a speculative glance.

"Yes, you will draw the visitors," he confirmed, but gave no further insights. Watching out the window, she tried to stifle her annoyance. Honestly; the least they could do was tell her what she should and shouldn't say to whoever was being drawn in. Apparently, this was not a concern, which was just as well; she was not good at duplicity—which was no doubt why she was not in Jost's confidence. I must not be a baby, she rebuked herself; this is deadly serious, and these men know what they are about. Turning, she smiled at Jost, and squeezed his hand, and he rewarded this sentiment by leaning to kiss her mouth in full view of the guards.

The Fleet Prison was a grim and utilitarian brick building, four stories tall, and surrounding a central courtyard. The warden ushered them to Juno's room which, he explained, was the most comfortable one on the premises, save his own. Juno was pleasantly surprised; coming in from the long gallery hall, there was an antechamber and then her cell, which boasted both a fireplace and a window. The furnishings were not luxurious, but were by no means shabby, and the room was fairly spacious. If the door to the cell had not been made of iron bars, it could easily have passed for a room at a respectable inn.

There were twenty other rooms on this floor on the Master's side of the prison, which were reserved for those inmates who could pay for more comfortable accommodations. "It will be quiet, my lady," the warden explained. "Most are on the common side, nowadays—we'll keep the riff-raff away from you."

Juno was introduced to a chambermaid who would see to her needs, and the turnkey who would act as a guard to her room. Juno noted that said turnkey met Jost's eye for a brief but significant moment, and concluded he was also a friend to the grey-eyed gentleman.

Despite the fact that it was not nearly as grim as she had envisioned, Juno found it very discouraging to hear the iron door slam behind her, and felt compelled to pull up a chair and cling to Jost's hand through the bars for a time. He took her mind off the situation by discussing what she would need, as she'd brought no clothes with her—not even a toothbrush. "Ask Landon to choose a dress," she suggested. "He has good taste."

The Dutchman cocked his head in apology. "Landon, he will be very busy."

"Everyone is very busy, save me," she complained. "I am slated to rot in prison."

"Horry, he is also not busy," he soothed. "And please do not rot."

Ashamed that she had complained, she subsided. "If you would just bring me a brush, Jost. And a warm cloak."

"Me, I will ask the girls who work at the shop to help me," he assured her.

"No flirting," she directed. "You are a married man."

He lifted her hand to kiss it lingeringly. "Me, I never forget. Not for a minute." He rose to leave. "*Ik houd u.*"

"*Ik houd u.*" She watched the turnkey escort him out to the gallery, unable to suppress a bleak feeling within her breast, as the door was shut behind him. Trying to cheer herself with the conviction that he would return soon, it suddenly occurred to her that—for all the stealth and secrecy that had been necessary, so far—her very recognizable husband was apparently going shopping in London, bold as brass. Struck by this, she was reminded of his comment in Fort St. George, when he had openly shown his interest in her to unseen watchers. He is making the birds beat their wings again, she thought; here's hoping he knows what he is about.

Once having started on this particular train of thought, Juno tried to pass the time by contemplating her situation, and piecing together what she knew. Although she hated to admit it, the discussion with the judge had made her uneasy in that it seemed evident he believed Jost's motives in marrying her were suspect. Indeed, even the grey-eyed man had conveyed the same impression—he was unhappy that Jost had secured title to the bridegift without his knowledge.

But there *is* no bridegift, thought Juno in exasperation—I am sure of it, and I should have been more adamant with the judge on the subject. Although, she acknowledged fairly, the fact that others thought there was a bridegift was what put her at risk—whether or not it truly existed was beside the point. And Jost did not seek an advantage for himself—she would swear to it. There was something else at play; it seemed evident they were setting some sort of trap for the Nabob—although a trap hardly seemed necessary, considering the man's despicable actions in falsely declaring her married, and then dead. He could not possibly escape justice, no matter his power, and the scheduled hearing would expose his perfidy to the world. Once the testimony was taken, the Nabob would be arrested, and her prison stay would come to an end—and not a moment too soon. Fingering one of the iron bars on the door, she tried not to think about having to sleep without her husband's comforting presence beside her.

Several hours later, the turnkey entered the door again to inform her she had a visitor, waiting in the gallery. "A Mr. Peyton, my lady."

"Oh," sighed Juno, who was still trying to adjust to her circumstances. "I do not know if I would like to entertain Mr. Peyton, just now."

The turnkey stood and regarded her with a wooden expression, unmoving. After watching him for a few moments, Juno ventured, "On the other hand, it is very kind of him to come."

This was apparently the correct decision, as the man continued, "I am to stand within the door while you entertain visitors—it is for your own safety, my lady."

"Thank you." She watched him open the outer door, turning over this development in her mind. Peyton, she thought in surprise, and remembered the recent scar on the man's temple. Be wary, Juno.

But Peyton's appearance was not at all ominous, and he carried a welcome armload of books. "Lady Van der Haar, I was so sorry to hear of your incarceration."

"Thank you—it serves as a reminder that I should take care to commit no felonies."

Smiling at her jest, he indicated the books, as he set them down. "I made so bold as to acquire some books from the lending library down the street; I hope you do not mind."

As he handed her the books one at a time through the bars, she thanked him. "I was just thinking of sending my husband for books—I appreciate it enormously."

"Is the Captain here? I'm afraid I missed out on all the excitement, and I have no standing orders."

"I'm not certain where he is," she answered in all sincerity, stacking the books in her cell. "I imagine he will return soon."

Peyton straightened. "And your brother? Is young Horry with the Captain? I had thought to give him a tour of London, if he is free."

The judge may have thought Juno naïve, and too trusting, but a small alarm sounded in her mind. "I'm afraid I'm not certain where Horry is, either—I wish I could be more helpful."

Her visitor demurred with his grave smile. "It is not your fault, certainly; it must be beyond vexing to be held here for no other crime than to command a fortune—one that may or may not exist, I might add, which only makes the whole thing even more unfair. Although Jairus tells me you were carrying a cache of diamonds on our journey, unbeknownst to the rest of us."

As this cat appeared to be well out of the bag, she answered honestly. "I confess it was a relief to turn them over—I am not certain to whom they belong, but I am certain they are not mine."

"Such honesty is indeed refreshing—and I must commend you; you have had a difficult time of late."

As this seemed self-evident, Juno decided to change the subject. "Will you visit your family now that you are in England, Mr. Peyton?"

Her visitor disclaimed with a small smile. "I have no family in England, my lady—perhaps now that I have some leave time, I will visit friends. Have you any relatives in the area?"

"I do not," she confessed with a small shake of her head. "Or if I do, I do not know of them—I left England when I was very young, and can scarcely remember."

"Then Horry would not be staying with them," he concluded, thoughtful.

"You are eager to track down my wayward brother," Juno observed with a smile, hiding a qualm at this realization.

But the man shrugged in a disarming gesture. "He is good company—such high spirits are impossible to resist, and since I am at loose ends, I thought I'd seek him out."

Juno made a wry mouth. "If you do run across him, let him know that I am here—he does not yet know."

"Certainly," the other agreed, his grave manner returning. "He mustn't neglect his sister, in her troubles."

At this juncture, voices could be heard in the gallery—one of them Jost's—and he entered, carrying parcels under an arm. "Peyton; you will break Juno out, yes?"

"If that is an order, I will do my best," the other replied with good humor, assisting with the unloading of the parcels.

"Mr. Peyton was kind enough to bring me some books," Juno explained.

"Good man," said her husband. "Me, I am not the one for books."

"But I see you have brought me some clothes." Juno smiled with gratitude.

"Many clothes," her husband added with a gleam. "The shop girls, they said much was needed."

Peyton chuckled. "I can see that I am *de trop*, and I shall take my leave. Good luck, my lady; I hope your stay here is a brief one."

As he left, Jost watched him go, amused. "*Vrijster.*"

"Me, I do not know what this means," Juno replied, imitating him.

"A woman who never married."

"Well, be that as it may, he did offer to marry me, on board the ship."

Her husband met her eyes in astonishment. "*Verdomme.* And yet you did not tell me of this?"

"It was out of chivalry—when he told me about Preya, and thought I might have need of a husband, since you were already wed." She eyed him. "I did not realize at the time that Peyton was not to be trusted."

But she was to obtain no insights on this very interesting subject, as Jost only noted,   "Me, I make the better husband, yes?"

Juno decided she was not going to be distracted, and continued, "He wanted to know where Horry was—he seemed rather persistent." She watched for his reaction to this revelation, but was again to be disappointed.

"Me, I look for Horry, too. He has my razor."

"Horry is shaving?" This was news to Juno.

Jost paused, his hands on his hips, and offered diplomatically, "Horry, he thinks so."

Juno had to laugh, and then found she was suddenly on the verge of tears. "I hate this," she confessed as he drew her to him through the bars, so that his hands cradled her face. "I miss you, and I miss Horry."

"Ach, Juno; I am sorry for it," he soothed. "I will sleep here, for the first night."

"You shouldn't have to sleep on the floor," she protested half-heartedly, wiping her eyes.

"Me, I have slept on the floor more than on the beds. It is nothing."

Ashamed that she had lost her composure, she rallied, "It will be like that first night at the school, remember? Only not quite as nerve-wracking."

"Me, I watched you sleep, that first night," he confessed. "I could not stop."

"Oh, Jost," she whispered, and began to weep again.

34

The court hearing was underway, and Juno's advocate leaned forward to ask, "And what, my lady, was the outcome of the hearing?" He turned to the judge in a rather theatrical manner, to emphasize that this response was particularly important.

"The judge at Fort St. George nullified both the marriage license, and the death certificate."

Before the hearing, the advocate had come to confer with Juno in her cell, and after listening to a detailed description of exactly what had happened in the Madras court, he had suggested—in a carefully neutral tone—that she testify only in broad generalities, and omit any reference to swordplay unless directly questioned on that subject. Juno thought this a good plan, all things considered.

"Move to accept the evidence, my lord," said her advocate, presenting the documents to the judge with the air of someone who has the case sewn up.

"Any objection?" asked Judge Moore, seated atop the bench, and wearing his full judge's regalia.

The Nabob's advocate stood. "None, my lord."

Juno carefully kept her lowered gaze on the wooden rail of the witness box whilst the clerk marked the documents. When she had been escorted into the court under heavy guard, she had immediately seen the Nabob, sitting at the Petitioner's table, and watching her entry with a sympathetic expression. Thinking of the man's involvement in her father's murder—not to mention his treasonous plans—she had to look away, and firmly turn her mind to something else. In the first row of the spectator's seats sat Jost, Jairus, and Peyton—Horry being nowhere in evidence. Toward the back of the court area were perhaps a dozen citizens, many of them elderly, whom Juno was given to understand were court-watchers who spent their spare time observing whatever proceedings were going forward. Juno glanced up quickly to meet Jost's eyes, and her husband gave her a slow wink of encouragement.

"And what did you believe was the purpose of the filing of these false documents?"

The Nabob's advocate stood. "Objection, my lord. Calls for speculation."

"I will allow it," said the judge. He then leaned to Juno. "You may answer."

Juno swallowed. "I believe the purpose was to lay hands on my bridegift." She corrected herself, "My supposed bridegift."

Her advocate turned to face the assembled spectators when he asked the next question. "But if, under Indian custom, your bridegroom would receive your bridegift upon your marriage, what would be the purpose of the false death certificate?"

Juno's gaze rested upon Jost's and she said as steadily as she was able, "I believe my death was planned so that I could not contest any falsely-claimed marriage."

There was an audible gasp among the court-watchers in the back, and then a murmuring of voices.

"Order," commanded the judge, tapping his gavel. "Quiet in the court."

The advocate turned back to her, tilting his head in studied concern. "That is a grave accusation to make, my lady."

"I cannot think of any other reason," Juno admitted in a small voice. "It is horrifying, indeed."

"I rest my direct examination, my lord," said the advocate, and he gave Juno a glance which seemed to convey that she had done well.

The Nabob's advocate now stood to conduct his cross-examination, and Juno mentally steeled herself. His questions, however, took an unexpected tack.

"I understand you attended a religious school in Calcutta, my lady."

"I did," Juno readily admitted. She added nothing further, having been cautioned by her advocate to answer each question as briefly as possible.

The advocate turned to glance at the spectators. "A Roman Catholic convent school, I believe."

"Yes," said Juno, wondering if he was hoping to prejudice the judge against her.

"You have been taught the basic tenets of the Christian religion, then, and you have sworn to tell the truth upon the Bible; isn't that correct, Lady Van der Haar?"

"Yes, sir," said Juno, at sea.

"Do you indeed know where your bridegift has been secreted?"

Juno was almost relieved, now that she realized what was afoot. Leaning forward, she replied with all the sincerity she could muster, "I honestly believe there is no bridegift, sir. My father never spoke of it, and I have no idea where such a gift could be." Hopefully, her face was like glass, because it was nothing more than the unvarnished truth. She leaned back, and could feel the intense regard of every person assembled in the court, even Jost. There, she thought; I hope that settles it.

The Nabob's advocate paced back and forth for a moment, gathering his thoughts. "When did you last see Mr. Finch, before today?"

With an effort, Juno refrained from glancing toward the large man seated at the Petitioner's table. "It was nearly four months ago, at the school in Bengal."

"Did the two of you discuss marriage?"

Juno could not like his characterization, and corrected him, "Mr. Finch did suggest a marriage between us."

The Nabob's advocate nodded thoughtfully. "Did Mr. Finch attempt to browbeat you, or threaten you in any way?"

"He did not," said Juno fairly.

"And what was your response to his offer?"

"I told him I would consider it," admitted Juno, and again, a murmuring of voices could be heard from the back of the court.

"But instead—" and here the man paused so as to draw attention to the question "—you married another within a very short span of time?"

Juno was almost stung into marshaling a heated defense of her actions, then remembered her advocate's caution. "Yes," she replied, and added nothing more.

"Order," said the judge, tapping his gavel again to quell the quiet crescendo of voices from the back.

The Nabob's advocate nodded thoughtfully as he paced before the witness box. "My lady, the court has issued a subpoena for your brother, Master Horatio Payne; however, we cannot determine his whereabouts so as to serve him, and bring him forth. Do you know where your brother is?"

"I do not," admitted Juno.

The man paused, thinking. "When was the last time you saw him?"

Juno's advocate stood. "I fail to see the relevance, my lord."

"Sustained," said the judge. "This is neither here nor there—have you further examination?"

"I will rest, my lord." The man stepped next to the Nabob, and leaned down to have a murmured conversation.

"The court discharges the witness," said the judge, and with no small relief, Juno descended from the witness box, and went to sit at the Respondent's table with her advocate.

"Next witness," the court directed.

"The petitioner would like to testify, my lord."

Juno watched as the Nabob stepped heavily into the witness box, his expression grave. Papa's financier, she thought; and apparently the lever of his disgrace, and death. She must have made an involuntary sound because her advocate laid a hand on her arm, and patted it in reassurance.

The direct examination commenced. "Mr. Finch; you are a Director with the East India Company?"

"I am."

There was a small pause to allow those observing to be suitably impressed, and then the Nabob's advocate continued, "Did you file a marriage license with the St. George court?"

"I did not," the Nabob proclaimed loudly and with an air of injury. Again, there was a collective gasp in the back of the area.

The advocate appeared suitably puzzled by this mystery. "Do you know who did?"

"I have no idea," the witness asserted. "I am as much a victim of this fraud as is Lady Van der Haar."

"And did you file a death certificate for this young woman?" The man's air of incredulity left little doubt as to the expected answer.

"Never," the Nabob maintained, ponderously shaking his head. "I sincerely wished to marry her—to take care of the poor young woman in her difficulties."

Incredulous, Juno listened to the testimony and realized there was little that could be proved; not without laying hands on witnesses who resided halfway around the world—and not to mention that those selfsame witnesses might very well testify however the Nabob wished them to testify. To ease her frustration, she tried to look on the bright side; surely he was now stymied—he wouldn't dare attempt any more skullduggery, now that the scrutiny of the law was upon him.

The Nabob's advocate put a hand on the witness box to emphasize the next question. "Did you have any idea that the young lady's father had bestowed a bridegift?"

"None," the Nabob testified in the same sincere tone. "My motives were altruistic, I assure you." He paused, and then added in a self-deprecatory tone, "Although the young lady is indeed very attractive; one such as I could not hope to do better." He made a self-deprecatory gesture indicating his great girth, and this sally was met with some sympathetic chuckling from the gallery. On this note, the direct examination concluded, and Juno's advocate rose to conduct a cross-examination.

He asked without preamble, "Mr. Finch; if your motives were altruistic could you explain to the court why you filed a Writ of Execution with respect to this young woman's assets immediately upon reaching London?"

"Objection, my lord," the Nabob's advocate cried, leaping to his feet as the whispering in the back reached a crescendo. "Assumes facts not in evidence."

Juno's advocate assumed a posture of confusion. "I withdraw the question, my lord; let us walk through the sequence of events, then. Mr. Finch, did you file a Writ of Execution immediately upon reaching London?"

But the Nabob had recovered his equilibrium, and replied with dignity, "I had heard word of her death, and sought to secure any inheritance for Horatio; their father had recently died, and I felt—as his friend and his financier—that it was my obligation; there was no one else to stand *in loco parentis,* so to speak."

Juno's advocate heard this explanation with a grave expression, as though seriously considering what he had heard. "I see. You could not know when you took such an action that Lady Van der Haar was, in fact alive—and indeed, had married."

"No," the witness testified with emphasis. "I could not know."

Juno's advocate spread his hands. "Then perhaps you will agree to withdraw your petition before this court; as these two events have indeed occurred, it must now be clear you can hope for no part of any bridegift."

But the Nabob would not concede, and replied in an apologetic manner, "I'm afraid it is not that simple, sir. Questions remain as to the young lady's marital status."

A dead silence met this remark, and with an inward sigh, Juno waited for the inevitable questions about her wedding ceremony, thanking providence that Jost had the foresight to have so many witnesses—there could be little question that she was well and truly married.

Juno could see that her advocate was wary, and did not frame a new question. The judge, however, was under no such constraint. "What is meant by such a remark, sir?"

The Nabob's advocate signaled to a bailiff who stood in the back of the court, and the man moved to help a reed-thin woman to her feet, and escort her forward. Juno gauged the women to be approximately thirty years of age, and of Middle Eastern descent; she was dressed in a modest walking-dress with her dusky hair arranged in a becoming coiffure under her bonnet.

"Preya," breathed Jost from behind Juno. "*Verdomme*."

"Lady Van der Haar," the bailiff announced.

35

"Order," cautioned the judge, tapping repeatedly with his gavel, while the gallery broke out in excited exclamations. "Will you come forward and be sworn, madam?"

Juno sat in shock, processing several factors at once; on the one hand, the surprise witness could only mean trouble, as it was clear the Nabob had some scheme in mind. On the other hand, Juno had to face the possibility that it was true—that Preya was the rightful Lady Van Der Haar. No, she thought immediately—Jost assured me he had never married Preya; that he said it only to protect her. It was the height of irony that his gesture had worked so well that the woman was now before them, safe and sound, and working with the Nabob to bring about Juno's disgrace. Unless it was true—Jost was indeed a bigamist—and in that case, the woman could hardly be faulted, and Juno's own future stood in smoldering ruins.

Preya walked toward the witness box as the Nabob exited, and Juno, along with everyone else, watched her progress with intense interest. She had imagined that Preya would be an older version of Aditi, attractive and sensual, and so was rather surprised that the woman did not have these qualities at all. Instead, she was almost painfully slender, and looked every inch her age, her skin tone rather sallow. Juno was reminded that she'd recently lost her child and her lover, and despite everything, felt a rush of sympathy. With quiet dignity, Preya passed by the counsel table on her way to the witness box, and turned her head at the last moment to look—not at Jost, but directly at Juno. Their eyes met, and Juno felt a strange sense of recognition; the woman's calm gaze reminded Juno of something--or someone. In any event, her demeanor was not hostile, or triumphant; but strangely serene—given the circumstances—and Juno, along with everyone else, was transfixed.

"Do you speak English, madam?" asked the judge as Preya was seated.

She nodded and said in a quiet voice. "Yes—some."

"Do you understand you must tell the truth?" Apparently, he had concluded that flourishing a Bible would not be helpful.

She nodded again. "Yes."

The judge indicated Jost with a gesture. "Do you believe you are married to this man?"

Preya turned to look at Jost. "Yes." Her gaze then rested briefly on Juno, once again.

Neda, thought Juno in surprise; she reminds me of Neda. A little girl of perhaps seven, Neda had been rescued by Sister Marie from slave traders. Juno had not witnessed the incident, but had been told that the diminutive nun had confronted the slaver as he beat his helpless charge. Sister had paid the man for the girl, and Neda had come to live at the convent for a short time, before she died of consumption. The little girl never spoke, but followed Sister everywhere, her devoted gaze never wavering from the nun's face. I don't understand, thought Juno in confusion; why would Preya look upon me with such profound gratitude?

"Did you live together as husband and wife?"

"Yes," Preya nodded. "We had a daughter—Bala—but she is now dead."

The murmuring in the gallery rose up once again, but the judge did not bother to attempt to regain order, instead giving a mighty sigh as he indicated Jost with a tilt of his head. "Swear him in, and let us get to the bottom of this."

Jost was asked to stand in place before the bench, and was sworn in. "Are you married to this woman?" The judge indicated Preya, who remained in the witness box.

"Which woman?" Jost's demeanor was one of guileless confusion, which evoked suppressed laughter from the back of the court.

But the judge was not in a joking mood. "None of your insolence, if you please; answer the question."

Jost indicated Juno, seated in front of him. "I am married to this woman."

"Objection, my lord," cried the Nabob's advocate as he leapt to his feet. "This man is a convicted felon, and therefore his testimony must be discounted."

But Juno's advocate also stood to protest, "I believe, my lord, that all past convictions have been expunged by command of the king."

Impatiently, the judge motioned for both to be seated. "No more interruptions, counsel." Leaning forward to continue his questioning, the judge asked, "Did you participate in a wedding ceremony with this witness at any time?"

Crossing his arms, Jost gave the appearance of thinking very seriously about this, but in the end, shook his head. "Me, I do not think so."

The judge's annoyance was betrayed only by the tapping of his fingers on the bench as the gallery tittered. "But you are not certain? How can this be, sir?"

Jost shrugged, and spread his hands in an apologetic manner. "Back then, there was much of the drink, much of the time." Again, suppressed laughter could be heard, a bit louder this time.

Having apparently decided this line of questioning was not going to be fruitful, the judge again turned to Preya. "Do you have your marriage lines, madam?"

"No," Preya said calmly. "I have lost them."

The Nabob started, and glanced at his advocate, and Juno had the impression this was a surprise; apparently they had hoped to present the court with conclusive proof of the marriage. Noting their reaction, Preya looked over to them, seated at the petitioner's table. "I must tell the truth."

Frowning, the judge thought over the situation, and then asked, "Are there witnesses who could testify to your marriage, madam?"

"Oh, yes," Preya agreed, nodding. "Many witnesses. They are in Algiers."

Dismayed, the judicial officer asked, "But is there anyone here in England, madam--someone closer to hand?"

The witness shook her head with regret. "No one in England."

The Nabob's advocate stood. "My lord, I am not certain this is true; allow us to investigate—"

"No," interrupted Preya firmly. "There is no one in England who was at my wedding."

So, thought Juno with extreme interest—this particular piece of false testimony was not going according to plan, it would seem.

The judge once again rested his sympathetic gaze on Juno, then cleared his throat and addressed the assembled spectators. "As Sir Jost Van der Haar and Lady Van der Haar—this one—" here he indicated Juno with a nod of his head, "—have each testified they are legally wed, the claimant—" here, he indicated Preya, "—has the burden of proof to come forward with credible evidence sufficient to overcome that presumption. The claimant believes such evidence exists, although it will take some time to marshal.

The claimant shall bear the burden of proving that the marriage between Sir Jost and the claimant was valid, and that it preceded his marriage to the current Lady Van der Haar. Therefore, I'm afraid the court must hold in abeyance the determination as to whether Sir Jost is entitled to the bridegift until a later date."

The Nabob sat back heavily in his chair as the judge addressed the bailiff. "Lady Van der Haar continues at risk, as long as her marital status remains unclear. Therefore, she must remain in protective custody." Addressing Preya, he asked that she leave her direction with the clerk, in the event the court needed to contact her. The proceedings were then adjourned with a tap of the gavel, and Juno was once again escorted by armed guards through the Hall, to go back to Fleet Prison, which was apparently to serve as her home for the bleakly foreseeable future.

Distracted by the enormity of the situation, Juno's gaze rested briefly on the spectators who watched for her reaction to these scandalous revelations. Startled, she recognized a familiar pair of grey eyes, peering at her from beneath the brows of one of the elderly pensioners. I am unsurprised, she thought as she walked past without showing a trace of recognition. Because nothing is what it seems, or more properly, no one is who they seem, including my erstwhile husband. Sighing, she thought over the significance of what she'd heard, and came to the unwelcome conclusion that one way or another, she had been thoroughly duped by Jost; it only remained to determine which of her theories was the correct one.

36

Juno sat in her cell, leaning against the wall by the gate and waiting for Jost, watching the shadows move on the opposite wall, and finding that she was having some difficulty putting two thoughts together. I am so weary of having the ground cut out from beneath me, she thought, and just when I think I have finally found my feet; it is of all things unfair.

The turnkey had taken one look at her face, and had bowed out to leave her alone. I wonder how much he knows of all this, she thought, tracing a finger on the iron bars. It would be the final straw if my jailor knows more about my marriage than I do. When the handle of the door to the gallery began to turn she sat up and straightened her skirts, wishing she could straighten everything else out as easily. Watching Jost hold the door to speak to the turnkey for a moment, she decided he looked unusually weary, and her heart turned over for him. He is so dear to me, she thought a bit fiercely. And there is no doubt we are truly married—there is that. I must not wail and gnash my teeth because I have a only a half a loaf, when I believed I had a full loaf—it is a very fine half loaf, after all.

Pulling up a chair on the other side of the bars, her husband's gaze searched her face. Horry must still have the razor, she thought—he has not shaved recently. Striving to keep her tone light, she remarked, "It appears you have one wife too many."

Her tone did not fool him, and his own manner was grave. "It is not true, *lieve*."

"Preya is lying?"

"Assuredly."

He offered no further explanation, and she thought about this. "Is she in danger, then?"

Tilting his head so that the braid fell forward, he said only, "Preya, she will help to solve the problems—I cannot tell you more."

Utterly perplexed, Juno said, "I suppose I can understand the desire to delay the decision about the bridegift so that the enemy does not have it, but since the bridegift has not been found, I fail to see how any of this is helpful."

"It is hardest for you to understand—me, I know this," he replied with true regret. "You say always what is true, and will not do the callous things."

But you will, she thought with her newfound sadness, thinking of what Preya's testimony had revealed about the lengths to which he would go. Shying away from thinking about it, instead she focused on his obvious dismay at causing her this particular heartache. "Were you expecting me to behave in a certain way—should I have had a more violent reaction? I didn't know."

He reached his hands through the bars, palms up, to hold her hands, and after the barest hesitation, she placed her hands in his. "No, you were very good. I am sorry for it, but we wanted you to have the shock, so that all could see."

She made a wry mouth. "Oh, I had the shock—never fear." Only not for the reason he believed.

His dark eyes were watching her carefully, unsure of her mood. "Do you believe me when I say it is not true? Me, I swear to you on the soul of my mother, Juno—"

"I believe you," she assured him, and fought the sadness that threatened to overwhelm her. "I wish I knew what had been planned, is all."

He squeezed her hands gently. "You are not the good liar, *lieve*."

"That is one of the first things you ever said to me, do you remember?" She couldn't control the slight quaver in her voice.

"Me, I do not forget anything," he assured her, his worried gaze on her face. "All will be well, my Juno—we will take Horry, and sail to Tortola; we will leave this place."

"Good." She dropped her gaze again. "England is too cold." You are such a coward, Juno, she thought; you have every right to know, and you must ask, or it will hang between you for the rest of your lives. Drawing a breath, she said, "There is something I need to ask you."

He lifted her hand to kiss it through the bars. "*Lieve*, there are those things I cannot tell you."

"I understand—but this is something else."

Gauging her mood, he bent forward, the dark eyes serious upon hers. "Tell me, my heart."

"I was thinking it over," she began, "—and I cannot imagine that you have seen Preya since you were in Algiers."

"No," he agreed. "A long time."

Juno paused so as to keep her emotions in check, and continued. "Yet she knew to come to London, and contest your marriage to me—it is no short trip, from Algiers, so that she must have been already on her way here, before we were married. It seems to me that this plan—or whatever it is—meant that you knew that it was necessary to marry me, even before you met me."

"*Lieve*—" he protested in dismay.

But she overrode him, and added before she lost her nerve, "And I must admit that it makes perfect sense—you are not a man to marry anyone, yet you wanted to marry me immediately, and did not rest until you had done so."

He shook his head in denial. "No; me, I will explain it to you—"

Very much afraid that she would believe whatever tale he told her, she interrupted him again to plead, "Please, Jost—I love you and I will always love you—but I would like to know the truth—whether it was all a sham—" despite her best efforts, her voice broke and she struggled on, "—and you married me for the express purpose of protecting the bridegift." She found she could no longer look at him, and retrieved her hands from his, so as to cover her eyes and weep; the pent-up emotions from the last few hours finally bursting forth.

His hands stroked and cradled her head as she buried her face in her hands and sobbed, wishing she could have maintained her poise and aware, all the while, that she would take whatever scraps he would offer her, because life without him did not bear contemplation.

"*Lieve,*" he whispered. "Do not cry—ah, do not."

Taking a deep breath, she wiped her cheeks with her hand, having left her handkerchief in the courtroom. Trying to gather up the shreds of her dignity, she concluded, "I do not doubt that you are fond of me, but I would have the truth from you."

Resting his forearms on the cross bar of the gate, he gently lifted her face in his hands. "Juno, you must look at me."

Stifling a sob, she raised her eyes to see that he was completely serious, the dark eyes intent upon hers. "Me, I do what I want, yes?"

But she could not agree, and pointed out in a watery voice, "Not always; there is the *niyama.*"

He made a sound of impatience as his thumbs brushed over her cheeks. "The promises among the men are each for the other. Me, I do what I want; *niemand*—no one—has the *om kracht*—the force—to make me do what I do not want to do—no one."

Watching him through her tears, she was convinced of his sincerity, because in his agitation he was fast losing command of the language.

"No one brings the power over me," he emphasized again, her head in his hands. He paused, his jaw working. "No one except you," he amended. "What you tell me to do I will do—always."

Raising her hands, she ran them along his thick forearms, to soothe him. "Yes, I believe you; I hadn't thought of it that way—you are the least likely candidate to go along with such a scheme. It is only that I don't understand— what of Preya, how did she know to come?"

He took a breath to calm himself. "Preya, she was going to be you."

At sea, Juno ventured, "I'm afraid I do not understand."

His hands still on her face, Jost leaned close and lowered his voice, even though the turnkey stood on the other side of the door, and they were quite alone. "Your father, he hid the diamonds and said they are Juno's, but the others—the ones we fight—they know this also. So I go to Bengal to see if you are still alive."

Nodding, she noted in a wry tone, "I was still alive, but only because the Rajah got greedy."

"Yes. If you are alive, then I must take you to London, to say there was no marriage with the Nabob. But if you are not alive, Preya goes to London to say she is you, and she is not married, so that it would take much time to prove she is not you."

"Oh—I see," Juno said slowly as the light began to break. "She was coming to London regardless, to help slow everything down. And when the grey-eyed man discovered you had married me, the plan was changed; instead she had to pretend to cooperate with the Nabob, so as to tell her tale today, but she crossed him up, and made it impossible for the court to decide who gets the bridegift."

"Assuredly. The court here is very slow; the more slow it is, the more it does not help Napoleon. And we have the time to find the bridegift."

"But Preya is quite a bit older than I," Juno pointed out with just a trace of feminine satisfaction. "And she is not English—no one would have believed that she was me in the first place."

"There are those who would come in to the court to swear that your mother, she was an Indian woman," Jost explained easily. "Many people."

"Oh," said Juno, a bit shocked. "I see."

The hard planes of his face softened. "No one tells me I must marry you. But I see you in Bengal, with your too-heavy gun, and your worries about Horry, and I think to myself, I must marry her—she is the finest woman."

Juno bent her head, because fresh tears had come, and he wiped them away with his callused fingers. "Yes?" He bent to look up into her face.

"Yes. I'm glad I understand, now."

"This, this is not good." He indicated the bars between them.

"Apparently it is necessary, so I cannot complain." Glancing up at him, she decided to raise her last remaining concern, and so ventured in a small voice, "I thought perhaps you married me because of Papa—because you admired him so."

The glint of humor returned to those dark eyes, and he weighed what he would say for a moment as his fingers moved gently on her face. "Your father, he says, 'Jost, you stay away from my daughter.'"

Juno had to chuckle; the imitation was pitch perfect. "Truly?"

"Yes," he admitted. "Me, I did not want to tell you he said this."

Lifting her hand to caress the side of his face, she felt the stubble of several days' beard and thought there was truly no finer sight in all the world. "He would be very pleased with how it all turned out, I think—now that you are decorous."

"You are the only one who thinks I am decorous," he admitted. Turning his face to kiss her palm, he added, "I marry you, Juno, because I love you. No other reason."

"*Lieve*," she replied, running a fond thumb over his mouth.

"You will not cry, anymore?" He wanted her promise.

"I will not." Which brought her to the next concern, in what appeared to be a never-ending list. "But I was thinking, Jost, if we delay too much, and too much pressure is brought to bear, wouldn't that make them think that the most expedient thing is to simply kill you, so as to make me a widow?"

He shook his head in disagreement. "If our marriage is good, the bridegift, it is mine. If I die, it goes back to your father, not to you."

"Oh," she said, thinking this over. "I forgot—it's not like an English dowry, it is a gift to the bridegroom. But in this case, Papa is dead."

"They must prove your father is dead." Jost shrugged his broad shoulders. "Who can say? Where is he buried? Again, there are the many witnesses who will say he is hiding from the legal troubles, only."

Staring at him, she noted with admiration, "I see. It appears every contingency has been stymied."

He tilted his head. "Me, I do not know what this means."

"It means your people have thought of everything."

His expression turned grave. "We will see, soon. I will not visit for several days, *lieve*."

She digested this piece of unwelcome news, and tried to hide her dismay. "Will you see Horry?"

"No," he said with regret. "Me, I do not know where Horry is."

"Right, then," she replied as steadily as she was able. "I will await your return, safe as a house."

37

As Jost had predicted, Juno found she was to entertain various visitors during her stay in the Fleet Prison. Peyton came again to exchange her old books for new ones, and stayed for a half hour to converse in a manner that made it clear he felt an obligation to help her through her difficulties. Juno hoped she struck the right balance of polite friendliness, and did not betray her conviction that Peyton was a despicable traitor, who probably should be hanged forthwith.

"I am certain the matter will be resolved to your satisfaction, and that the other woman is mistaken," he assured her in his understated manner. "I am only sorry that you are embroiled in such an awkward situation."

"Indeed." She noted that Peyton was another who appeared to need some additional sleep. "I suppose it is fortunate that I have no relations in England, to be mortified by the situation."

"Save Horry," he corrected with his grave smile. "Have you had comfort from your brother?"

Juno decided it was past time to turn the tables. "No—have you seen him? Do you think I should be concerned that he hasn't been to visit?"

There was the slightest pause before he assured her, "No, no, my lady—I would read nothing into it; he is a young lad, and loose in London for the first time. I am certain he will turn up shortly."

"I hope so," said Juno with genuine anxiety, and believed that she had carried off the deception.

Her next visitor was slightly more august. "Sir James Brenthaven, my lady," announced the turnkey, handing her a calling card. "A member of the Board of Directors for the East India Company."

Juno's heart sank, but then she rallied, thinking she could defend her father, and explain that the *Minvera* was not sunk, but was currently docked in the Blackwall Yard. Eying the turnkey, she ventured, "I suppose I should entertain this one, also?"

"Certainly, my lady," the man said without missing a beat, and went to open the entry door.

Sir James was revealed to be a white-haired gentleman, dressed in a very fine suit of clothes, who bowed elegantly upon making her acquaintance. "Lady Van der Haar," he intoned in a dry voice. "I hope I do not intrude."

Juno smiled. "I am at my leisure, sir."

He acknowledged the jest with his own slight smile, as he drew up a chair. "May I begin with my condolences upon the unfortunate death of your father."

Folding her hands in her lap, Juno matched his grave expression. "Thank you, Sir James,   I shall miss him acutely. Did you know him?"

He bowed his white head in regret. "I did not have that pleasure, but I am informed that he was a very engaging man."

Feeling that she may as well grasp the bull by the horns, she added, "He was also an honest man, also, sir—despite what you may have heard."

Her visitor offered delicately, "I understand there are other factors to consider, with respect to his purported actions."

Juno decided she probably shouldn't speak of the secret work for the Crown, and so merely nodded in agreement. "I am certain that when the truth of the matter is revealed, my father's good name will be restored."

Nodding, the gentleman then cleared his throat, and glanced at her from under his brows. "I understand, my lady, that you smuggled a cache of diamonds back from India."

Ah, she thought, here's the meat of the matter. "Yes— in my Papa's pipe, in fact; they have been turned over to the court, until a determination can be made as to whom they belong."

Shifting in his seat, the man chided her gently. "I do not mean to deprecate your actions, my lady, but surely these diamonds should more properly have been delivered to the Company—any assets your father acquired in the course of his trading rightfully belong to the Company."

This seemed a bit deceptive, as it seemed to Juno that the diamonds should be handed over to Lloyd's of London, who had paid out insurance proceeds under false pretenses. Juno fell back on her status as a wife, and replied, "It was my husband's suggestion to deposit them with the court, sir, and I followed his direction."

Into the pause in conversation, her visitor scraped his chair even closer to the barred wall that separated them. "My lady, I confess I have come to speak with you confidentially, upon confidential matters."

"I keep no secrets from my husband, Sir James," Juno warned in a mild rebuke, worried about whatever was to come.

"Of course, of course—indeed, Sir Jost is no stranger to these matters, and no doubt would approve of my request wholeheartedly."

Sighing inwardly, Juno conceded, "I suppose you wish to speak of what will happen with the bridegift."

"Not precisely a bridegift," the man corrected her. "Rather, a subterfuge to expedite the transfer of purloined outlay."

Poor Jost would have no idea what he is talking about, thought Juno, and I am barely keeping up. "Yes, I completely understand that the bridegift does not truly belong to me—or Sir Jost, more accurately. That aspect is not disputed, I assure you. "

The man bent his head for a moment, gathering his thoughts. "Economic matters in England are currently in a precarious state."

Juno nodded, remembering that the wealthy men who paid out insurance claims for Lloyd's could not help England's Treasury, because all their money was going to pay out the false insurance claims from India.

The gentleman leaned forward, his manner intent. "It is a delicate matter; if word gets out that—" he paused, trying to find the right euphemism "— matters were not aboveboard, with respect to the Company, the result could be cataclysmic—worldwide commerce could grind to a halt."

"Surely it is more important that the truth be revealed?" asked Juno, slightly shocked.

The man tilted his head in an equivocal manner. "Upon first blush, certainly. But you must consider the dire results, if worldwide trade is disrupted. Why, Napoleon would have prevailed in bringing down England, even though his scheme would not have been successful. We are a nation of traders, after all."

Knitting her brow, Juno thought this over. "I should think we are past such considerations—it is Mr. Finch who should have considered the harm he would do England, and to the Company."

The gentleman nearly choked, and leaned toward her with some anxiety. "I beg you, my lady; pray make no such accusation—Mr. Finch is a fellow Director."

But Juno was having none of it, and retorted with some fire, "Mr. Finch planned to murder me, and he probably arranged for my father's murder, Sir James. I am past caring about your cordial relationship with him."

The man stared at her for a long moment, aghast. "You are convinced of this?"

"I am," she averred in a grim tone, but then added fairly, "Although I do not know if it can be proven in the Court of Chancery. Perhaps, Sir James, you should be more concerned about the damage to your industry that would occur if Mr. Finch was arrested for treason and my father's murder."

"It is indeed a grave situation." The other leaned back, clearly shocked. After a small pause, he made a conciliatory gesture with his hands. "Do you think we could—at the very least—work together, Lady Van der Haar, to see that the sensational details—whatever they may be—are kept to a minimum? It would be to both our advantages."

Juno couldn't help but smile, and made a gesture indicating her circumstances. "What am I to do, Sir James? I am under the court's protection, and must testify when compelled—I have no choice but to speak the truth."

Nodding in understanding, he continued, "Quite right, of course; well, it was just a thought. You will aid us in our efforts to return the funds to their rightful owners, though?"

"I will," she agreed, willing to grant him this. "I have no claim, certainly."

There was a delicate pause. "I must point out, my lady, that it is not your claim that concerns me—indeed, technically speaking, you have no claim."

Seeing what he meant, Juno assured him, "Sir Jost and I are as one mind on this subject, sir."

The gentleman raised his eyes to consider the view from the window for a moment, then said in a neutral tone, "It is a great deal of money—indeed, a fortune; and—although I am loath to cast aspersions, my lady—your husband's past livelihood does not bear close scrutiny."

Juno could only shake her head and smile. "Then I suppose our only option is to trust him, you and me; it seems we have little other choice."

Although he acknowledged her point with a dry smile, her visitor persisted, "As a new bride, you may have influence."

"I do," she agreed, thinking he didn't know the half of it. "But I think the greater influence is my husband's hatred for Napoleon, and those who serve him."

"Oh?" The gentleman raised his brows. "Is that so?"

"I am not at liberty to relate the particulars, but rest assured; Sir Jost wishes for nothing more than to bring the enemy down."

Juno could see that this revelation was met with some relief. "You ease my concerns, then, and I shall say no more. However, I would be more sanguine, my lady, if we knew where the funds were hidden. Perhaps we could circumvent any further unpleasantness in court, if we could simply lay hands on the diamonds." He made an attempt at a friendly smile, which she could see was foreign to his nature.

Juno hid her annoyance only with an effort—it seemed he was openly suggesting that they operate without the consent of the court. Coolly, she replied, "I can't imagine how I can help you in this aim, Sir James."

But the gentleman persisted, even in light of her unbending attitude. "Perhaps—if you would—you could influence your brother; convince him that there is no point to keeping your father's secret any longer."

Juno stared at him in surprise. "I'm afraid you are mistaken, Sir James. My brother knows no more of this than I."

But the gentleman disagreed, and leaned forward again, speaking softly. "No, my lady. One of those who worked closely with your father is now here in London; he is adamant that your father said the funds were on deposit under your name, and that Horry is the one who knows where they are located."

Astonished, Juno now understood the impetus behind everyone's sudden interest in Horry's whereabouts. She could only stammer, "Sir James—I assure you that Horry knows no such thing. He would have no reason to keep such a secret from me, or my husband."

After a moment's hesitation, Sir James offered, "Could it be he does not trust Sir Jost? Young Master Payne may fear that anything he tells you will reach Sir Jost's ears."

Adamant, Juno shook her head. "That is not the case, sir; Horry trusts Sir Jost—I am certain of it."

There was a pause, while Juno and her visitor thought over this particular stalemate. "If I may ask," the man ventured, "—do you indeed know of Master Payne's whereabouts?'

"No, I do not," said Juno in a tart tone uncharacteristic for her. She then stood so as to bring the conversation to a halt, signaling to the turnkey to see her visitor out.

Juno's third visitor this day was more welcome than the other two; the turnkey announced Judge Moore, and as the older man approached, Juno held out her right hand through the bars to shake his, until she corrected her gaffe, and switched hands. "I beg your pardon."

"Happens all the time," he assured her as he settled into the chair recently vacated by Sir James. The judge indicated the empty sleeve pinned to his chest. "Lost it to a cannonball in Spain. I was a battlefield surgeon at the time, and had to come up with a new way of earning my bread." With a twinkle, he added, "At the very least, I hoped to be mistaken for Admiral Nelson by the ladies but alas—it never happened."

As Juno smiled at him, he leaned forward to ask with all sincerity, "How are you, my dear? Is it bearable, here?"

"I miss my husband, but I understand the necessity."

Nodding thoughtfully, he disclosed, "I'm afraid pressure is being brought to bear—and from more than one source."

"Yes," she agreed with empathy. "I entertained Sir James Brenthaven, just now."

"Ah." He raised his brows. "Then I tell you nothing you haven't already heard."

Juno recited what she knew. "The company's Board of Directors would like to see the matter resolved discreetly, and they want the diamonds handed over with no further ado. Apparently the impact of a prolonged scandal may have a catastrophic effect on trade."

"Indeed—although, are you aware—" he asked carefully, "—that there is an international interest in your bridegift, also?"

"I am," she admitted, and was not certain whether she should say anything further.

Focusing his gaze on the grated window, he said almost idly, "I have been presented with a marriage license, and a witness who will attest to your husband's first marriage to the pretender."

Juno could only shake her head. "I am not surprised; it must have been extremely annoying when they discovered that the putative first wife was not going to cooperate, at the hearing."

Nodding slowly, he agreed. "I confess that is what struck me as strange, also. I wonder why she testifies so adamantly that there are no witnesses and no marriage lines in England; it would be to her benefit—one would think—to instead say that there were."

"That is true," Juno agreed, knowing she mustn't say anything further about Preya's role in the scheme to thwart the Nabob.

"What is she like, can you tell me?"

Juno shook her head. "We have never met, my lord."

This brought his gaze back to her in mild surprise. "Is that so? I had thought she looked upon you as a dear friend."

"Isn't that strange? I had the same impression." Juno knit her brow in puzzlement. "But we have never met, and indeed, it seems unlikely—given the circumstances—that she would look upon me with any favor at all."

Stroking his chin with his good hand, the judge offered, "You and I, it appears, are at the pressure point of immensely powerful competing interests—and through no fault of our own, I might add."

"What will you do?" Juno was genuinely curious. "If it is indeed a matter of national security, as Sir James suggests, perhaps the matter should be resolved discreetly." Catching herself, she remembered that she mustn't disrupt whatever plan Jost and the others had put into play, and tempered her comment accordingly. "Although I imagine you'd like to be certain, and not influenced by those perceived as influential."

"*Fiat justitia ruat caelum,*" he agreed.

"I'm afraid I do not know what that means," she admitted.

"'Let justice be done, though the heavens fall,'" he translated, a twinkle appearing in his eye. Reaching into his inner waistcoat pocket, he pulled out a well-worn deck of cards. "May I offer a game, to help pass the time?"

38

They were once again in court, and the Nabob's advocate gestured toward Juno, who was sitting in the witness box. "It is understandable, certainly. A young woman, raised in a convent school and then thrown into close company with a foreign mercenary who has a certain—allure."

Not going well, thought Juno, blushing hotly at the insinuation. Wishing for the hundredth time that Jost was here, she listened to the advocate's insinuations of sexual subjugation. The new judge who was presiding over the matter listened with acute interest, nodding in agreement and giving Juno the occasional pitying glance.

That morning Juno had awakened to the alarming news that Judge Moore had been attacked, and now lay gravely injured and under the care of his physicians. His chambers had been ransacked, and the cache of diamonds, locked within a strongbox, had been stolen. Heartsick over these events, Juno concluded that the heavens had indeed fallen. The news was made even more alarming because it was given to her by a new turnkey, who had replaced the old one without explanation; the new one spending much of his time surveying her with a leer.

Juno brought her attention back to the hearing, which had been hastily convened to discuss these latest alarming developments, and their impact on the pending matter.

". . . a Barbary pirate, after all; it must raise grave concerns for any right-minded person."

Exasperated, Juno interrupted to point out, "If Sir Jost wished to steal the diamonds, he had plenty of opportunity, for heaven's sake—indeed, he held them safe for me, whilst we sailed to England."

"My dear," said the new judge in a gentle tone, leaning in to her. "You must not speak out of turn."

Juno subsided, and wondered if anyone else had noticed she had no advocate to represent her, this time.

Spreading his hands, the Nabob's advocate continued, "Where is Sir Jost? It cannot be a coincidence that he is missing, along with the diamonds. Instead, he abandons his too-trusting young bride to face disgrace alone."

"Indeed," nodded the new judge, shaking his head in sorrow. "Deplorable."

A fool, thought Juno with angry contempt; he must have been hand-picked, and I can only hope that the powers-that-be have everything under control—otherwise I might be tempted to think I am being thrown to the wolves.

Heartened by the judge's comments, the Nabob's advocate continued, "His first wife is also not present, and perhaps we may draw the obvious conclusion--reminded of his obligations, the gentleman has now abandoned this poor young woman, whom he has ruined."

Ah; so at last I am ruined, thought Juno. And I imagine I will soon receive a chivalrous offer of marriage to resolve the situation—from the Nabob, or perhaps even Peyton, again. Where, oh where is Jost?

"My client—" here the advocate indicated the Nabob, who nodded solemnly in acknowledgment from the counsel table "—stands prepared to forgive the witness her breach of their engagement—"

"We were never engaged—" Juno protested, but the judge leaned over to her again, shaking his finger in a gentle admonishment. "Will you not let me speak?" Juno asked him in bewilderment. "You must see that this is all very untoward."

The advocate and the judge exchanged a glance that spoke of the inability of a female to grasp the basic truth that she was incapable of making any judgments for herself. With a sigh, the judge pronounced, "I am given documentation—uncontradicted documentation—to the effect that Sir Jost's first marriage was indeed valid, and that his alleged marriage to Miss Payne was a nullity. I admit I am inclined to release this poor young woman from her current confinement, and send along with her my sincere wish that she consult wiser heads in the future."

I wish I had a blunderbuss about me, thought Juno in a fury—or even a knife, to throw. "You make a grave error, my lord—if you would only listen—"

Sensing victory, the advocate made a deferential gesture with the palm of his hand, and said in an aside to the judge, "I imagine there is a pension connected with her father's service to the East India Company; I can look into the situation, and report back to the court."

Whatever response the judge was to make, however, was interrupted by the sound of raised voices and the sudden tramping entrance of a dozen constables, some of whom came forward and some who remained standing guard around the perimeter of the courtroom area.

"Order," ventured the judge, tapping his gavel, and gazing about him in timid bewilderment. "My heavens—what is the meaning of this?"

A magistrate came forward, flanked by two constables. "Pardon the interruption, my lord, but I come from the Central Criminal Courts, and I must serve an arrest warrant for Mr. Finch."

The Nabob sprang to his feet, or sprang as quickly as his bulk would allow. "Outrageous," he thundered. "I assure you, you will not hold your job by this time tomorrow."

But his wary advocate signaled to him to stay silent, "An arrest warrant? Surely there has been some mistake; my client is attempting to aid this young lady in her difficulties."

"He must come along to the Old Bailey, to be arraigned forthwith," the magistrate declared. "Does he plan to resist arrest?" The man glanced at the waiting constables, who looked as though they were looking forward to a set-to.

"Hold, hold—let us be reasonable," offered the advocate in a conciliatory tone. "Perhaps there has been some mistake; what are the charges?"

With a flourish, the magistrate produced a parchment and handed it to the advocate, who held his pince-nez to his eyes and read the document as the magistrate recited the charges aloud. "Grand theft; conspiracy to commit a burglary; conspiracy to inflict grievous bodily injury on an Officer of the Crown; perversion of justice."

Juno could hear the gasp of shock that reverberated throughout the court; the charges were serious indeed, and suddenly Juno's sorry marital status seemed of little importance to the court watchers, who craned their necks in the back.

Blustering, the Nabob made to speak again, but his advocate again signaled him to stay silent, and instead gave voice to his own outrage. "You cannot contend that Mr. Finch was involved in any way with the attack on Judge Moore? Good Lord, man—think over the repercussions of such an accusation."

After a dramatic pause, the magistrate played his trump. "The stolen diamonds were discovered an hour ago in Mr. Finch's home safe."

"Ridiculous," blasted the Nabob, unable to stay silent. "I store gold, diamonds and precious gems in that safe as a matter of course; how dare you—how *dare* you imply they are the stolen diamonds."

"Not diamonds," the magistrate corrected him. "Mere paste."

There was a small silence. "Paste?" asked the advocate, and Juno noted that the Nabob drew out a handkerchief, and held it to his lips.

"Paste," the magistrate confirmed. "And specially marked, besides." Turning to the constables flanking him, he directed them to manacle the suspect, which they did by roughly turning him about, and pulling his arms behind him. "I would much enjoy hearing an explanation as to how the marked false diamonds came to be in your safe, Mr. Finch."

"Say nothing," the advocate instructed the Nabob, himself a bit pale as he accompanied the group out of chambers. The court-watchers, anticipating a much more interesting session in the criminal assizes, followed them out, leaving only Juno and the judge in the courtroom, flanked by a few remaining constables.

"Well, fancy that," said the judge, in some shock. "Poor Will."

Juno imagined he referred to Judge Moore, but she was still staring at the retreating group of men, and marveling at the trap that had been sprung. So; the diamonds entrusted to her by the dying priest—or faux priest— were indeed planted, and not diamonds at all. It would be impossible to directly implicate the Nabob in the insurance scheme, so Jost and the others had done the next best thing, and set up a situation where he would be desperate to seize whatever diamonds he could—only these ones could be traced, and were not diamonds at all. It was damning evidence indeed, and one would think all the money in the world could not purchase mercy from a court seeking vengeance for an attack on one of its officers. The Nabob was finished, and there would be no more nefarious schemes—indeed, he may well hang.

Was it over? Juno wondered as she thought it through. Could she go to Jost now, wherever he was?

The answer, unfortunately, presented itself almost immediately. One of the constables came forward to stand before the still-stunned judge, and explain deferentially, "I've been instructed to take the lady back to her cell, my lord."

Juno saw, with an inward sigh, that the erstwhile constable was actually the grey-eyed man. Without waiting for permission from the incompetent judge, she rose and stepped down from the witness box and then willingly accompanied her escort and another constable back to her cell—and now that she was paying attention, she recognized the constable as her former turnkey. They entered the transport coach, and as soon as the driver had been given direction, Juno decided these people owed her some answers, after the humiliations of this day. "Where is Sir Jost?"

The grey-eyed man answered without looking at her. "He is otherwise engaged. As for myself, I would prefer to be watching the assizes, but I was required to give my solemn oath that I would escort you back to your cell, personally."

Her escort seemed disinclined to speak further, as the transport coach rattled up the Strand. Nevertheless, she asked in a quiet voice, "So; it is not yet over?"

"It is never over," he replied cryptically. "And you are better off in your prison cell, believe me. The bridegift remains undiscovered, and you remain at the center of this mystery."

"I am given to understand that it is Horry who is at the center of the mystery, and not me."

But he would neither confirm nor deny. "Perhaps, but marrying Horry will win no one a fortune."

Sighing, Juno reflected, "I used to be no one of importance."

"The perils of war," her companion agreed. "Chin up; it is entirely possible you will retreat back into obscurity very shortly—although obscurity is probably no longer an option, given who you've married."

Juno retorted with defiance, "I wouldn't change a moment of what has happened, if it meant I wouldn't have met my husband; not a *single* moment."

But her companion only made a sound of impatience. "Spare me the sentiment, if you please; you have no idea what you have married into."

"On the contrary," she retorted with some heat, "I have every idea, and I will not listen to you disparage him."

"Don't make her angry," cautioned the turnkey, in all seriousness. "I heard tell that she killed a tiger with her bare hands."

"Oh, for heaven's sake; I *did not* kill it with my bare hands, I speared it with my umbrella," Juno corrected him crossly. "Honestly, I don't know how such stories get started." A sudden silence settled over the coach's interior, and nothing more was said for the remainder of the journey.

When they arrived at her cell, the grey-eyed man indicated to the leering turnkey that he had been relieved, and the man seemed very surprised by this news. "Are ye sure? I bin tole..."

"Oh, I am sure. Come along." He then turned to say to the original turnkey, "Report any visitors to me through the usual channels."

Puckering her brow, Juno watched him leave from behind her grated door, and wondered at the command—apparently she was to continue in her role as the bait in the trap, even though one would imagine the trap had already been successfully sprung. Sighing, she settled into her chair and took up a book, awaiting the next dire event.

She didn't have long to wait. In a short while, the turnkey entered to announce that Peyton waited without. "Oh—oh, of course; do show him in." If Peyton was aligned with the Nabob—or the French—he must be very uneasy about the latest turn of events; indeed, she wondered that he'd come at all, instead of choosing to flee with all speed.

"Mr. Peyton is accompanied by a young woman, who claims your acquaintance," the turnkey added, his expression carefully impassive.

Preya, thought Juno in some surprise, and decided there was no harm in hearing what the woman had to say. Rising to greet her visitors, she was astonished to behold not Preya, but Aditi; only Aditi was clinging to Peyton's arm, and gazing upon Juno with a triumphant, spiteful expression.

Trouble, thought Juno with a sinking heart, and wondered if the grey-eyed man knew of this particular disaster.

39

Juno addressed Aditi in a pointed tone. "Mrs. Landon; where is your husband?"

"You do not ask the questions," retorted Aditi at her most insolent, tossing her head. "You will answer the questions." She then ran her fingers down Peyton's arm in a proprietary manner, and leaned into his shoulder, looking up to him with a seductive smile.

Thoroughly shocked, Juno admonished the girl, "Aditi, you are a married woman, now; recall that you have your ring."

"And you are a stupid, *stupid* girl," Aditi declared, stamping a small foot as her temper flared. "You lecture me—you! You who let Jost take you to bed every night before you were married."

"Aditi," breathed Juno in embarrassed dismay.

But the girl was unrepentant, and lifted her chin. "Mr. Landon does not have money; Mr. Peyton has money. It is simple, and you are *stupid*." With a full measure of spite, she emphasized the adjective once again, nearly hissing in her triumph.

"Please," interpolated Peyton in his calm voice, patting Aditi's hand on his arm. "Do not be unkind, my dear—I must ask my questions, remember?"

"Hurry," urged Aditi as she wound her arms around his neck with a sensuous motion, and Juno wondered in horror if she was, in fact, drunk.

His ears turning pink, the man gently drew her away. "You must forgive her," he apologized to Juno. "She was not raised as a gentlewoman, I'm afraid."

But Juno was having none of it. "I confess I am shocked by your behavior, Mr. Peyton; I thought you a friend to Mr. Landon."

He bowed his head in acknowledgment of the justness of her accusations. "Yes; but I'm afraid matters have reached the sticking point, and I must reassess my plans—indeed, I fear I must depart England immediately, and I cannot resist the offer of such pleasant companionship. You must agree that I cannot claim your husband's prowess with the opposite sex."

Aware that he was trying to wound her with the innuendo, Juno didn't flinch, but instead reiterated, "You are no gentleman, sir, to play such a trick."

Petyon watched her narrowly for a moment. "I am only too happy to take my leave, madam, but first, I must know whether the remaining diamonds—the ones from your father—are also paste. You will save me and many others a great deal of time and trouble."

But Juno held firm, unwilling to give him any advantage. "I will tell you nothing. Take Mrs. Landon and leave, please."

With an apologetic smile, the small man played his trump. "Perhaps you will reconsider? If you won't tell me, then Aditi has agreed to lead me to your brother. She knows where he is, if you'll remember."

Horrified, Juno advanced to the bars and said in an urgent tone to Aditi, "You mustn't; whatever he has promised you is false—he is not a good man, Aditi."

Tossing her head, Aditi turned a shoulder to her, and refused to answer.

Trying to quash her burgeoning panic, Juno addressed Peyton again. "Horry knows nothing of this; the rumor that he has knowledge of the diamonds is simply not true."

"My concern is not whether Horry can find the diamonds—I am certain he can. My concern is whether I will wind up with a bagful of paste, for my trouble," Peyton explained patiently. "You will tell me what you know, and then we shall see if Horry is worth my time."

Sickened, Juno struggled, wishing she knew what she was supposed to say. I imagine everyone is expecting me to behave as I normally do, she decided, and so she admitted honestly, "I have no knowledge of whether the diamonds are real or paste, or indeed, if they exist at all."

Watching her, Peyton nodded, apparently satisfied. "I see. Then I must pursue them."

"*Please* leave Horry alone; Aditi—"

"Enough." For the first time, Juno heard a touch of steel in the man's voice, beneath his normal courteous tone. Addressing Aditi, he turned to leave. "We must go see to the boy, my dear."

Desperate, Juno clutched at the bars, and begged, "Aditi—oh, *please*—"

But Aditi was not to be moved, and instead followed Peyton toward the door, swinging her hips in an insolent manner. Whirling, she paused to mock Juno once more in parting. "Aditi, Aditi," she imitated in a sing-song, scornful tone. "That is not even my true name, you stupid girl—my true name is Judith."

Juno stared in shock, as the Indian girl's gaze held hers for a long moment. The reference was to Aditi's favorite Bible heroine—the one who had seduced, and then beheaded the enemy general.

Peyton signaled to the turnkey to open the door, and said in parting, "Farewell, Lady Van der Haar; I doubt we will ever meet again."

As Juno watched him go—presumably to his death---Aditi followed him out the door. Just before she left, the Indian girl turned to Juno one last time, and dropped the perfectly executed curtsey that Juno had taught her.

The door clanged shut, and Juno was left in the profound silence of her cell. "Well, then," she said aloud, and sank back into her chair. Impossible to puzzle out how Aditi had come to be with Peyton, but one thing seemed clear; Horry was safe, and Peyton was not. I wonder how many more are to be lured into a trap, she thought, and kicked the leg of her chair with her heel in frustration. I am heartily sick of this cell.

Juno had no more visitors that day—even the turnkey did not enter again. However, she was awakened later that evening when she heard the key turn in the outer door. Juno had gone to bed early, to avoid wondering when her errant husband would return, and her first thought was that he had finally appeared. "Jost," she whispered in profound relief.

"Not Jost, I'm afraid," the grey-eyed man responded, his lean figure outlined against the moonlight that streamed in through the window. "Please prepare to depart."

"Where?" she asked warily, noting that the turnkey stood with him. It seemed an odd time to make a departure.

"I shall take you to this husband of yours; we leave in five minutes."

But Juno knew a moment's qualm, considering the various crosses and double-crosses she had witnessed this day. "Perhaps I shall instead await him here."

He crossed his arms and regarded her thoughtfully. "You are an untrusting soul; I am to tell you 'the frizzen is fixed.'"

It was the first thing Jost had ever said to her. "I'll be ready in three minutes," she exclaimed, leaping up. Finally, *finally*, she was to leave this wretched place—and not a blessed moment too soon.

A short time later, Juno stood beside the grey-eyed man in her cell, and watched as he and the turnkey yanked the cage of bars from the window— the bars having been neatly severed, at some earlier time. After he leaned to look out over the mews two stories below, her companion turned to the turnkey, "Go below, I will send her down first." He then produced a rope and began to loop it in preparation. "Do not be alarmed—" he began.

"I am to be carried on your back—yes, I know," interrupted Juno with impatience, hiking up her skirts in anticipation.

He glanced at her, as he completed his preparations with unhurried movements. "As inviting as such a course of action would be, instead I shall ask that you place your foot in this loop—" he paused to demonstrate "—and wrap this other loop around your arms, so that I may lower you down."

Juno dropped her skirts back down in embarrassment. "Oh—I see. Sir Jost usually puts me on his back, when we stage an escape."

Taking her waist in his hands, her companion boosted her up on the window ledge. "I am beginning to understand how this extraordinary alliance took place."

"I held a blunderbuss on him," she reminisced as she threw her legs over the brick sill, and secured her foot on the loop. "And he felt compelled to marry me."

"Spare me the details, if you please. Over you go."

"You are not a romantic, I fear," she observed with a small smile, as she wound the rope around her arms.

"On the contrary." He peered over the ledge to make certain the turnkey had appeared below. "I consider myself bound by a long-term understanding." He then raised the hood of her cloak over her head, and carefully lowered her down the wall to the mews below, Juno using her feet to keep from knocking into the building.

"Here you are, my lady," said the turnkey as he caught her in his arms. "Hurry, now." He disentangled her from the loops, and then held the end of the rope as the grey-eyed man rapidly followed, with quick hand-over-hand movements.

"This way," that gentleman instructed upon landing, and they moved across the street to the Fleet River, keeping to the shadows. "You have served your purpose, and it is time you were removed to a more secure place."

In a fever of curiosity, she asked, "Is Mr. Peyton still at large?"

After carefully checking to see that their way was clear, he replied, "No longer; in fact, the two of us held a very civil conversation."

Juno thought she heard the turnkey chuckle, and decided she didn't want to know the particulars. She followed him along the river bank for a few minutes in silence, careful to keep up with his rapid pace. "How did you know to put Aditi to use?"

He slowed for a moment, so as to walk beside her, his sharp gaze scrutinizing the shadows. "A very useful sort of young woman—I questioned her at length, and you can imagine my surprise when she let drop the interesting fact that Mr. Peyton had offered to pay for her—services—during your voyage."

Juno made a sound of disgust. "When he was not offering me marriage."

"Yes; a busy man. But with a fortuitous weakness, as it turned out. And apparently, he is also a desperate man; the Nabob is not one to stand bluff, and his cohorts are no doubt very uneasy about what he will disclose to the authorities."

"The birds are flapping their wings," Juno noted, in a knowing tone.

He eyed her askance. "God in heaven; you are beginning to sound like him."

"Where is he?" she demanded, hurrying along beside him, as they continued to make their way along the river bank. "And why is it always so cold in this miserable country?"

"Patience," he instructed without sympathy. "And a pox on your father for not making himself clear—my only comfort is that the enemy knows as little as I do."

"It *is* very strange; Papa was always so straightforward."

"Indeed."

Juno suddenly caught the scent of sea air, as the Thames came into view. Her companion did not hesitate, but made a right turn along the embankment. "Do we head to the dock again?"

"Perhaps. As we may not meet again, I wish you well in your future endeavors—and pray do not mention to your husband that you displayed your legs to me."

"I won't," she promised. "Are you leaving?"

"No, you are." He grasped her beneath the arms, picking her up bodily. Juno knew a moment's horror, thinking she had indeed walked into a trap, and that he was going to throw her into the Thames. But instead, he lowered her quickly over the side of the embankment and into Jost's waiting arms, raised to receive her from where he stood, balancing on the floorboards of the *Juno*. As she was crushed in a bear hug, she looked over her husband's shoulder to see the welcome sight of her grinning brother.

40

"Easy, my dear—I cannot breathe," Juno gasped, and Jost loosed his hold on her only to kiss her full on the mouth, despite Horry's amused presence.

"*Mijn hart,*" her husband exclaimed, which she interpreted as a sincere accolade.

But Horry didn't have much patience for this display of conjugal affection. "I say, Juno; Sir Jost says you've been in prison."

"Like a common criminal," she affirmed. "And where have you been, Horry?"

"The opposite, I suppose. I've been posing as a sexton at a church."

"With *Aditi?*" Juno could not contain her surprise at the picture thus presented, as Jost settled her into the bench at the stern.

"No, she was taken elsewhere—they told me Aditi was too conspicuous to be seen with me."

Juno could well believe it. "Yes, they found another use for Aditi. Is Mr. Landon nearby?"

Jost answered as he pushed one of the oars against the embankment wall so that they were away. "Landon, he has been on the docks, watching."

"And you? I have missed you mightily." Unable to help herself, Juno leaned to place a hand on Jost's knee, as he plied the oars.

She saw his white smile flash in the darkness. "Me, I lead the birds up the river—they think I go to fetch the diamonds."

"A wild goose chase," Horry pronounced with satisfaction. "Capital; I wish I could have gone."

"There are no wild gooses, here," Jost explained patiently. "It is not the right time of year."

Juno could not resist laughing aloud, she was so happy to see them both.

"Hush, *lieve*," cautioned her husband. "You must stay quiet, until we are aboard."

"Do we board the *Minerva*?" Juno wasn't certain, but it seemed to her they were headed away from the Blackwall Yard, instead of toward it.

"No, we board a coal barge. We stay quiet for a few days."

"Thank heaven; I would very much like to stay quiet." Juno hoped she would share a private cabin with her husband—she was finding it difficult to refrain from touching him, and besides, it would be such a relief to no longer be an object of scrutiny.

"I am sick of staying quiet," Horry complained. "And I am sick of answering questions about Papa's bank accounts."

"Poor you," said Juno. "Everyone seems to think we know more than we do."

"These people, they are not fools." Jost glanced over his shoulder to correct his course. "And the diamonds, they are somewhere."

"At least the enemy doesn't have them," said Juno, repeating what the grey-eyed man had said. "There is that."

"And the Nabob is in prison," Horry added. "Serves him right, the blackguard—trying to murder us."

"It wouldn't have done him much good, with the diamonds still missing," Juno pointed out. "All his scheming was for naught." Reminded, she asked Jost. "Does Horry know about Peyton?"

Rowing, Jost shook his head, as Horry asked with interest, "What about Peyton? Was he killed?"

Juno leaned forward, happy to be able to impart something of interest to another, for once. "He was working with the enemy."

Horry was suitably astonished, and stared at each of them for a moment, speechless. "Peyton? I wouldn't think he had it in him; he seemed such a dull, milk-and-water fellow."

Juno nodded in confirmation. "It was all an act."

"I did see him lose his temper, once," Horry remembered, gazing ahead at the lanterns that were now visible from the looming barge. "He had a row with Jairus, of all people."

Jost suddenly paused, and lifted the oars. "What does this mean—'row'?"

"A quarrel," Horry explained. "It seemed so unlike him; I thought perhaps he'd been drinking, or something."

Jost sat very still, and Juno could sense his wariness as he asked softly, "When was this, Horry?"

Realizing that Jost thought it significant, Horry considered. "It was about a week before we made landfall."

Jost leaned forward and said quietly, "Both of you must stay down—now." Juno obeyed the urgency in his tone without hesitation, and slid off the bench to curl up on the floorboards, Horry beside her. Jost scissored one oar so that the skiff abruptly turned around, and then made in the direction from whence they had come, rowing rapidly and dipping the oars with a powerful rhythm.

"Is it a trap?" Horry concluded in a soft tone.

Jost looked over his shoulder to see where he was headed. "Jairus should not be in the quarrel with Peyton. It may be nothing, or it may be something; we shall see. Can you swim, Horry?"

Juno could not like the tenor of the question, and she clasped her hands to keep them from trembling as she listened to the water slough against the bottom of the boat.

"Yes, sir," Horry answered without a qualm.

"And you, Juno? Can you swim—swim strong?"

"Yes," she whispered, and hoped she sounded more confident than she felt. Surely he didn't expect them to swim in the cold river in the middle of the night?

"Good." He was slightly out of breath from his exertions. "They think we go to the barge, so we will run to the shore and disappear instead, yes? But if they come after us, Juno must go into the water, and hide among the boats while Horry swims to get help. He goes to the tavern on the pier—you remember the one?"

Horry nodded, his face close to Juno's. "Yes, sir."

"Speak to the tavern keeper—but no one else; yes?"

"Yes, sir."

Although Juno very much wanted to ask where Jost would be, she held her tongue, trying to emulate Horry's steadiness. Fortunately her husband knew her well, and said to her, "I will lead them away."

Jost cautioned them to stay down, as the skiff silently bumped up against one of the boats that was docked along a dark, narrow pier. Lifting his head to peer over the boat toward the shoreline, he quietly stored the oars, and began to pull the skiff along the sides of the tied-up boats, his actions wary and deliberate, as they slowly came closer and closer to the shore. He whispered, "We land here, but Juno, be ready to run back into the water."

She nodded from her position on the floorboards, and watched what she could manage to see over the gunwale, as they advanced upon the shallows. It was low tide, and the seaweed lay on the exposed shore, all the way up to the wooden palisade that acted as a seawall. There were crude steps built onto the palisade for the boarding of boats when the tide was higher, and it appeared that these steps were their object. First, however, they must cross the exposed shore, and Juno nervously gathered up her skirts in her hands and made ready, hoping that she wouldn't slip on the slick seaweed.

Suddenly, there was a loud crack to the left, and several things happened almost simultaneously. Jost grunted in pain, and immediately threw his weight toward the right side of the skiff, so that Horry and Juno were unceremoniously dumped into the cold, shallow water. Then, with a mighty heave, Jost lifted the skiff so that it was balanced on its side like a shield, just as another shot rang out, and hit the bottom of the skiff with a thud.

"Go, Horry," said Jost softly, drawing one of his pistols, and peering over the top of the tilted skiff into the darkness.

But Horry hesitated, crouching beside Juno in the dark, shallow water. "No—give me a pistol."

Jost did not look at him, but said in the same soft tone, "You will obey orders."

Horry sank down into the water, and silently disappeared.

Juno watched in shock, as Jost braced his pistol with careful deliberation on the top edge of the tilted skiff, and fired. A startled exclamation could be heard from the neighboring pier. "Go hide between the boats, *lieve*, and stay low in the water; we wait for Horry to bring help."

"You are hurt," she whispered through stiff lips, watching the bloodstain spread on the back of his left shoulder.

His gaze never leaving the opposite pier, he spoke to her in a reasonable tone, as though nothing extraordinary was unfolding. "We will have the pact, *lieve*. You will go, and I will catch up to you. But you must go, yes?"

"I can tell them I know about the diamonds," she whispered, trying to control the quaver in her voice. "I—I can make up a tale—I want you to be safe."

But he only repeated, "You must go, *lieve*. I will catch up to you."

Another shot rang out, and another thud hit the bottom of the skiff. Trembling violently, Juno emulated Horry, and sank down into the cold water, backing away between the pilings under the pier, and moving soundlessly away from him. But then she stopped, unable to obey her orders, because if she knew nothing else, she knew that she could no more leave him to face them alone than she could have left Horry to face the tiger alone. So instead, she clung to a piling, shivering in her sodden clothes, and trying to force her paralyzed mind to think.

41

After a few minutes, Jost began to move toward the shore, holding the propped-up skiff like a shield, and firing another shot in the direction of his attackers.

Juno wondered at his strategy, and then realized that several dark figures were moving along the seawall—around toward the pier over her head, which was behind Jost. They sought to surround him, she realized, and so he needed to make a dash for the shore; to lead them away from her. Think, Juno; think—there was so little time.

Behind her, on the opposite side of her pier, a small fishing boat was tied, with a platform protruding from the stern for the purpose of hauling in the nets. Juno shed her cloak, and waded under the pier toward the boat as quickly as she was able in her wet skirts, making her way to the platform. As she clambered up, her arms trembling with exertion, she could hear shouted instructions and more gunfire from the opposite side of the pier. Hurry, Juno; as soon as Jost ran out of ammunition, they would be upon him.

Once aboard the fishing boat, she scrambled to the far side, keeping her head low, and removed a shoe, leaving it on the boat's walk-around. Racing back to the platform at the stern, she grabbed hold of a short wooden spar, and then sank down once again into the cold water, grateful that Jost's stand on the shore served as a distraction. Fighting her sodden skirts again, she half-swam under the pier toward the shore, watching through the pilings to see that Jost was indeed out of ammunition, and that the others were circling around him.

"Don't kill 'im yet," one of them instructed. "They'll want 'im to talk."

Juno fell forward, to crawl through the shallow water with her hands in the mud and the spar under her arm, watching in horror as four men advanced upon Jost. With his back to the seawall, he held them off with his slashing sword, until a man dropped from the seawall onto his back, knocking him out with the butt of a pistol.

Juno watched no more, but instead rose far enough out of the water to throw her other shoe so that it hit the fishing boat with a bang, and then let out a sharp shriek, that echoed along the pier's wooden trusses. Quickly sinking back down into the water so that only her eyes and forehead were exposed, she watched the men's reaction.

They paused in surprise, looking over toward the fishing boat. "Wot's that? It sounded like the girl."

"Go, go—she's over there. I'll stay wi' 'is lordship." The man emphasized his words by forcefully kicking Jost in the ribs. The others scrambled up onto the pier, and Juno could hear the boots tramping above her head, as they searched for her. She crept forward on her hands in the shallow water toward the remaining man, who stood guard over Jost, and--placing her cold fingers in her mouth--she issued a soft whistle.

The man on shore turned in surprise, and peered into the dark water under the pier. "Whoosat? Is summat there?"

Again, she whistled softly, so cold that she was afraid her lips would not obey. Warily, the man walked toward her into the shallow water, his pistol held before him, whilst Juno's hands closed around the wooden spar. Taking a breath, she lunged upward and smacked it into his chin with all the force she could muster; the man's head snapped backward, and he dropped like a stone.

Frantic, she scrambled out of the water and headed toward Jost, hearing the excited exclamations behind her, as the searchers found her shoe.

Dropping to her knees beside him, she shook him, hard. "J-Jost," she whispered, her teeth chattering. "Quickly."

He lay, unmoving, and Juno could hear the others making excited exclamations from the fishing boat to the effect that she must had escaped by swimming away.

Desperate, Juno grasped Jost's legs, and dragged him toward the water; the slick seaweed aiding her efforts, and ensuring that no tracks were left behind. As she dragged him down the shore, she backed into the *Juno*, lying propped up where it had been discarded, and decided it was as good a hiding place as any. Dragging Jost beneath it, she pulled the skiff upside down over both of them, just as she heard the tramping boots on the pier signal a return of the searchers.

"'ere! Where's Jem?"

"Gawd—where's t'pirate?"

Juno lay under the skiff on top of Jost, terrified, and shaking uncontrollably. With a gasp, she realized that a portion of her petticoat was exposed outside the boat, and carefully pulled it in as she listened to the alarmed men draw their guns, and survey the area. One spotted the hapless Jem, and she could hear them pull him out of the water, with curses and exclamations that conveyed their certainty that Jost must have been feigning, and had managed to cosh Jem so as to escape.

"Should we look fer 'im?" one asked tentatively, his tone wary.

There was a small silence. "Better iffen we look fer t' girl," another suggested. The others fell upon this suggestion with alacrity, and Juno could hear them vacate the area with all speed.

Nearly lightheaded with relief, Juno rested her head on Jost's chest, listening for a heartbeat. "Don't you *dare* die," she hissed at him furiously. "Do you hear me?" He was warm, and his heart was beating—thanks be to God. Now what? Horry was presumably going for reinforcements, and would look for her here. However, the enemy may return—perhaps exhorted to do so by Jairus, or whoever was giving them orders; especially when the search for her came up empty. Best to escape to a safer place.

Gathering her strength, she rose to her hands and knees, straddling Jost, and inched the skiff against her back into the water, sliding him along beneath her as best she could. Once in the water, she clasped her inert husband under his arms and, with the skiff bottom-side-up over their heads, floated him against her as she crept along in the water, occasionally knocking into a piling, since she couldn't see where she was going. Her plan, such as it was, was to navigate thus to a safe distance and then look for help—she was so cold that she feared her limbs would soon cease to function, and Jost needed a doctor.

In this clumsy fashion, she inched her way along the shallows for a considerable distance, unable to see, but careful not to wade any deeper, and hoping no one would take any notice of an overturned skiff floating along in the water at this time of night. Just when she thought she'd reached the limit of her abilities, she felt a knocking on the skiff's bottom over her head, as though someone was knocking on a door. Pausing, she assessed the situation, and decided there was nothing for it, so she lifted the edge of the skiff and peered out.

Her eyes met those of a young boy--perhaps ten--who bent down to stare at her with some suspicion, up to his knees in the shallow water.

"Hallo," said Juno.

The boy nodded, clearly of two minds about embarking on a conversation with a woman skulking in the shallows, and carrying a skiff over her head.

"Are you alone?" she asked.

Again, he nodded.

"Can you help me lift the skiff? My husband needs help."

The boy, after hesitating for a moment, helped her to lift the overturned skiff, revealing the unconscious Jost.

"Cor!" exclaimed the boy in wonderment.

"He is hurt," Juno explained unnecessarily. "And I am freezing; is there some place we can go?"

The boy looked at her, then at Jost, then balanced on one foot in a posture that Juno recognized as preparing for an escape. Desperate, she added, "I will pay you *handsomely.*"

Ah, this caught his attention, and she could see him reassess the situation, his little features sharpening.

"He is a pirate," she added in a dramatic whisper, aimed at enticing a ten-year-old's sensibilities. "Do you see?"

Eyes wide, the boy stared at Jost, and nodded. "Cor!" he said again.

"He has a great deal of treasure hidden away—how much would you charge to help?"

Her companion considered it, silently. "A bob; nuffin' less."

Juno had no idea of which he spoke, so she trumped him. "Well, I shall pay you fifty pounds." Immediately, she realized her error, as the boy's expression became closed and wary; apparently this sum was beyond the realm of comprehension, and he now doubted her sincerity. To rectify the situation, she added, "And I will give you this skiff." Prudently, she didn't mention that there were musket holes that would need repair.

The boy stared at her in disbelief, and so she held out her hand, shaking from reaction, and the cold. "My promise on it."

He solemnly shook her hand, then said with some excitement, "Me da'll be that ginned."

"That is excellent," Juno replied. "The skiff was my Papa's, so it is only fitting."

"Oi'm in t' watch shed. Ov'r 'ere." He pointed to indicate a small guard shed, located at the entrance to a nearby pier

"Is your father there? Perhaps he will help us." Juno wasn't certain they could carry Jost's heavy figure, between them.

"Me da's at t' Blue Gull," the boy explained. "Gittin' 'is tipple."

"Ah," said Juno, and withheld her opinion of a man who would desert his job to leave his small son with his responsibilities. "Then I suppose we shall have to manage it ourselves."

"'ere; we'll each take an arm," suggested the boy, "an' drag 'im."

"You must be careful," Juno cautioned. "He's been shot."

"*Cor*," exclaimed the boy again, suitably impressed. "'E's been done over by oth'r pirates?"

"Absolutely," affirmed Juno. "Let's hide him, shall we?"

Between them, they managed to roll the heavy man onto a cargo pallet, and then drag it to the shed, the progress necessarily very slow. Juno had contemplated seeking help, as there were surely people about the docks even at this time of night, but she realized it may be best to keep their presence as secret as possible; if a description of Jost began to circulate, their enemies would be upon them in short order. Panting with exertion, she dragged Jost the final few feet to the shed, and asked the boy, "What is your name?"

"Li'l Bob," he gasped, out of breath himself. "Me da is Big Bob."

"I am Juno, and I am pleased to meet you, Li'l Bob. You must tell no one we are here, do you understand?"

"A' course," he replied with some scorn. "Oi'll not grass—filthy beggars."

"Exactly," Juno agreed. "It was not a fair fight, I assure you."

The interior of the shed was cramped and crude, but Juno nearly wept with relief to see a brazier, emitting a glow of heat. A small lantern rested upon a ramshackle table, and a cot in the corner revealed a blanket, which Juno snatched up to tuck around the prone figure of Jost. His wound should be washed, but Juno had her doubts about the purity of any available water, and decided that the best procedure would be to seek a rescue, as soon as possible. Besides, the bleeding had slowed to a sluggish ooze, undoubtedly due to the immersion in cold water.

Wringing out her skirts, she asked the boy in a solemn tone, "Are you ready for your assignment?"

He nodded, tearing his gaze away from Jost's exotic figure; the long, wet braid having left a soak mark on the wooden floor.

"You must go to The Nob's Fancy, on the big pier," instructed Juno, thankful that she had been paying attention. "Speak to the tavern keeper—no one else. Tell him Juno sent you."

Filled with importance, the boy matched her serious tone. "T'Nob's Fancy. Oi'm t' speak t' the keeper, an' say Juno sent me."

"Very good; now, hurry."

The boy darted to the door, then paused, remembering his responsibilities. "Keep yer eye out on t' dock."

"I will," lied Juno, and watched him slip out.

42

Juno knelt beside Jost, and gingerly moved her fingers over his head, feeling the lump, and noting that this hair was matted with blood around the wound. Head wounds bled, though, so it probably appeared worse that it looked. In reaction to her fingers, he frowned, and moved his head, muttering for a moment. Heartened by this sign of returning consciousness, she stroked his forehead with her palm—he was pale, but seemed to be breathing regularly. I hope our allies find us before our enemies do, she thought, and thus reminded, looked about the shed for some sort of weapon. There was nothing to hand, so she checked Jost's boots, looking for his knife. It was there, and she placed it on the floor beside them, just in case she'd need it—although it would be desperate times indeed, if she did.

Any moment now, she thought, trying to give herself some much-needed encouragement. Horry or Landon or the grey-eyed man would come through the door, and they would be rescued. No one knew they were here except Li'l Bob, and as long as he didn't speak to the wrong people by mistake, they were safe.

Pausing, she realized that there was one indicator that would betray their presence—Jairus would recognize the *Juno*. After looking about her, she grasped a burlap potato sack that had been propped in the corner, and dumped out the few blackened potatoes that remained within. With the sack in hand, she carefully slipped out the door, holding the knife at the ready. Holding up her wet skirts, she hurried down the bank to crouch beside the *Juno*, thinking to cover the nameplate with the sack. Her hands paused, and she ran her fingers gently over her father's carved accolade to her. I wonder if I could take it with me, she thought; then Horry could have his pipe, and I could have this nameplate. Using the knife, she began to pry along the edges and found, to her surprise, that the nameplate popped out easily.

Papa, she thought with a rush of emotion, and held it against her breast for a moment. I hate to leave your skiff behind, but it is going for a good cause, believe me. Gazing at the forlorn and abused vessel, she noticed that there was a dark area behind where the nameplate had been—a cavity of some sort. Tentatively she ran her hand along the edge of it, and then reached inside.

As soon as her fingers touched the object, she knew exactly what it was, and caught her breath. Carefully, she drew out a small sack that was securely tied at the neck—a sack that felt as though it contained several pounds of small pebbles. At long last; the diamonds.

Galvanized, she stuffed the sack into the burlap bag, and fled back to the shed to slam the door behind her, and lean against it, her breath coming in gasps. They had misunderstood—all of them; Papa had put the diamonds under Juno's name—literally--and Horry must have known that the hidey-hole existed, but no one had thought to ask Horry where Papa would have hidden something valuable, that only Horry would know. Instead, everyone had assumed Papa meant the diamonds were on deposit in a bank under Juno's name—disguised as a bridegift. But there was no bridegift, and never had been; instead, confusion had reigned because there were two Junos—and no one had asked Horry the right question.

Hearing footsteps approaching outside, she crouched down next to Jost, tossing the potato sack into the corner. Her mouth dry, she brandished the knife, and waited for whatever was to come, wondering if she had the wherewithal to try and stab someone. The door cracked open, and she could see two rough-looking men peer into the interior of the shed with some trepidation.

Now what? she thought in irritation; honestly, I shall have no nerves left, after this night. "Go away," she said in a firm tone.

"Where's Li'l Bob?" asked one, his voice slightly slurred.

Coming to the conclusion that the two had been drinking, Juno responded, "I sent him on an errand. Pray shut the door, it is cold."

"Oi sees ye take sommat from t' boat," accused the other suspiciously. "What've ye done wi' Li'l Bob?"

"An who's this?" asked the other, indicating Jost on the floor. The door opened wider and the two made as if to enter, so Juno said the first thing that came to mind. "You mustn't approach—he has yellow jack." Turning to Jost, she deftly lifted an eyelid, as she had seen him do with Horry. "Do you see?"

For once, Juno was a good liar. Scrambling, the men exited in disarray, and couldn't shut the door behind them fast enough. Speaking through the door, one said, "Cor, lady—iffen e's got t' yellow jack, yer a goner."

"Not I," she explained in a loud voice. "I am immune. But you must keep everyone away until he recovers."

But the two had already determined that the shed represented a hazard, and she could hear them stumble away. Letting out a long breath, she turned to see Jost watching her, the dark eyes slightly unfocused.

"*Waar ben ik?*" he muttered.

She dropped the knife with a clatter and knelt beside him. "English," she prompted with a delighted smile, her hands cradling his face. "Do you remember English?"

"No," he said. "But me, I remember you."

"Thank heaven you are awake—I am heartily sick of being brave."

His eyes focused on the interior of the shed, assessing. "Do I have a weapon?"

"Only one knife," she replied with regret. "But—but I think we are safe for the time being—I—I said you had yellow fever, and I sent Li'l Bob to The Nob's Fancy."

He made no comment in response to this disjointed explanation, and instead propped himself up on an elbow, grimacing as he tried to gather his bearings. "*Verdomme*, my head hurts."

"They--they kn-knocked you out." She found that she was having trouble catching her breath. "And—and then I knocked him out and I—I found the diamonds and here we are." Unable to control it, she placed the back of her hand against her mouth and began to tremble violently. Pulling himself upright, Jost put his good arm around her, grunting in pain when he moved his left shoulder.

"C—careful," she warned, her teeth chattering. "You—you've been shot."

"Who is this Li'l Bob?" he asked gently, his cheek against hers, while he stroked his right hand across her back.

"A—a boy who went for help. I said you—you would give him fifty pounds, although—although he seemed to think this excessive and didn't know whether to believe me. I-I said I would give him Papa's skiff, also, which seemed to interest him more although—although I--I didn't tell him about the holes in the bottom—" With a deliberate action, she clamped her teeth together, and made a mighty effort to stop gabbling.

"Tell me, Juno," he soothed. "Do not stop."

Instead she began to cry, relieved beyond words to weep onto his capable chest. "I—I didn't know what to do—I was so—so very afraid they had killed you."

"Me, I am hard to kill."

She pulled back to look up at him, shaking like a leaf. "I—I planted my shoe to make a false trail—just as you did at the Rajah's palace—it worked *wonderfully*."

"Juno, you are larger than life," he observed in wonder, taking a tendril of her hair and smoothing it behind her ear. "Here, *lieve*—let me put the blanket around you."

"I-I am sorry I am acting like a peagoose, but I was *so* very afraid, Jost. I whistled, and—and he didn't know I was in the water and—bang!—I knocked him out."

"In the time of nick." He wrapped in the blanket tightly around her.

Smiling through her tears, she agreed, "Yes, in the time of nick." In a few moments her trembling subsided, to be replaced by the occasional shudder. "I feel much better—thank you."

"Me, I did not know you could whistle."

"Papa taught me. Who killed Papa?" She shuddered again.

"Peyton," he answered without hesitation, his hand running along her back.

She thought about it, unsurprised. "And you knew all along?"

"Me and Landon, we guessed this. Someone close killed your father, and Aditi's brother. But I didn't know about Jairus."

"Despicable," she breathed. "To betray one's friends."

She could feel him tilt his head. "The money, it makes men think wrong."

"Yes—but now we are the ones who have the money."

Embracing her again, he rubbed his bristled cheek against hers. "Hush, *lieve.*"

Pulling away from him, she insisted, "It is *true*, Jost; I have found the diamonds. They were hidden in the skiff—beneath the nameplate—do you see? Papa said they were under my name."

"*Verdomme,*" said Jost, much struck. "Are they there now?"

"No." She gestured to the potato sack. "I put them in there."

He reached for the sack and with quick fingers, unlaced the bag, and poured a few diamonds into his hand.

"Oh," Juno gasped as they glittered brilliantly in the lantern light. "They are *beautiful*—not at all like the paste ones."

With a smile, Jost picked up one in his fingers and gently tucked it down into her cleavage. "The children, how many do you think we will have?"

"Jost," she protested, laughing, "—we cannot *steal* the diamonds."

"Four, I think," said her husband, ignoring her and tucking three more down her bodice. He then leaned forward and kissed the hollow between her breasts. "Me, I will negotiate my price—do not worry; I am the honest man."

"So there was no bridegift, after all—perhaps you should never have married me."

"*Vloek zij,*" he complained, as he rose stiffly to his feet. "Me, I need a new woman; where are my dice?"

"Oh? Then where's my blunderbuss?"

"Hush," he said suddenly, and raised his hand in caution, as the sound of men's voices could be heard outside on the dock.

43

Jost went to lean heavily on the wall next to the door, his knife held at the ready. "Come behind me, Juno, and if I tell you to run, you must run and scream—loud, yes?"

Juno dutifully positioned herself behind him, but confessed, "I don't know if I can leave you. I couldn't, before."

Placing an ear against the door, he listened for a moment, then said matter-of-factly, "If they hold a knife to your throat, I will tell them anything they wish to know."

"Oh—I see; then I suppose I must run."

They heard two sharp whistles, and Juno closed her eyes in relief. "It is your men."

But he held up a cautioning hand. "Hold; it may be Jairus. Be ready, and wait for me to say."

For the second time this night, Juno nervously gathered up her skirts in her fists, and waited, her heart beating in her throat.

"Who is within?" asked a man's voice.

Jost did not respond, but waited.

"Juno?" called Horry.

"Horry!" Juno called out in relief, but Jost stayed her with his hand.

"Horry, who is with you?"

"A Mr. Greeley," called Horry. "And a boy who says you gave him Papa's skiff." This last in a tone of great injury.

"If the young lady remembers," said the man's voice. "I caught her from the window in the prison."

"The turnkey," pronounced Juno, and Jost allowed them entrance. Horry threw an affectionate arm around Juno and told her she looked a fright, whilst Jost held his blade to Greeley's throat, and suggested he turn over his pistol.

As the man readily complied, he offered, "I was aboard a man o'war at the Battle of Lissa, Captain, so I know something of your work."

"Report, then." Jost tucked the man's pistol into his belt.

Indicating Horry, Greeley complied. "When the young master turned up, a contingent was sent to reconnoiter, and another man was sent to sound the alert. I stayed behind to guard the young master—"

"Ridiculous," retorted Horry with full scorn. "*I* was the one who knew where you were--"

"Horry," interrupted Jost, his tone sharp. "Enough."

Horry subsided, flushing, and Greeley continued, "And then this young lad appeared, insisting he speak to the tavern keeper, who had gone to raise the others—"

"Yer bruvver says I can't have t' skiff," Li'l Bob interrupted angrily. "Tell 'im, Juno."

"No one has the row with Juno," declared Jost in a tone that would have frightened Juno, had she been its recipient. "Me, I will give you fifty pounds and a new skiff. Horry, he keeps his father's skiff—yes?"

Mollified, Li'l Bob agreed with a sniff, "That's jakey—Oi'm chuffed."

Greeley offered, "I think it best we return to the Fancy; the cat will be among the pigeons when the young master comes up missing."

Jost considered this, his gaze on Juno. "We go by the river, then."

Juno noted with some delicacy, "The skiff may not be seaworthy."

Shrugging, Jost winced at the movement to his injured shoulder. "Then we take another."

"'Ere now," protested Li'l Bob in alarm, "Oi can't let ye steal one o' the boats."

"You will follow orders," said Jost, in the same tone he'd used with Horry. "No more of the mutiny."

Li'l Bob shot him a darkling look but was silent, and Juno had the impression Jost was amused, as he took the burlap sack and tucked it down the front of his shirt. "Come; we go outside—Juno stays between me and Greeley."

And so the small party cast off in a stolen rowboat, with Greeley manning the oars, and Jost silently watching the shoreline. I hope I am not going into the water again, thought Juno, still shivering, despite being wrapped in the threadbare blanket and Greeley's coat; I truly believe I will never be warm again.

Horry had been subdued ever since Jost rebuked him, and he now spoke into the silence. "I am sorry, sir."

"You are like your father," Jost replied without rancor, "—with the hot head. But you must wait and listen; wait until you have more—" he thought about the right word.

"S-seasoning?" suggested Juno, shivering.

He tilted his head, his gaze never wavering from the shoreline. "I do not know what this means."

"Experience," she explained. "J-judgment."

"The seasoning," he agreed. He then turned his head to Li'l Bob. "You, also."

"Oi'm s'posed to watch o'er t' boats," the boy insisted stubbornly. "Not let the pirates do a bunk wi' 'em."

Horry started chuckling, and in a moment they all were chuckling, even Li'l Bob.

"May I tell Horry about what we found?" asked Juno, aware that she should be circumspect in front of the others.

"Horry," said Jost. "If your father, he wanted to hide something, and said Horry will know where it is, where would it be?"

Horry thought about it for a moment. "He hollowed out a hole in the stern of the *Juno,* to hide his purse when we went out fishing."

"*Verdomme.*" Jost shook his head with a grim expression.

Horry stared at him in disbelief. "The bridegift? Truly?"

"Not really a bridegift," Juno explained. "We were distracted by the wrong Juno—Papa meant the skiff, not me."

As the realization sank in, Horry grinned. "Lord—think on it; we sailed half way around the world, and it was with us the whole time."

"Me, I do not think it is funny," Jost replied.

"Papa would think it was," Horry countered, and they all chuckled again.

They arrived at the pier without incident, and Greeley scaled the ladder first, to ascertain if it was safe to enter the tavern. Thankfully, the area was deserted, and in short order Juno found herself seated on the hearth before a roaring fire at The Nob's Fancy, a better blanket wrapped around her shoulders, and Jost seated beside her, pretending to examine Greeley's pistol, although Juno knew he was actually watching the door. The cook had thrown together bread and cold meats, and Horry and Li'l Bob sat at a table, devouring the repast as though they hadn't eaten in weeks.

Softly, Juno addressed her husband. "You need to see a doctor—does it hurt?"

"Soon," Jost replied. "First, we will see that you are made safe."

Embarrassed, she laid a hand on his leg in apology. "I am sorry to worry you so—I can't seem to help my hysterics. I do not make a very credible pirate's wife."

His gaze slid toward her for a moment, a gleam of amusement contained therein. "Juno, when I think of what you did—my heart, it stops."

"I had no choice," she confessed in all honestly. "It is not brave when you have no choice."

His reply was curtailed by the approach of voices and footsteps outside, and Juno could hear Jost cock the pistol on his lap. No further heroics were needed, however, as first Landon, then the grey-eyed man entered, accompanied by several other rough-looking men.

"Lady Van der Haar," Landon greeted her with a nod. Then to Jost, "I have something for you." He tossed Jost his sword, which was deftly caught with much appreciation. "Took it off one of the men we swept up."

"Landon, you are the good man—do you know of Jairus?"

"We managed to seize him," said the grey-eyed man, who Juno noted was dressed once again as a common sailor. "Although your arrival on the scene disrupted the proceedings to no small extent."

Jost was silent, trying to decipher what was meant, and so Juno helped him out. "Do you mean you had set up a trap for Jairus and the others?"

"Indeed; originally, we had planned to lure them into the Blackwall Docks, and seize them there. In the end, however, there was no harm done."

Juno gasped as Jost sprang up, his sword flashing in the lamplight to rest against the grey-eyed man's throat. The threatened man held out his hands to each side and carefully backed away from the point of the sword, but Jost advanced also, with the result that the other found himself pinned against the wall, the tip of the blade pressing into the hollow at the base of his throat. In the sudden and profound silence, no one moved.

"Hold," said the grey-eyed man with what Juno thought was admirable calm. "You forget yourself, Sir Jost."

"You knew of Jairus, and did not tell me?" Jost's soft tone was no less menacing for its volume.

"I didn't want to give away the game," the other explained, his hands still raised. "How was I to know you would go to shore, instead of to the barge?"

Incensed, Jost ground out, "My Juno is not now a widow, only because she has the heart of a tiger. I should slit your throat, yes?"

"No," said Juno, who felt it incumbent upon herself to interject. "You are making yourself bleed again, Jost. And recall that everything worked out for the best, after all—if I hadn't given the skiff to Li'l Bob, I would never have pulled the nameplate."

Jost did not move for a moment, and the cornered man took the opportunity to acknowledge, "I must beg your pardon; Jairus was your man, and you had every right to know."

Slowly, Jost lowered the point of his sword and reached into his shirt. Pulling out the burlap sack, he tossed it to the grey-eyed man. "Your diamonds," he said with a hint of scorn. "Juno found them."

The other stared at Jost then stared at the bag in his hands. "God in heaven."

"My husband needs a doctor," ventured Juno, who felt it an opportune time to make some demands.

44

"How was your curtsey? Did Mr. Landon's mother approve?"

Juno was sitting with Aditi in the parlor of their temporary residence on Cutler Street. The East India Company had given them the use of the residence, the staff, and a carriage; the Company's Governors being very pleased with the *denouement* of Juno's latest adventure.

"She is very nice to me—she puts me in bed with a hot brick." Aditi had been suffering mightily from morning sickness. "She thinks the baby is a boy, because she had a dream."

There was little of the *houri* to be seen in the demure young woman seated across from her, and Juno could only marvel at Aditi's easy transition from one role to the other. "Did she make any inquiries about your former life?" Juno could easily imagine the outspoken Aditi reciting chapter and verse to the horrified woman.

Aditi's amber eyes gleamed. "I was raised in a convent school outside of Bengal."

"Were you indeed?" Juno smiled, very much amused.

Landon says she will not ask about it because she is not Roman Catholic."

Juno had to laugh aloud. "An excellent strategy." Let the woman think misguided religious beliefs were Adidi's worst sin—it was also a handy way to explain away any gaffes. Aditi had come a long way, but Juno was not fooled; the girl would be a handful, and Landon would no doubt be led a merry chase—although perhaps motherhood would have a steadying effect; stranger things had happened.

"What did Preya say to you—did she admire your ring?" Aditi had been reunited with Preya the day before; Juno was told the woman was also enjoying the generosity of the Company's Governors, who were as happy with her as they were with Juno—it was much better for business that the Nabob was awaiting trial on charges of theft and assault, than on charges of treason, and Preya had been instrumental in achieving this aim.

Jost had also gone to visit Preya this morning, which is why Juno had sent for Aditi—it was best to have Aditi visit when Jost was away from home. Her husband was a loyal friend, but Juno had come to the conclusion that once you lost his good opinion, it was lost forever. Juno had asked if he'd like her to accompany him on his visit, but he had shaken his head. "No, *lieve*—it is better that I see her alone."

Juno respected his decision, and felt she could understand; Preya would wish to see her old lover without Juno present, to remind her that time and events had moved on. On the other hand, she hoped Jost wouldn't stay overlong—one shouldn't tempt fate, after all.

Lost in her thoughts, Juno realized that Aditi was hesitating in her answer. "What do you know of Preya?" the girl asked cautiously.

Puzzled, Juno said, "I know of what you told me; that she was Jost's—paramour—then your brother's, before he was killed. And that she was captured in Algiers with you."

Her brow knit, Aditi contemplated Juno thoughtfully. "I do not know what to tell you."

Juno was surprised at the girl's reticence, especially now that there was no longer a need to pretend that Preya was married to Jost. "I hold no grudge against Preya, Aditi—she testified at my trial, and was very helpful in setting up the trap for the Nabob."

"Preya has the wasting sickness," Aditi disclosed in her abrupt way. "She dies, soon."

"Oh," breathed Juno in dismay. "Oh—I am so sorry, Aditi."

No stranger to life's hardships, Aditi simply shrugged, and Juno reflected that women of such a profession rarely lived to old age—it also explained why Preya had seemed so thin to Juno. "It is heartbreaking, such a series of tragedies," Juno continued in a subdued tone. "First your brother, then her daughter, and now she is slated to join them—all in such a short time."

Aditi's sharp gaze darted to Juno's face, then lowered to her lap, as she nodded without comment. Juno watched her narrowly for a moment, contemplating a sudden and unbidden thought, and decided to change the subject. "Did you kill Mr. Peyton like Judith, wielding her sword?" Truthfully, she would not be at all surprised.

With a slow, reminiscent smile, Aditi gazed into the fire. "I take him to the bed, and I say I must leave for a moment—then the others run in, and seize him. He was naked." It was clear that she relished the memory.

Juno contemplated how best to raise the question that she was most curious about, then decided there was no point in being discreet with Aditi. "Did you—service him?"

"Never," Aditi retorted with a full measure of scorn. "But I made him think I would."

"You fooled me," Juno admitted. "You were very good."

"Yes," Aditi agreed without conceit. "Landon says they wanted to use me again, but he told them no, because of the baby."

"I suppose you must obey your husband, now," Juno ventured. "It must seem strange to you, after the life you've led."

But Aditi showed no sign of discontent, and smoothed her skirt over her knee, her face softening. "Landon takes care of me like—like I am a *ranee*. He is the one teaching me to read, now." She paused. "And he tells his mother lies, so that she will like me."

"An excellent trait in a husband," responded Juno, hiding a smile.

The girl raised her face, and leaned forward in a confiding manner. "And he is like a Brahman bull, in the bed."

"Oh," said Juno, her cheeks pink. "How very gratifying."

Fortunately for Juno's composure, any further confidences on the subject were interrupted when the maidservant entered with a tea tray that featured freshly baked macaroons.

"Agh." Aditi quickly averted her eyes. "I must be sick." She then fled to the retiring room under Juno's ambivalent gaze; Juno was beginning to suspect that she and Aditi shared the same condition, and she couldn't like this display of the consequences.

Aditi eventually returned, her lips a bit pale. "Shall I ring for anything?" asked Juno, unsure of how to help. "Tea, perhaps? I could probably find some of Horry's chinchona bark."

"The ginger root is better—have you ginger root?"

"Perhaps," offered Juno in a dubious tone, and asked the maidservant to inquire of the cook.

"Where is Horry?" asked Aditi. "Landon says he saved you, by swimming across the big river."

"Today he is at the docks with a little boy who helped us; they are buying a new skiff." Li'l Bob had been returned to his shanty on the river, after Jost had urged him to join his crew. The boy had refused, explaining that his father needed him, and after Jost had assured him he would always be welcome if he changed his mind, the two had parted with no further animadversions on either side. Jost had shaken his head as they walked away, expressing his opinion that men of the father's ilk usually did not live long, and the boy was foolish not to take the chance to better himself.

Juno had observed fairly, "He is loyal to his father—you can respect that, I think." But Jost, who had willingly gone to sea at a tender age, could not think it a good choice.

"When do you leave?" Aditi interrupted her thoughts.

"Soon, I hope," Juno admitted. "I can't imagine living here in London, and Horry is pestering Jost to leave. We are only waiting for Jost's shoulder to heal a bit more—I'm afraid he will not give it rest on a ship."

"You go to Tortola?" Aditi's speculative gaze was sharp upon her again.

"I imagine—at least I haven't heard otherwise. And what of you, Aditi? Will you stay in London until the baby is born?"

"Yes—Landon says there is much work to do." She tossed her head. "He is very important."

Nodding, Juno was willing to offer support for this accolade. "He is very good at what he does—he terrified me, when first we met."

"He says I am much prettier than you." Aditi fired off this salvo with a great deal of satisfaction.

"As well he should—and you are indeed beautiful, Aditi," Juno offered in all sincerity.

With the same triumphant mien, the Indian girl continued, "His mother wishes me to meet her friends. She says they have many grandchildren, and now it is her turn."

"You are to be paraded around like a prize, then," Juno teased, and hoped Aditi would behave herself; although perhaps now that she carried the much-desired grand-child, she could do no wrong.

To Juno's surprise, the kitchen managed to serve gin-ger root tea, and after Aditi carefully sipped a cup, the visit came to an end. "If I write to you, will you write me back?" asked Juno as they walked to the door. "Landon could help you."

"If I am not too busy," replied the other girl, with her usual lack of tact. "Then perhaps."

Juno watched her enter the waiting carriage, and spied her husband's tall figure approaching at the same time. She waved Aditi away, relieved that Jost did not have to encounter the girl. As she met him at the door he bent to kiss her. "Me, I hoped you would push Aditi down the steps."

"Next time," she promised. "Come in and have some macaroons; the cook has some fresh-baked." The quantity of food her husband could consume never ceased to amaze her, and she rang for the tea tray to be re-introduced.

Jost accompanied her to the drawing room, and paused by the window for a moment, gazing out, and lost in thought. He then winced as she helped him remove his coat—he was supposed to wear a sling, but scorned such a sign of weakness.

Assessing him, Juno gauged his mood. Troubled, she decided, and small blame to him; it couldn't have been easy to visit Preya, and be reminded that so many who were dear to him are now dead—or near dead. Fortunately, she knew the cure for what ailed him. Walking up from behind, she ran her hands around his waist and up his chest, pulling him against her. "Come with me, husband—I have a mind to inspect your dragon."

In response, he tilted his head back to consider the ceiling, a smile playing around his lips. "Ach, Juno; you make the demands on me—again and again."

"Let us try not to re-open your wound, this time," she murmured, and he turned to hoist her up against him, bad shoulder notwithstanding. Nothing loath, she wrapped her legs around his hips, her skirts ruched up, and as he carried her toward the bedroom she could see the maid, coming in from the kitchen with the tea tray, retreat in embarrassed confusion.

45

Juno laid drowsily content after lovemaking, and had to acknowledge that London offered at least one advantage—this roomy bed; it was not an easy thing to share a ship's berth with her large-framed husband. Her head on his chest, she contemplated the weak light that slanted in through the curtains. It was gray and misty outside, as usual; when it rained in India, it rained in no uncertain fashion, and then was done with it. Here, the light never seemed bright enough; the sun never in the right place in the sky. If Mama hadn't died, I would have lived here all my life, she thought in wonder; how strange life is.

"You have saved the world, *lieve.*" Jost lay against the pillows, his right arm cradling his head.

"Have I? Will they give me a commendation, do you think?" she teased. "Or perhaps a small country?"

"Me, I am serious. The war, it will be finished for good this time. Napoleon is out of money."

"Did the underwriters get their money back?" Juno traced his dragon tattoo with a desultory finger.

"Not yet; now they buy the bonds from the Treasury, for the war. The French, they are done."

"Napoleon never seems to be done," Juno noted with some skepticism. "Will you be needed?" She was thinking about what Aditi had said—that Landon had more work to do.

He shifted slightly. "Not here; back in Algiers, maybe."

Ah, thought Juno.

Misinterpreting her silence, he leaned to kiss her temple. "Me, I will be careful. I am married, now."

"Yes," agreed Juno with a great deal of irony. "I am certain you will be a pattern-card of caution, now that you are married."

"Juno," he chided. "You do not believe me—I am safe as a house, now."

"Except that you will kill that dangerous gentleman, whose name I have forgotten."

"Except when I kill Rochon," he agreed. "But you will not know of it, so you will not worry."

"That is excellent; you relieve me no end."

They lay together, content, and listened as the rain begin to patter against the window. "Your father, they will give him—" he searched for the word, holding up his hand to make a circle with his fingers.

"A medal?" Juno lifted her head in interest. "Like an award?"

"Yes—a medal. They will give it to Horry."

Squeezing her husband's chest, she pressed her cheek against him, and confessed, "I never should have doubted him—no matter the evidence against him. Horry never did."

But he would not allow her to be at fault in any respect, and kissed the top of her head. "Ach, *lieve*—the problems, they should not have happened. I did not understand about the other Juno." He paused for a moment, then added, "Me, I will give you something, also."

"I think you have already given me something," she teased wickedly.

"Juno, you must not always think of the bed sport," he chided. "I will give you a medal." He lifted a finger and traced a small circle between her breasts. "A big diamond, you will wear it on a chain, here."

"Do you indeed have such a diamond? It is a rare wonder there were any left to give back to England."

"Me, I took the biggest one," he confessed. "I could not help it."

And she could not help but laugh, and he laughed right along with her. She rationalized, "I suppose they are very pleased with your work, and will not begrudge yet one more diamond."

Gingerly, he turned to raise himself on an elbow, so as to look down upon her. "We will need one of the others soon, I think."

Juno blushed and laid a hand against his face. "I was going to tell you as soon as I was certain."

He leaned in and kissed her gently. "Juno, you have been very busy."

She laughed again. "My life was very dull before the day I met you, but events since have more than made up for it."

"The finest day." He kissed her again, not as gently this time.

"It's a bit like being in a typhoon," she teased. "One can only try to keep one's feet."

"You have very pretty feet," he noted, his mouth traveling to her throat. "You must try to keep them."

To reward this sentiment, she lifted her head so as to kiss him, and he responded as she knew he would. We are well-matched, she thought as she arched against him, and tried to avoid wrenching his shoulder. I can't get enough of him, and he can't get enough of me; thank heaven we found each other in Bengal, on that finest day that didn't really seem so, at the time.

Later, she decided they had avoided the subject long enough. "Are you awake?" she whispered.

"No," he whispered, sleepy.

"Can you wake up long enough to tell me of Preya? How does she? I understand she is quite ill."

There was a pause, whilst his fingers moved on her back. "Juno, do not die."

"All right, then—I won't," she promised. "When are you going to tell me about Bala?"

She could sense his sudden caution. "What of Bala?"

"That you only pretended she had died, so as to keep her safe from the killers of children, but in reality, you secreted her away on the *Dragon* and promised Preya that we would raise her as our own."

His hand stilled on her back. "Juno, sometimes I think you are the witch."

To let him know she was not upset, she nuzzled his throat. "At the trial, she looked upon me with such gratitude—then Aditi told me she was dying. I put two and two together, and decided you had hidden Bala away."

His hand under her chin, he gently raised her head to meet his gaze, and said with all sincerity; "You do not need to do this, Juno. Me, I can put her with my overseer's family on Tortola, and give her a bridegift."

Juno shook her head. "No, it is only fitting, Jost—now it is my *niyama*, too. And she may be your daughter, after all."

"Perhaps not," he admitted. "She has the eyes like Aditi."

Juno rested her cheek against the broad expanse of tattooed chest. "It doesn't matter—you are so magnanimous, certainly I can be just as magnanimous."

"Me, I do not know what this means," he confessed.

"It means I love you," she explained simply.

"*Zeer goed*," he replied, and kissed the top of her head.

Made in the USA
Middletown, DE
11 March 2020

86179043R00227